2/18

P9-DKD-596

MONSTER

Also by Shane Peacock

Eye of the Crow
Death in the Air
Vanishing Girl
The Secret Fiend
The Dragon Turn
Becoming Holmes
The Dark Missions of Edgar Brim

the Dark Missions of
EDGAR BRIM

MONSTER

SHANE PEACOCK

tundra

Tundra Books, an imprint of Penguin Random House Canada Young Readers,
a Penguin Random House Company

Library and Archives Canada Cataloguing in Publication

Peacock, Shane, author
Monster / Shane Peacock.

(The dark missions of Edgar Brim)
Issued in print and electronic formats.

ISBN 978-1-77049-701-6 (hardback).—ISBN 978-1-77049-703-0 (epub)

I. Title.

PS8581.E234M65 2017   jC813'.54   C2016-906911-7
                                                C2016-906912-5

Published simultaneously in the United States of America by
Tundra Books of Northern New York, an imprint of Penguin Random House
Canada Young Readers, a Penguin Random House Company

Library of Congress Control Number: 2016956779

Edited by Tara Walker and Lara Hinchberger
Jacket images: (roots) koMinx/Shutterstock Images; (skeleton and bolts)
Pepin Press—*Graphic Ornaments* + L'Aventurine—*Animals Animaux Tiere Animales*
Designed by Jennifer Lum and Rachel Cooper
Printed and bound in the USA

www.penguinrandomhouse.ca

1 2 3 4 5 6   23 22 21 20 19 18

Penguin
Random House
tundra | TUNDRA BOOKS

To Sam, a young man of many talents,
who grows more fearless every day.

I

The Creator

Art is long, life short, . . .

∞

Johann Wolfgang von Goethe,
Wilhelm Meister's Apprenticeship

1

Aftermath

Edgar Brim is running for his life on the dark streets of London after midnight, Tiger Tilley by his side and fear in his heart. A demon is pursuing him: the creature that has just murdered Lear. Edgar can hear its footsteps thudding behind him, feel its presence in dim alleys, sense it peering down from the rooftops of buildings, but he cannot see it, cannot even imagine it or what it might do to him. And as he runs, the shriveled arms of the supernatural old woman who has terrorized him since he was in his cradle are squeezing his chest so he can barely breathe. He had thought this was over—the fear, the visitations of the hag, and the monsters. But it is all here again: as real as the thick London mist.

Edgar's flame-colored hair is like a spotlight in the darkness as he rushes past the weird denizens who populate the night like actors in a dream—ragged, staggering women, swerving swells and deformed beggars. This is where civilization has brought us in the greatest city on earth, thinks Edgar, this is progress. The shop windows are black, some boarded up for the night. Whispers and shouts and screams echo up and down the streets. Edgar feels the monster getting closer. Tiger moves at lightning speed, quick in her black trousers and loose shirt. She flies around a corner and up Drury Lane in front of him and he is desperate to keep up. His breath comes in heaves. The Crypto-Anthropology Society of the Queen's Empire and the madman who operates it are just a few doors away. He has their guns.

They had left Jonathan and Lucy at the Langham Hotel, one-armed Professor Lear growing cold in his bed and his face whiter and stiffer by the hour, as if it were becoming a mask. The moment before he died, his eyes had stared at them as though he had seen the devil and he had spoken in a croak from dried lips, his larynx quivering in a mutilated throat marked with red lines like the imprints of a huge hand. "*Monster*," he had whispered. And then: "*Worse!*" The creature that had been in the room had frightened Lear more than the living-and-breathing vampire they had destroyed two days before!

Then the old man had gasped, "*It is coming for you all!*" before lying still.

Lucy had wept while they had all sat around the professor's bed, unable to move. Finally Edgar had stood up and proposed a plan to get them through a day or two.

"We can't tell anyone what really happened here. We need to remove the corpse from the room and suggest a believable cause of death. We might say it was a fall against something, his neck striking a hard surface, a bureau, a bathtub edge? But first, we need protection from this beast. Tiger and I need to make a run for the weapons. Jonathan, you and Lucy stay with your grandfather, on guard."

Jon was holding his face tight and had trouble even answering, but his sister had risen and taken a thick iron poker from the hotel room's fireplace and put it into her brother's hand. When Edgar and Tiger left at three in the morning, they heard the door bolt shut behind them.

The Crypto-Anthropology Society's door is locked too. Edgar puts his back to Tiger and surveys the dim street, sure that the monster is near, while she pounds on the entrance hard enough to wake the entire street. The lights are already on in the downstairs chambers.

Little William Shakespeare comes to the door fully dressed for the day, wearing a frilly Elizabethan blouse under a purple smoking jacket, rubbing his eyes, but his huge sagging face not betraying any sleepiness.

"You were awake?" asks Edgar, glancing at him and then back into the street.

"I had offered myself to the arms of Morpheus but had not yet entered his distant realm of—"

"Let us in, now!" says Tiger. "Something may be after us! Lear is dead!"

She shoves the short man aside and enters, and then locks the door behind them after Edgar goes past. Shakespeare stands frozen. But he doesn't look upset, at least for a moment. Then there are tears, great blobs of them, falling down his hound-dog cheeks and wetting his shirt.

"Oh, my God, my God, my God," he keeps repeating, "another has come for him, for all of you, has it not?" His voice cracks a little, as it does when he is excited . . . which is often.

"Downstairs, now!" exclaims Edgar and nearly picks up the diminutive man as he descends the steps with him.

"Where are the weapons?" demands Tiger the moment they enter the august meeting room with its big round oak table and its many place settings for the men who are never really there. "We need them NOW!"

"It won't matter," sobs Shakespeare, "this one will destroy you all. And then it might come for ME too!" He utters a little scream. "And these dear men . . . Messrs. Sprinkle, Winker and Tightman!"

"The guns!" repeats Tiger, advancing on him.

Shakespeare hesitates, then motions limply toward the weaponry, hidden in the darkness of his hallway.

They leave the distraught little man standing at the foot of the stairs and rush back into the night. It is raining now. Edgar has Alfred Thorne's extraordinary rifle in hand, not even trying to hide it. Jonathan had fired everything in the gun at the other creature when it had menaced them. They will have to steal more bullets from Thorne House. Tiger is pulling the little cannon behind her and it is thundering along on the cobblestones, fully loaded.

They reach the hotel safely, soaking wet, Edgar holding the rifle by his side as he slips through the lobby, but Tiger is unable to disguise her weapon. She simply moves briskly, drawing looks from the doorman and desk clerk who aren't exactly sure what the red contraption is that she is rolling along.

They knock three times—once hard, twice soft—as agreed, and Lucy opens the door and locks it once they enter. Edgar is relieved to see that nothing has tried to break into the room since they left, but the scene is grim. Jonathan and Lucy stare out at their friends from what seem like deep sockets now, their backs to the corpse, Jon gripping the poker tightly in both hands, his knuckles white. Finally, Edgar breaks the silence.

"It followed us, back and forth."

"No," says Tiger, "I imagined that too, for a while—but this thing would have struck if it had been out there. The hour was ideal. Remain calm, all of you. Do not make anything up; react to what is real. Remember, Edgar, you had a plan. Let us hear it again."

He gathers himself. "We have to do as we said. We must tell the authorities that your grandfather has had an accident. The fall in the bath is the best idea. He needs to be taken from the room."

Lucy is sitting on the edge of the bed and, though her back is still to her grandfather's corpse, she has reached behind and is gripping a cold white hand. Edgar steps toward her and gently removes it, taking her hand in his.

"All right," she says softly.

The big-bellied hotel owner wears an elaborate black suit and carries a black bowler hat, his cadaverous assistant a tall top hat that seems from another time, his cheeks powdered red as if it were he who was being prepared for burial. The two men are sour and suspicious, but after notifying the police, they allow the body to be removed. Lucy won't look as it goes out the door.

"What's next?" asks Jonathan when they are alone again. "Shall we search the streets and go into the pubs with our weapons and shoot off the head of any tall chap who prefers blood to ale?"

"It won't be a vampire," says Tiger.

"We don't know that." Jon is pacing.

"Lear saw it," says Edgar. "He said it was worse."

There is silence again.

"We need to go home," says Lucy.

Jon stops. "Home?"

"We need to bury grandfather properly. Staying here won't keep us safe. We need to divide up the weapons, stay vigilant, and figure out how to save ourselves. And we need to do that quickly."

"Going home might be fatal," says Edgar quietly. "We need to stay together, with all the weapons."

"Perhaps it will just leave us alone," says Jonathan. "Perhaps killing grandfather . . ." He swallows. "Will be enough for it. Perhaps it will see that as a sufficient warning. Maybe all it needs is for us to keep quiet *about what we know*." He nearly shouts that last sentence, as if he wants it to be heard beyond the walls.

"Lucy is right," says Tiger. "We need to take courage and separate for now."

"One can be too brave, my friend," says Edgar. "We should stick together."

"Hear me out," says Tiger, stepping closer to him and putting her hand on his shoulder and then sliding it down to his arm, which she squeezes. "I not only don't think this thing followed us in the streets, Edgar, I doubt it is still lurking around here. If it wanted to kill every last one of us, it would have done that by now. Instead, it murdered an aging man, whose death might be explained away, and left. That is indeed a warning. If we gather together and barricade ourselves with weapons, it might take that as evidence of our intent to fight it, perhaps soon pursue it, a

8

declaration of war. I don't think that's what we want. Not yet, anyway." Her eyes flare for an instant. "We need to act normally, at least on the surface: return to our residences, but as Lucy said, with precautions, fully armed. The Thornes are expecting you to come home anyway, Edgar. It would be difficult to explain staying away any longer."

"She's right," says Jon, looking more like his old self. "Let's just be ready for anything." He smiles at Tiger.

Lucy drops onto the bed again. Edgar sighs and sits beside her. He doesn't take her hand this time, but lets his leg gently touch hers. For some reason, this gives him strength. During the silence that ensues, Tiger walks to a window, pulls back a curtain and peers out onto the street.

"All right," says Edgar finally. "If this is what you all want, then Lucy and Jonathan should take Thorne's rifle and Jon's pistol too. And Tiger," he adds, and looks up at her as she turns to him, "you take the cannon."

"That leaves you defenseless," says Lucy, now pressing her leg against Edgar's.

"No," he says, "I'll be at Thorne House where I may be able to steal more weapons from the laboratory. I'll get some bullets too, for whatever I find, and for you. I don't think this thing will go there. I'm guessing that if it attacks it will choose either of your locations first . . . for you are the ones that are more alone." He turns to Tiger again. "Especially you." He thinks of her wide awake in her little abode in Brixton, her back to the wall, her face set with determination, the cannon primed and at hand in the middle of the night.

"Don't worry about me," says Tiger, her hands on her hips, her eyes narrowed. He can see the bump on her nose and the little scars left from it being twice broken.

"She can protect herself," says Jon.

Edgar rises and goes across the room to where Professor Lear's portmanteau sits on a luggage rack and opens it. He sees what he is seeking, lying on top of two shirts with the left arm-sleeves pinned to the shoulders.

Edgar thinks of the creature they confronted at the Royal Lyceum Theatre, the undead revenant, its shaved head, the sickly white pallor of its skin, its long teeth for driving holes in human chests and drawing out their blood. He thinks of its cold hand across his face and of those long bony fingers caressing his chest when it ripped open his shirt. He thinks of its big head in the guillotine, the blade slamming down, the head severing from the trunk and rolling onto the soil on the stage, the eyes staring up. He cannot imagine a monster that is worse. Professor Lear had told him that the vampire was after *him* more than any of the others. Perhaps that is true of this one too.

These thoughts fill him with fear, his foe since childhood, the thing that debilitates and unhinges him, that brings on the hag. He thinks of his early years and the terror in his little heart when his father read the sensation stories that came through the heat pipe to him in his bed in their broken-down home.

He can hear the hideous old woman outside the door now, waiting for him in the hall. She used to only come when he slept, but now she can be anywhere. Edgar wants to run, forever and ever.

But he picks up the thing in Lear's luggage.

"And I'll have this," he says, holding it up.

Lear's huge blade glistens in the dim light.

Edgar follows Tiger home, keeping his distance, carrying the big sword-like knife inside his bag. The sun will soon be up and a strange dim glow is infusing the London streets. It is the sort of lighting that Edgar imagines exists in the other-worlds of the scientific romances of the brilliant young novelist H.G. Wells. Working people are beginning to appear, pulling carts, carrying heavy satchels and tools in rough hands, their ruddy faces cast down toward the stones. Edgar reassures himself that monsters seek and need anonymity, the shadows, secrecy. But still, he keeps his senses alert. Up ahead, Tiger's strong, lithe figure is impossible to lose despite the growing crowds as she crosses Waterloo Bridge trailing her cannon, unconcerned (as always) about the way people look at her. She never once glances back. He follows her all the way to the end of Mordaunt Street and then observes from there, making sure she gets through the door and into the safety of her home.

But is she really safe there? he wonders.

As soon as he leaves, her door opens again, and she stands on her porch watching him, her dearest friend and perhaps more someday, walking away in the distance.

2

Refuge

"My dear boy!" cries Annabel Thorne the instant she sees Edgar Brim on her doorstep. She takes him into her arms. But he feels a different sensation from the usual sense of safety and love that he receives from her embrace. He is suddenly afraid for her. It sends a shiver through him and he immediately wants to protect her.

"Mother," he says, "I am *so* glad you are well."

"But, why wouldn't I be?" She pushes him back, gripping him by the shoulders, looking up at her now-tall adopted son, with her light blue eyes on his darker ones. "You look pale, Edgar."

As they speak, Alfred Thorne is standing halfway down the stairs that descend to the hallway past the vestibule, no more than a dozen strides away. But he is in a shadow at a corner and partially out of sight, the scar on the left side of his face turned from the light. He is listening.

"Has everything been . . . all right here?" Edgar asks Annabel, stepping by her and into the hallway with its glistening black-and-white checkerboard floor. He looks up and down the corridor, glancing anxiously behind an open door, the suitcase with the sword inside still in his hand. He notices Thorne on the stairs with a start.

"Of course it has," says his adoptive father in his stern voice, staring at him.

"Sir, I did not see you there."

"Evidently, or you would not be uttering such drivel."

Edgar walks up the stairs and edges past Alfred Thorne without looking at him, though he knows his adoptive father's eyes are on him. "Excuse me, sir," he says, "and mother, but I am exhausted and should retire to my room for a while." He must stop searching the house while being observed. Nothing would come here anyway, he tells himself—the thing that attacked Lear couldn't know where he lives, at least, not yet.

Edgar has a bad night, listening for an intruder, and thinking about Tiger alone in her home and Lucy and Jonathan in theirs. He feels a coward for not staying with them, for not insisting that they all keep together. Sleep is not an attractive option. He knows if he drifts off his nightmares will come and the hag will be on him when he wakes. So, as he did on the first night he came to this house as an orphaned little boy, he lies awake for hours and then gets quietly to his feet, goes out the door and sneaks up the creaking steps to the laboratory at the top of the house.

This time, he knows how to get in. He has been watching Tiger, who grew up on the streets and knows how to break into any building, and could get herself inside the rooms where the sweets were kept in their student days at the College on the Moors. A simple piece of wire can do the trick and he often carries one of hers now.

The door has a complicated lock, designed by Thorne himself, but in minutes, Edgar has it open.

He is inside with the entrance closed behind him in a flash. There is something about this place that is electric to him. The big ceiling window that stretches nearly the length of the room is partially exposed tonight. The long blind is not fully drawn shut and the stars are twinkling in the clear black sky above, casting soft light onto the floor and on the tables, on Thorne's big desk and the books that line the wall—those unexpected works of fiction.

Edgar steps carefully, intent on getting what he needs quickly and then leaving. He wonders if he dare steal another weapon.

"Find the rifle bullets and get out," he whispers to himself.

And there in the center of the room is the table he is seeking. And there on it, as if left for him, is a scattering of the big bullets. He sweeps them into the pocket of his dressing gown and turns back to the door, his pulse racing.

He hears something, as if someone were in the room with him. Then he sees a shadow on the wall, glimpses it peripherally to the side and nearly behind him.

A figure is coming forward, tall and thin. It emerges out of the darkness and approaches the squares of light on the floor. Edgar thinks he sees something behind it: a body, a big human one lying on a table.

"Stop right there!" A hand seizes his elbow in a steely grip.

"Good evening, Edgar," says Alfred Thorne. "I see you have returned to my laboratory."

"Re-returned?" sputters Edgar.

"I believe you have been here before. Do you know, by the

way, that someone, or perhaps a pair of someones, stole two valuable items from my arsenal, just within these past two weeks?"

"No . . . no, sir, I did not know that. I am sorry to hear it."

"Well, never mind, I have informed the police and they shall be found out before long." He releases the boy and takes a step back.

"And so they should be." Edgar can't help glancing at the scar on Thorne's cheek.

"You have grown industrious, Edgar."

"Should that not be admired?"

"If it is for good. One might argue that breaking into laboratories through locked doors is not quite an altruistic thing."

"Good is hard to define these days, sir."

"Perhaps in any day, Edgar, though I would put it to you that something which advances human knowledge cannot be anything but admirable. And that is what I am attempting to do daily in this room."

Edgar glances toward the thing lying on the table behind his adoptive father. He thinks he can see a head turned on its side and is unsure if it is attached to the trunk. "Said like a true man of science, sir."

"There is nothing more important than science, my boy, nothing! Look out on the streets these days at these new motor vehicles. They will change our world and improve everything about life on earth: there is a kind of goodness in them." He advances toward Edgar, causing the lad to back up. Edgar stumbles and nearly falls into the bookshelf with those rows of sensation novels.

"Be careful, Edgar."

"Might I go, sir?"

Alfred Thorne pauses. "Why, yes, of course." Edgar turns to leave. "But do not come back."

"Yes, sir."

"Unless you are invited and I am prepared for you."

Edgar wishes he had a clearer view of what is on that table at the back of the lab, but Thorne seems to be standing so as to block his view. And with those bullets in his pocket, the theft of which he is almost sure Alfred did not see, Edgar is anxious to get away. He opens the door and begins to close it behind him, but it won't shut. When he looks back, he sees Thorne is holding it.

"You know, Edgar, you are not entirely unwelcome in this place now. Science is also a calling, an admirable one, in fact, the greatest of vocations."

"Yes, sir."

"And you must choose your calling soon." Thorne turns in the direction of that thing on the table for an instant.

"I . . . I am considering literature."

Thorne's face had been white and porcelain in the dim light but a sort of rose color quickly invades it. He grimaces, as if to keep himself from shouting, and turns on Edgar.

"I was not finished!"

"Yes, sir."

"That prospective hobby of yours, which you just mentioned, will *not* be your calling."

Edgar says nothing.

"You may choose from among the sciences. I have friends and I shall consult them and find you a position soon."

Edgar turns his back on him and slips out the door.

In the morning, there is no message from his friends—no telegram, nothing. But he tells himself that makes sense—anything arriving at Thorne House, even if addressed to him, would first be read by Alfred or Annabel, since he is still their ward. His friends must have considered that. But he wonders. Images of his comrades' gruesomely murdered bodies flash through his mind and he desperately tries to banish them.

He fidgets during breakfast under the glittering chandelier in the dining room, anxious to get away. Annabel pushes scones and jams and tea at her beloved adopted son and carries the conversation, asking Edgar questions about his final school year and what his plans are for the future. He, of course, says nothing of the terrible things that transpired at the College on the Moors during his last days there, and is careful to seem uncommitted about his prospects. Alfred says almost nothing, though he watches Edgar closely whenever he answers.

"You still don't look well, my son," adds Annabel.

"He is fine."

"I believe he has a tongue to answer for himself, Mr. Thorne."

"I am fine, mother."

"So, dark circles under your eyes indicate health, do they? You seem sad, morose. Is anything wrong?"

Edgar gets abruptly to his feet.

"No, nothing at all. But . . . mother, sir, might I be excused? I have an appointment late this forenoon."

"An appointment?" asks Thorne.

"I am meeting three acquaintances from school."

"How wonderful!" cries Annabel. "I shall have Beasley set out the appropriate clothes. Something with some color in it?"

"Uh, no, mother, dark would be better, and somewhat formal."

"Dark?"

"We, uh, we shall be attending a . . . lecture . . . by an esteemed gentleman."

"And who would that be?" asks Thorne.

"Uh . . . Professor T.H. Huxley."

Thorne smiles, a decidedly unusual thing for him. "Why, that's lovely, Brim! He is an excellent man. A scientist, biologist, Darwin's bulldog they call him . . ." But then Thorne frowns. "Did he not die, just last year or the year before?"

"I . . ." stammers Edgar, "I may have the wrong name. It is my friends who are hosting me. Perhaps it is Mr. Huxley's brother? Or son?"

Alfred's frown doesn't leave him.

"Well, I think that is marvelous," says Annabel, "whoever is speaking. Science is a wonderful vocation, you know, Edgar, but perhaps there are others for you to consider as well. After all, science can be a little dull. All that proving and proving—do we need proof for everything? Love, for example, can you hold that in your hand?"

Alfred Thorne drops his utensils with a bang onto the white tablecloth.

"Did I say something wrong, my dear?"

"Mrs. Thorne, we clearly have not yet had our chat about Edgar's future."

"His future is up to him, Mr. Thorne."

"That is unacceptable, you well know that."

Edgar backs toward the door, hoping they won't notice. Their eyes are locked on each other's, Annabel wearing a bright and daring dress that shows her stockings nearly to the calf and her husband without a spot of color on his person. But as Edgar reaches behind his back and feels for the doorknob, Annabel suddenly raises her voice.

"Beasley!"

The door opens from the other side and the butler's quick entry nearly knocks Edgar down. Beasley is a small man with a pronounced ridge for a brow.

"Yes, my lady?"

"Please lay out Master Brim's black suit coat and trousers for him, dark necktie, dress shoes, thank you."

She is still glaring at her husband.

Within an hour Edgar is on the street, almost running north from elegant Mayfair, the fistful of bullets for Jonathan and Lucy's rifle in the pocket of his dark suit coat. He has to get them to his friends. That is, if they are alive to receive them. Spooked by Alfred's presence in the laboratory last night, Edgar hadn't made an attempt to return there to steal a weapon, so other than employing Lear's big sword-like knife, which he has hidden under his bed, he will be defenseless should anything come after him when (and if) he returns home to Thorne House.

As he scurries along, he keeps looking back, knowing that he is leaving Annabel vulnerable too. He isn't worried about Thorne.

The inventor seems well equipped, both in spirit and in resources, to fend off anything, to arm himself with some extraordinary weapon with gruesome capability in an instant and destroy anything that might threaten him. But the inventor is always up there in that laboratory—even in the middle of the night, it seems—seldom at Annabel's side. Should something come after her, it would take her life with ease.

Edgar knows he must try to get back to her as soon as he can and somehow defend her, perhaps even tell her everything, so she is at least prepared. But he can't be everywhere at once. First, he must help his friends.

He boards an omnibus on Regent Street, advertisements for soap and ladies' items and Sainsbury's grocer splashed on its exterior. He goes up the spiral stairs to the roof and in minutes is moving past big Regent's Park, folks strolling about on its green inner-city acres without a care in the world.

If all has gone well, his friends will be at the Lears' house in Kentish Town, their first time together since they left the hotel with the professor's body in a coach, Edgar and Tiger standing silent on the footpath, Lucy and Jonathan both solemn in the hansom cab behind their grandfather. They had agreed the funeral would be today. The corpse would have spent yesterday and this morning in the Lear home and a coroner would have been there to inspect it by now. But what if that official, likely stern and humorless, didn't believe the story of the fall in the bathtub? Edgar tries to imagine the quiet house last night, the sound of a clock ticking, or perhaps no sound at all, as his friends waited out the darkness, their dead grandfather for company, terrified of a monstrous intruder, worried about facing the grim coroner in the morning, and then the funeral. He imagines them sleeping in the same room for safety, taking turns with Thorne's unloaded rifle pointed at their door as if its very appearance would be a sufficient deterrent, with their backs against the wall, hoping this new creature will let them live just one more day.

Did it? he asks himself.

And what of Tiger, he thinks, absolutely alone in her little home in Brixton, going without sleep, the cannon primed and ready. He wonders if she is alive too.

I let her go home alone.

The omnibus deposits him in the slightly upscale northern end of the Lears' working-class neighborhood, just south of the much more elegant Highgate with Hampstead to the west. Professor Lear couldn't afford a house in either of those areas, well known as home to great writers and artists, to the great of all sorts. It is as if the terrain acknowledges this, for here, near the foot of Highgate Hill, the land rises up to Hampstead Heath and Highgate Cemetery and the houses of the wealthy. Mary Shelley's immortal husband often visited other poets up there, and just recently the novelist Robert Louis Stevenson lived in its environs, he whose mind conjured up the monster in the terrifying *Strange Case of Doctor Jekyll and Mr. Hyde.*

"Where did that creature come from?" asks Edgar out loud. "Did the author actually see the demon Hyde walking those leafy streets after midnight?"

But the street Edgar is on now is much more humble than those. Many of the houses are attached to one another, built of sturdy brick, mostly just two stories high and tightly stationed near the footpath. Edgar is so anxious about what he will soon find that he starts to run toward the Lear home, remembering the number—66 Progress Street. He spots a black coach outside, two black horses hitched and ready, a man in a tall black top hat and black clothes up on the box with reins in hand. *The undertaker.*

Either the coroner has been to the house and swallowed the story about Lear's phantom fall in the bathtub and the professor's coffin lies in the coach ready for its trip to the cemetery . . . or this black conveyance is there for someone else, for two others, perhaps even three.

Edgar reaches the front entrance out of breath and doesn't bother to knock. He pulls open the door and enters, nearly colliding with Lucy. She is emerging from the little front parlor into the vestibule carrying a single red rose, dressed in black from head to foot, her pale face and copper-colored hair in great contrast to her black bonnet. Jonathan appears behind her, dressed in dark clothing too.

"You are alive!" Edgar nearly shouts.

Lucy brings a finger up to her thin lips. There are three other men behind Jonathan: a clergyman and two who look working class, all in black. Edgar wonders if they are undertaker's mutes hired to accompany the funeral procession.

Lucy takes his arm and leads him back through the doorway toward the street. Behind them, Jonathan speaks under his breath.

"No intruder, no creature, came here. We had grandfather washed and prepared. The coroner believed us, though he asked many questions. The five quid I paid him may have helped."

They walk out into the late morning, clouds gathering above, their hard shoes clacking on the stones. It smells of onions and wet clothes on the foot pavement. Perhaps the poor vegetable mongers have been past with their wares.

"I have chosen to walk with the procession," says Lucy. "I know it is unusual."

"Who are the other two?"

"That's the gravedigger and the undertaker's boy—they will walk with us too. We couldn't afford much and we had to keep this quiet. Grandfather had few friends anyway, most were from the college. Though we've invited no one, I've had a gravesite dug in Highgate Cemetery. I wanted him to lie up there. He deserves it." She begins to cry and Edgar finds a handkerchief for her in his trouser pocket. Annabel always thinks of everything.

"Where is Tiger?"

The other two say nothing and Edgar's heart sinks. He stands still behind the hearse, paralyzed, and feels a drop of rain hit his shoulder and another strikes the top of his head. He wants to run south, back down into London, across the Thames and into Brixton, to Tiger's house. He needs to see her answer the door.

"She must simply be late," says Jonathan. But he looks as if he doesn't believe it. He appears to be holding back tears. Edgar has never seen such an expression on his face.

If Tiger could crawl she would be here, thinks Edgar. He imagines her dead, her throat crushed like Lear's, torn apart by whatever attacked the old man in the hotel, some wretch, "worse" than the first. When the hearse moves forward he follows woodenly.

"It's my fault," he whispers.

They walk solemnly out of Progress Street and then pass the southern end of lush Hampstead Heath. Edgar wishes he could take Lucy by one hand and Tiger by the other and walk under the beautiful trees along the paths on that big, beautiful green heaven, London below them at their feet. But instead, they turn up Highgate Road and begin the climb toward the cemetery, Edgar's mind boiling.

"I have to leave," he whispers to Lucy. "I have to go to Tiger. She might be wounded. She may need me." Lucy glances at the hearse in front of them, and then back at Edgar and nods. They are now passing the cemetery's brick wall with its gated entrances, the grounds on the other side verdant like an English jungle. Edgar touches Lucy gently on the shoulder and steps away from the procession, but as he does, he sees someone coming up the road toward them: a girl dressed in black from her bonnet to her long dress and shoes, limping. Her short black hair curls out from under the hat and her black eyes stare in his direction.

"Tiger!" he says out loud.

He realizes she isn't actually limping. She is in high-heeled boots, which isn't her fashion, and it gives her a labored gait. She is rushing, hobbling toward them. Jonathan has stopped as well and begins to hold out his arms to her, but then drops them and simply smiles.

She falls into step beside them, drawing a glare from the undertaker up on the box in front of them, who now leads a motley little procession with two women in it.

"Good day," says Tiger, her voice weak, which isn't like her either. Edgar expects her to say more, but she immediately grows silent, her expression grim.

They move through a black wrought-iron gate set in the cemetery's brick wall, along a gravel path and keep walking at their solemn pace for another half mile, past the cedar trees and flowers and undergrowth that line the avenues. Shadows loom over them. It is difficult to believe that a place can be this eerie in the middle of the day. Edgar thinks of *Dracula*, that horrifying novel by Bram Stoker that he intends to burn in the Thornes' fireplace at the first opportunity—it was here in this very cemetery, he is almost certain from the description in the book, where *Dracula*'s woman-turned-vampire was staked in her crypt by her husband while three other men looked on. They had cut off her head and stuffed the mouth with garlic. Edgar remembers their own revenant, the one that had pursued them, its head severing from its body when the guillotine came down—he remembers putting that head, big and skull-like, between that creature's feet to keep it from rising again.

They stop at a deep grave positioned tightly between two others in a row with many stone markers, several tall and ornate. Edgar fingers the big bullets in his pocket as the clergyman speaks softly and quickly, as if to get things over with. "Ashes to ashes, dust to dust . . ."

The coffin is lowered and Lucy stares down at the ground. Jonathan, his face set like he is sitting for a funereal photograph, puts his arm around her. Edgar and Tiger step closer to each other. When the brief ceremony is done, Lucy goes to her knees and reaches down into the grave, almost falling into it. She drops the red rose onto the coffin.

"Good-bye," she says.

The gravedigger takes off his jacket and begins to throw the dirt into the hole, the spitting rain coming harder now. He has a black mustache like the tip of a thick finger and stubble on his cheeks. There is something about him, beyond his occupation here, that Edgar doesn't like. He is a big brute, but it isn't that. He seems to work in a calculated way, as if he were sizing up something about the grave, remembering it.

Moments later, Jonathan guides Lucy away and Edgar walks behind them, sticking close to Tiger. He can see now that there is a bruise on the side of her forehead stretching almost to her temple. It is red and angry and meant to be hidden under her bonnet. Something isn't right about her eyes.

3

Monster in the House

"What is wrong?" Edgar asks Tiger as they leave the cemetery. "Tell me the truth." The four friends are alone now. The undertaker, his apprentice, the clergyman and that gravedigger had abandoned them the minute the grave was covered.

Tiger staggers and Edgar catches her in his arms. He helps her to a wooden bench nearby and sets her down. He sits beside her, his hand on her shoulder, and then turns her face gently toward him, while the other two stand over them.

"I'm . . . I'm fine."

"You are not fine," says Lucy. "Oh, Tiger, what's happened?"

"I've taken a blow to the head. It aches. I didn't want to bother you, not now." She lowers her face into her hands. Edgar knows that if Tiger says her head aches, it must be absolutely pounding. He gently unties her bonnet and takes it from her head and sees the wound fully now. Lucy gasps. Though Tiger isn't cut, the contusion appears dreadful. It is swollen and looks like a piece of hard flesh surgically attached to her head. It's the size of a fist.

"I . . . I must have blacked out, that's why I'm so behind. I went last night to a draper's and bought this dress. I had it laid out to wear this morning. When I woke I knew I was late, very late. I put it on and came straight away."

"What happened last night?" asks Edgar. His dear friend has always been an early riser and never oversleeps, no matter what.

"Something came into my house."

"Something?" asks Jonathan. He sits beside her on her other side, making the bench creak, rests his broad shoulders against the back, and takes her hand. She doesn't pull it away.

"I don't know. I can't remember. I just recall lying in my bed, my clothes still on, listening. I had the cannon next to me, primed. I was trying to stay awake. Then something entered and was on me like lightning. It must have struck me. I don't remember anything else. My room was dark. I couldn't see its face, its body, anything, but I think . . . it was very large. I have the vague sense that it put its hands around my throat too."

"This is good," says Edgar.

"Good!" shouts Lucy. She looks as though she wants to hit him. He has never seen her angry at him before.

"Because it didn't kill her."

"It could have, instantly," says Jon. "The question is, why didn't it?"

"I'm not sure," says Edgar after a while, "but in the meantime, take these." He pulls the bullets from his suit coat, a fistful of them, and hands them to his big friend. "They're for the rifle."

Jon looks relieved. "I'll take off its head if it comes near us again," he says. "I won't miss this time!" In two months, he will be at Sandhurst Military College. He looks ready to leave now.

They walk Tiger back to the Lear home and she leans on Jonathan's arm most of the way, her head at times on his shoulder. Edgar knows how much that must bother her—she never likes to show any weakness.

When they arrive the Lears' front door is ajar. They halt on the footpath.

"Oh God," says Lucy, staring at the entrance. Her hands are shaking as she puts them up to her mouth.

"We can't go in," adds her brother. "We are unarmed. It would have us at its mercy in an enclosed space."

"Is there a back way?" asks Edgar.

"Only through our neighbor's house, from their yard," says Jonathan. "All the buildings are attached here."

"They aren't at home during the day," says Lucy, "and we keep a key."

"All right," says Edgar. "Let's go through the neighbor's house and out their back door. Jon, you and I will climb their wall into your yard and enter through the rear of your home. Lucy, you stay with Tiger, and if all is well, we will let you in through your front entrance. We are going to try to make it to the rifle."

"It's in my room," says Jonathan, "under the bed. I'll get it."

"We have bullets now!"

"I'll come with you," says Tiger, her voice barely audible, trying to stand on her own.

"You will stay with me." Lucy takes her from Jonathan.

They move through the neighbor's house silently and the boys are soon over the short wall without a sound. Jon opens the Lears' back door as quietly as he can, though it squeaks a little. They move through the scullery and into the back hall. They hear a sort of groan and a shuffling. Whatever is near is waiting for them.

"It's in the parlor," whispers Jonathan. "My bedroom's just ahead. I'll get the rifle. Wait here."

Edgar nods. But Jon seems to be gone for a long time, so Edgar takes a couple of quiet steps forward and peers into the parlor. There is something in there all right. Edgar can hear it breathing. And he can see it, or at least a tiny part of it—its feet. It appears to be sitting in one of the chairs!

The feet seem awfully small and they are encased in slippers, bright gold ones that turn up at the ends as if they are the footwear of a little genie from *The Arabian Nights*. Edgar takes a step forward and turns into the parlor.

"You!" he exclaims.

William Shakespeare starts so violently that he appears to elevate straight off the parlor chair toward the ceiling. He comes down and hits the cushion with his little rear end and vaults straight up again. This time he lands in a heap on the floor, staring up at Edgar Brim.

"Oh MY LORD! My LORD and all his disciples! You have given me a start, my boy! You have shaken me to the very foundations of my magnificent and munificent soul! Could you not simply enter the front door and bid me hello?"

"Could you not wait for us on the doorstep like a normal human being? And how did you get—"

Jonathan turns the corner, the rifle pointed straight at little Shakespeare's big head.

"OH!!" he screams. "Put down that blunderbuss, you rapscallion, you clod of wayward marl!"

Jon lowers the gun.

"Am I too late for the funeral?"

They get Tiger into the house, give her tea and put her in Lucy's bedroom with a cold compress over the wound and the lights out. Then they huddle in the parlor.

"What's next?" asks Jonathan.

"I think—" begins Edgar.

"Well!" says Shakespeare. "The first thing we must do is establish the identity of the creature that is in injurious pursuit of us."

"Us?" asks Jonathan.

"And I just so happen to have brought a book along with me, a novel of some repute, and it seems to me that it is from this particular tome that our monster has come, given its beastly attacks, its blunt ways." He draws a book out from the yellow waistcoat he wears beneath his purple suit coat, a curious outfit even for him to have worn to a funeral. "Now!" he exclaims. "I believe our monster is—"

"We must continue to stay out of all of this," says Edgar, "despite what happened to Tiger. Think about it: it's likely that attack was a second warning, and though horrific that's all it was, there was no attempt to kill. The best we can hope for is that there won't be anything more to this from here on. We are armed now, so let's keep to ourselves and make it seem absolutely clear by our actions that we have no interest in pursuing this . . . creature in any way."

"But, but—" sputters Shakespeare.

"That sounds cowardly after what happened to Tiger," says Jonathan. "This thing seems to be active right now, right here in London, so it may be killing others."

"Yes! An excellent point, young Lear!"

"Or maybe it isn't doing anyone any fatal harm," says Lucy. "Maybe it just wants to be let alone."

"I'm for fighting it now," says Jon. "We need to pursue it aggressively. We know where it was last night, so perhaps we can pick up a trail."

"No," say Lucy and Edgar together. They glance at each other a little sheepishly. "It seems to me," continues Lucy, "that there are three of us deciding on this, Jon. It's two to one."

"Two to two, my dear," says Shakespeare. "For I, leader de facto and de justo and de realistico of the Crypto-Anthropology Society of the Queen's Empire, shall take up my suffrage and cast my vote in glorious favor of—"

"We are only counting the people who would actually be willing to fight," says Lucy.

"But Messrs. Sprinkle, Winker and Tightman would also be—"

"And those whose actual existence can be verified."

Shakespeare goes quiet.

"Tiger would side with me," says Jonathan.

"I'm not so sure," says Edgar.

"How do you know what she feels?"

"I have known her since we were children, how about you?"

"She and I are more alike, Brim."

"Jon," says Lucy, "there may be a time to fight, and it may come very soon, but for now, I think we need to be cautious. Why invite more violence?"

Jonathan doesn't answer for a moment. "All right," he finally says, "but sometimes safety comes from fighting, not from sitting back and being afraid. I won't wait for long."

"I'm not afraid," mutters Edgar.

Jon sneers at him.

"We all are," says Lucy, "or we are fools."

Edgar motions for Shakespeare to put his book away, which he does with a long face. Then he turns to Lucy. "Tiger should stay with you two for a while. See if you can convince her to do that. Perhaps you can bring the cannon up here, then you will be more than sufficiently armed, and you can take turns sleeping."

"Did you steal another weapon from the laboratory, Edgar?" asks Lucy.

"No."

"Then what will you—"

"Remember, I have the sword. And I also have Alfred Thorne."

Edgar doesn't sleep well again that night. He doesn't dare go up into the laboratory, not two nights in a row. Instead, he lies awake listening, trying to resist dozing off. There is a deep fear within him that feels like his old terrors, like a disease that he cannot rationalize away with the argument that this thing that murdered Lear and attacked Tiger is only interested in warning them.

When he finally does drift off, a nightmare comes. The hag slips through the door and comes for him. She climbs on top of him and the pressure on his lungs is unbearable. When he awakens she is still there! All his limbs are paralyzed and he remains unable to breathe. He closes his eyes and tries to calm himself, repeating internally that this isn't reality, the hag is not real, but it's no use. The old woman's toothless mouth is inches from his; he can smell her breath, like the odor that comes from the sewers, and he can feel her red eyes glaring. He gets up and walks blindly around the room, but she clings to him, wrapping her bony legs around his torso, climbing up onto his shoulders, her thighs still pressed to his chest, piling her weight onto him to drive him to the floor. He falls to his knees and the shock of hitting the hard wood surface seems to wake him fully, and when he opens his eyes again she is gone. All that is left is the pounding of his heart and the sweat on his face, the sweat all over him.

She was so real!

It is dead quiet in the dining room when he enters for breakfast. Both his adoptive parents are waiting for him and neither has touched their toast or tea. Annabel is dipping her knife in the jam and drawing doodles on her napkin, remarkable images of her son's face. Edgar greets them and sits.

"You screamed in the night," says Alfred Thorne.

"I did?"

"Is there anything wrong, dear?"

"There is simply nothing that can be wrong enough for a grown man to scream in his bed."

"He is not a grown man, Alfred."

"He shall be soon."

"Edgar," says Annabel, ignoring her husband. "Your father and I have discussed your future and have come to a—"

"A conclusion."

"A compromise."

That sounds better to Edgar. He looks at his adoptive mother with anticipation.

But it is Alfred's big voice that re-enters the fray. "Here is the state of things," he says with some force, "and I would appreciate your full attention." Edgar looks back at him. "Mrs. Thorne and—"

"Your mother."

"Mrs. Thorne and I have decided that you are to enter upon a scientific career."

"But not a severe one, instead one with promise and creativity and—"

"A scientific career!"

"But not in a laboratory, in a dusty, old, boring situation like your father's."

The inventor's face has gone red. Annabel looks a little concerned, as if she may have gone too far.

"You, Brim, shall become a doctor," mutters Thorne.

"Oh, it will be ever so interesting and challenging and you shall be doing good in the world."

Edgar doesn't know what to say. He is wondering how he might get out of this.

"I see," he finally says.

"Your father wants to send you to the University of Edinburgh this autumn, but I have asked him to kindly allow you to stay with us for another year or two in London. You are still so young."

She pauses and looks as though she is anticipating an explosion of disagreement from her spouse, but when Alfred speaks he seems calm, though his teeth are held tightly together.

"We have agreed to have you apprentice, as it were, with a physician in London, a respected surgeon, for ONE year before you proceed to Scotland to enter the esteemed medical school there and work industriously to receive your degree. Then you will return and take up your practice here."

"You will be close to us!"

"At the London Hospital, one of our finest, and the best part is that the surgeon is your own uncle, Vincent Brim. He has agreed to take you under his wing for this year. You are a fortunate child."

"Imagine that, a child," says Annabel, "and just moments ago he was a man."

The silence in the room hangs there for several seconds.

"You are fortunate, Brim."

But Edgar doesn't feel that way. This is not what he wanted in life, and right now, he has so many other things with which to grapple. He doesn't want to be pushed toward a vocation right away.

"You shall start tomorrow!" exclaims Thorne.

"Tomorrow?"

Annabel gets up and puts a hand on his shoulder. "Well, you know, Edgar, you must make a start of it sometime. You need to get used to all those horrid things that doctors must do. All that blood and sawing of bones and—"

"That is enough, Mrs. Thorne. We do not need to discuss this any further. I shall wake you at five in the morning, Brim, and you will be on your way. You can walk to the hospital. It is not terribly far and brisk constitutionals in the morning are good for young fellows. Simply report to the Receiving Room or Accident Department, whatever they call it, at the main entrance, and ask for your uncle. Mrs. Thorne will have Beasley lay out the appropriate clothing."

Edgar spends the day feeling anxious, about his friends in Kentish Town, about something entering Thorne House and attacking, and this new worry: what will he encounter tomorrow at the hospital? He has always hated Vincent Brim. His uncle had disliked his father, thought him flighty and irresponsible, and had always been jealous that (the older) Allen Brim had inherited Raven House and then let it fall into such disrepair, especially while pursuing his "childish" interest in literature. When Vincent was given the old mansion upon Allen's death, he had drawn up a statement for nine-year-old Edgar to sign renouncing all claims on it and then immediately sold the place and purchased a luxurious home for himself and his loathsome, social-climbing wife Carmilla, in Kensington. Edgar remembers the few times he had seen her, got up in elaborate dresses, her face pancaked and white; and the single time he had been in their house, told in no uncertain terms to "NOT touch anything!" Edgar had been repelled by the very sight of Uncle Vincent too, short and thick, ridiculously clean, always inspecting his fingernails and pushing back the cuticles, with wide black eyebrows and a charcoal mustache and goatee—all dyed from their original red—with gleaming circular glasses and a way of holding his nose in an upward direction when he spoke to you. There was something else about him too, difficult for Edgar to put his finger on. Uncle Vincent always seemed to be scheming, to have secrets, as if he were plotting something and that something had to do with you. Sometimes Vincent Brim looked at Edgar as if he were examining him, planning his dissection.

4

The Surgeon

Edgar's adoptive father is right about one thing. The walk is indeed brisk, mostly because he has several miles to cover and has to arrive before the clock strikes 8 a.m. A hard knock came on his door just past five, and that was the last that he heard of Alfred Thorne that morning. Annabel greeted him at breakfast, made sure he ate fully from the choice of eggs and devilled kidneys and kippers. Then she made certain he was properly dressed, in his gray suit and tie, pocket watch attached, and sent him off with an apple and pound note in hand.

He heads south alone, down to Piccadilly, then to Regent Street and through Trafalgar Square, along The Strand where he passes the Royal Lyceum Theatre, barely able to look at it. On he goes, keeping up his pace, past St. Paul's Cathedral and through the Old City to Aldgate and then into Whitechapel. Even at this hour the streets are jammed, carriages and hansom cabs and omnibuses going pell-mell, the odd motor vehicle sputtering and smoking in and out of the masses, pedestrians running for their lives as they cross the street. The sounds are like a roar in his ears at times—thousands of horses and wooden wheels and the shouts of newsboys and mongers and the buzz of the crowds. It smells of that thick London smell—of human body odor and animals and manure and coal. When he reaches the East End, the people he encounters are mostly poor and some much more dangerous looking than any he has seen so far. Here, where Jack the Ripper had struck down this neighborhood's narrow alleyways less than a decade ago and might indeed still be at large, there is most definitely a more desperate sort of Londoner. It is a strange place for such a prominently named and important hospital to make its home.

It appears to his right with just ten minutes to spare, an enormous building, longer than a football pitch and wider too. It stretches along the south side of Whitechapel Road, four stories of brown brick with a dozen steps leading up a stone staircase to five arches, and an enormous clock presiding over everything. He stands for a second staring up at it and then has the feeling that he is being observed from behind. He turns and surveys the crowd. But he can't spot anyone watching.

Up the steps he goes with the other rushing employees and patients, through the big doors and into the receiving room. It is a spacious place with a tall ceiling and rows of wooden benches filled with patients, all of them anxious, some of the young ones crying. Edgar approaches a reception counter where a dour-looking nurse dressed in a long pale blue dress with a white pinafore apron and cap stands speaking to a mother and child. The nurse glances at him as if he is a disturbance then returns her concentration to her patients, barking out questions. But he notices another option—young nurses, obviously assistants, working at other desks behind the counter.

"Excuse me," he says rather loudly to one of them, the youngest and prettiest of the lot, "I have an appointment with Dr. Vincent Brim at eight. Might you direct me to him?"

The matron stops speaking when she hears the doctor's name. She turns to Edgar, seeming almost cowed for a moment, but she recovers quickly.

"Up these stairs to your right, Ward C on the first floor, room 1818!"

The steps are wide and wooden and worn in the center. They creak as he ascends, a noise that is barely heard among the thumps of doctors in lab coats over high collars and ties, uniformed nurses, and patients either moving very slowly or nearly running up and down the same broad boards.

He finds a hall with a painted brown floor and white walls and that medical smell that hospitals have—either chloroform or ether or perhaps simply the smell of disease. It is quieter here—just the sounds of low conversations and the odd cry from an unseen source. He passes many doors. Some are open, allowing him to see that most rooms seem fully occupied, their many beds, usually in two rows against opposing walls, filled with patients. The sick lie there with forlorn, sometimes desperate expressions.

Edgar has heard many stories about this famous hospital, not all of them pleasant. It was said that the Ripper's victims were brought here—or at least what was left of them. This was the closest hospital to his horrible crime scenes and the mutilated bodies were examined here and taken apart by surgeons, perhaps with coroners hovering over them. These corpses, all women, had been opened up and disemboweled by the murderous fiend. The famous freak called the Elephant Man had been in this building too, in fact, had *lived* in the basement and died here just seven years ago. Edgar was a child when that human creature was brought in for examination: a man with a head like an elephant's, his forehead bulging as if it were a balloon of flesh, lips swollen and one arm the length of a gorilla's, a limping monster with his face often covered by a linen bag to hide his hideousness, two eye-holes cut in it so he could see out. It was said that he died of a broken neck, having tried to lie down to sleep one night "like a normal human being," only a few floors below where Edgar now walks. One day long ago, when he and his father had come into London from their home in the country to visit the British Museum Library, Allen had told Edgar that he had seen the Elephant Man on the street, cane in hand, masked and cloaked, a well-dressed surgeon by his side, the famous Dr. Treves. It had given Edgar the shivers when his father described the scene, though he knows now it shouldn't have. Not all monsters, all aberrations, are evil.

Edgar keeps striding down the hall and pulls out his pocket watch, seeing it is past the 7:59 mark and inching toward eight o'clock. He is almost certain now that someone is following him, and when he turns he actually sees a man who appears to be in pursuit, tall and thick, heading directly toward him, his gaze set on him. It's a doctor, wearing a white lab coat and bearing a stethoscope, middle aged and handsome with broad shoulders. But Edgar needs to get to his Uncle Brim without a second's delay. Room 1810 appears, then 1813, there it is—1818. The door is closed. He knocks. No response. He knocks harder. The doctor who was observing him from behind is now within a dozen strides, though he slows. But before Edgar can confront him, he hears a shout.

"ENTER!"

He knows his Uncle Vincent's voice immediately. It is often loud and always frightens him. But Edgar is still surprised to see his hand shaking as he reaches for the doorknob.

Dr. Brim is sitting at the far end of a room that seems far too large to be his office. He is behind a big oak desk staring at his nephew. There are numerous skeletons of varying sizes nailed by the head or the limbs, hanging from wooden supports. Two flank Dr. Brim. Diagrams of the human body, the muscular and skeletal systems, the nervous system and systems Edgar didn't even know existed are glued to the beige walls. Dark, plain books, none of them looking like novels, fill a tall bookcase. On a black-topped table near the desk are test tubes and bottles containing liquids and powders. There are a few long serrated knives and something that appears to be a saw and other ghastly looking instruments on a metal tray. There isn't a scrap of decoration or color anywhere, not even a solitary flower.

"You are . . . almost late," says Brim, snapping his pocket watch closed. "Sit." He points at one of two wooden chairs that are facing the desk. The doctor's own seat is plush leather. It squeaks whenever he moves in it.

"Yes, Uncle Vincent."

"None of that, you will call me Dr. Brim or simply Doctor, and I shall address you as Master Brim. Is that understood?"

"Yes, Uncle . . . Dr. Brim."

"Master Brim." Vincent Brim pauses for a moment. "Let me make one thing perfectly clear. I did not ask for you to be apprenticed to me and that is a ridiculous term anyway. There are no apprentices in the medical world, in the world of science. You should be readying yourself to attend medical school like any other young man, but Mr. Thorne asked me for a favor and I was . . . not able to refuse. Family should count for something, not that it did to your father, who destroyed our family's legacy."

"That isn't—"

"You are to LISTEN to me and not QUESTION me, do you understand?"

"Yes, sir."

"It is your privilege to be here!"

"Yes, sir."

The doctor gets up and paces behind his desk between the two skeletons, examining his fingernails. Edgar now notices two books that had been near his uncle's right hand before he rose, both looking well-thumbed: *Frankenstein* and *The Island of Doctor Moreau*. Edgar has a good nose. His uncle smells of some sort of perfume. As Vincent Brim strides with his white laboratory coat undone, his spectacular dark suit is evident underneath—a stiff white color with black tie, a black coat and trousers with pin stripes, a gray waistcoat and a gold chain looping across his abdomen. His dyed black hair glistens with some sort of lubricant, as do his perfectly trimmed mustache and goatee.

"I do not know what I shall have you do for me. I cannot trust an untrained youth with any of my work. I am an operating surgeon, you know, one of the best in London, and I save people's lives. Most of my work is conducted in the operating theater, where the slightest error can mean death, and some of it is secretive because I employ groundbreaking techniques on desperate cases. I can give or take life from others with the touch of my hands. It is not a place for a child. Perhaps you can sweep the floors in here, tidy up, that sort of thing." He sits down again.

"Or he could aid me!"

The two Brims turn. The tall, good-looking doctor has somehow soundlessly entered the room.

"Forgive me, Dr. Brim, but I heard some of your conversation. I believe I have the pleasure of meeting your nephew? I noticed him in the hallway making a beeline for your door."

Vincent Brim gets to his feet immediately and smoothes down his already perfect hair and mustache and goatee. He almost bows. "I . . . I didn't know that I had mentioned his relation to me, Dr. Godwin."

"It is my pleasure to meet you, young man," says the newcomer, extending a hand. Edgar thinks there is something familiar about this man's name.

Godwin is remarkable to behold: stunningly handsome, his unwhiskered face broad and clean without a single wrinkle, his nose perfect, his eyes dark and smiling, and the hair on his head as black as midnight. His grip is strong and masculine, his hands large.

"I have been in search of a young man for some time," he says. "You are from an excellent family, Edgar Brim, and I am sure you will be a fine assistant." Edgar finds the doctor's speech mannered—he takes care with each impeccably pronounced word, as if he were an actor trying to get the words and the emotions that go with them correct.

"That sounds like an excellent idea," says Vincent Brim, a wide smile emerging on his lips. "Edgar, I work closely with Dr. Godwin and I can assure you that he is a man of great esteem. Please appreciate the honor that is being bestowed upon you. Well, don't let me keep you two, take him off to the dungeons."

"What, might I ask, sir, did my uncle mean by the dungeons?" says Edgar as he and Dr. Godwin turn out of the room and into the hallway.

"Well, your uncle is not known for his sense of humor, my good man, to say the least, but even he goes along with the little joke about my office and laboratory. You see, my rooms are in the basement, thus the others say I work in the dungeons. It is a marvelous jest!"

Godwin offers a laugh of a sort but it seems awfully forced, as if he doesn't quite get the humor to which he is referring. Pretty nurses smile at him as he passes, but he barely seems to notice.

They descend the stairs at the other end of the hallway and go down two long flights, the second of which is stone and takes them below the ground floor. The medicinal smell gives way to a slightly different odor, one tempered with what can only be described as "basement." Here the walls too are stone. It is difficult to tell how long the basement hallway is for it is lit only for a hundred feet or so and then is obscured in darkness. They move silently along, passing no one, deep into the bowels of the hospital. There are no windows here either. A growing sense of fear, the old fear, begins to invade Edgar and he tries to keep himself from trembling. He can't stop from looking behind and thinks he sees an old woman peering out from under the stone staircase.

"This is a sort of dreary place, Edgar. Might I call you Edgar?"

"Yes, sir, of course."

"Dreary, but only in appearance; it is really a place of great opportunity. I am fortunate to be the chief experimental surgeon in the hospital and thus I have funds to do all sorts of scientific research into the healing of heart and brain problems and of grievous wounds, into the origins of diseases, into the origins of life itself. My laboratory," he says with a smile and a gesturing hand as they stop at a large wooden door, "is a sort of scientific wonderland."

He sticks the key into the lock and opens the door as if he were opening the entrance to heaven, with a flourish and another winning smile.

The room is large and filled with the sorts of bottles and tubes and tables that one would expect in a laboratory, but also with something that surprises Edgar. Animals.

"Voila!" cries Godwin, turning on the electric lights.

Monkeys chatter and rats squeal and then there is a sort of growl. Edgar walks into the room and sees the animals in tight cages along the walls. He can smell them too. They seem to smell even stronger than the creatures he has seen at the London Zoo. He remembers reading that animals give off stronger odors when they are frightened. In a large cage on the floor is a big cat, the size of a large dog, black and sleek—it looks like some sort of panther. There are rabbits too, some of which whistle at him.

"Why the animals, sir?"

"For experimentation."

Edgar can't stop a frown. They are still walking and are now near the center of the room where a high table just slightly longer than an average man and about twice as wide is positioned. An array of light bulbs hang above it and a stand sits near its head with a broad metal tray on it. In it is an arsenal of instruments larger and more complicated in appearance than the few Edgar had seen in his uncle's office—big knives, four saws and things that look like pick axes.

"Have no fear, Edgar, this is all for good. It is science at its best. Yes, I am a vivisectionist. I cut up and work upon these creatures, but I am a doctor too, and my mission is to help humanity and ultimately to aid the animals themselves. I am learning things here that will change the world for the better!"

"What do you want me to do, sir?"

"You can keep the animals happy and fed, you can clean up around here, but I also will have you assist during experiments."

"On . . . the animals?"

"Yes, that and human cadavers. Do you have a strong stomach? Can you bear the sight of blood?"

"I think so, sir."

"A great deal of blood?"

"I—"

"The cutting of skin, slicing of arteries, the sawing and fracturing of bones?"

"I don't know, sir."

Godwin smiles and slaps him on the back. "I love a frank man. I am sure you will do just fine. One must do these things to become a surgeon of any sort!"

Edgar notices a door in the far wall, sealed shut with a particularly large lock.

"What is that?" he asks without thinking, pointing at it.

"That?" asks Godwin. For a moment he seems to resent the question. "Oh, that is a marvelous thing. It is the entrance to another room, a sort of holy place around these parts. It is where Joseph Merrick used to live."

"Who is he?"

"The Elephant Man."

5

Alfred and Edgar

E dgar comes home feeling exhausted, but not because of the amount of work that Godwin asked him to do—he did very little that was taxing. The great surgeon had, instead, nearly talked his ear off, querying him about his life, his interests, his home and his guardians. They had even eaten together, food provided by Godwin, laid out on the operating table. Then the surgeon had disappeared after telling Edgar to feed the animals and clean up around the lab. Each creature had shrunk back from him as he approached and the panther, or whatever it was, had roared when he dropped two dead rats into its cage.

"Tomorrow will be a big day for you," Godwin had said when he returned. "We have a fresh corpse to work on and I want you to help."

"Hello, dear," says Annabel as Edgar enters the drawing room, having been brought there by Beasley upon her instructions. "I am just going out. In my role as a *new woman of the modern age . . .*" She pauses, smiling to herself. "I love that phrase, since it upsets your father so much—I am attending a meeting tonight populated exclusively by ladies where we shall debate the apparently *outrageous* idea that we of the so-called *weaker sex* should be able to cast a vote. Imagine that! Not but an hour ago, I also terrorized Alfred with the news that I am about to become a full member of the Fabian Society, with all those vegetarians who believe in the proper treatment of animals. He was not pleased. What a moment; it made my entire week. How was your day?"

"It was fine," he says. "How have things been here today?"

She is fixing a hat with a flower on it and smoothing down her dress, a navy blue one with only a small bustle. She believes the larger ones make women look like simple objects of desire for men. Edgar had blushed when she had told him that right in front of Alfred. She stops fussing with her outfit and gives him an exasperated look.

"Just fine? Is that all you have to say about your big day? What was it really like? Do tell. Was Dr. Brim mean to you, was there blood and the sawing of bones, was it too horrible? All that scientific stuff conducted by stiff scientific men. Your father is really not like that all the time, you know, Edgar. He is truly a lovely man, underneath, very tender with me."

Edgar clears his throat. "I shall be working with a Dr. Godwin, not my uncle."

"Godwin? I know that name. Oh, yes, some say he is the greatest surgeon in England, in the world. That's wonderful, Edgar. But he is a vivisectionist too, is he not?"

"Yes."

"Well, I do not much like that. Mr. Bernard Shaw of our Society has protested it, as has that young novelist, that fascinating man who writes those scientific romances that are all the rage,

The Invisible Man thing and that one about the time traveler . . ."

"H.G. Wells," says Edgar. "Dr. Godwin actually seems like a nice man. He was very nice to me. I shall describe him at length later, but I don't want to keep you. How have things been here, really?"

"Edgar, you have asked me that about a thousand times since yesterday. Why do you keep inquiring?"

"No reason."

"All is well. Well, well, well, well, well. There, is that good enough for you?"

It is time to tell her, thinks Edgar. He has to explain. She and Thorne need to be prepared. "You see . . . I . . . it's just that . . . have you noticed anything unusual—"

"Edgar, I am going to scream. These sorts of questions are all that come out of your mouth these days. There is NOTHING unusual around here . . . other than your deliciously unusual father. He is a man, you know, who both upsets and fascinates me. He bores and intrigues me."

Edgar doesn't want to hear more about that, so he embraces her and bids her farewell.

"Oh," she says as she picks her umbrella from a hook on the wall, "your father wants to see you later, up in the laboratory."

"Are you sure you have that correct, in the laboratory?"

"I know, rather strange, that. Beasley will set out your dinner at eight o'clock, and then you are to proceed to the lab for a meeting at nine o'clock, a *manly* meeting I am sure! And it will take place just as darkness falls!" She says the last few words in a mock-scary voice. "Alfred is such a nut! I like to pinch his derriere, you know, when he gets too serious."

Edgar blushes. Annabel Thorne leaves him with a kiss on the cheek.

Edgar eats alone in the dining room. He hears strange noises, but that is a regular thing in Thorne House. Their home seems to feel every gust of wind, every drop of rain, as if it were a human being groaning and shivering.

At the appointed hour he climbs those creaking stairs and comes to a halt in front of the laboratory door. There seems to be dead silence throughout the house now. *No Entry* reads the old sign directly in front of Edgar's face. He can't believe Thorne is actually inviting him in. A sudden loud sound explodes the quiet— a gong, going off nine times. It's the grandfather clock on the ground floor. When it finishes, Edgar knocks, and hears his adoptive father's voice ushering him in.

Alfred is standing halfway across the room, appearing unsure if he wants to approach his son or stay put. It is almost alarming to see the scientist looking uncertain. Without a word, he motions for the boy to follow him to his big desk. When they get there, Alfred makes as if he will go around it to sit in his chair, but then stops and leans clumsily against the bookcase. Edgar sees an entire row of novels near Alfred's head. He has never been able to figure out why his adoptive father, professed hater of fiction, has such books in his laboratory.

There is an awkward silence. Edgar realizes that none of the weapons he has twice seen in this room are there anymore. The tables are cleared off. But that other table, the one at the back in the shadows, still seems to hold a body. Edgar thinks he can smell it. He tries not to glance its way but does, and Alfred appears to notice.

"My boy, I called you here this evening in order to tell you something."

"Yes, sir."

"Edgar," he begins again. He never addresses his adopted son by his Christian name. "Edgar, I . . ."

Edgar can't help looking back toward the body, and it appears to move. Surely it was just the shadows playing tricks on his mind.

"Yes, sir."

"You and I . . . we seldom talk." Thorne pushes himself up from the bookcase and walks toward Edgar at a measured pace. "I hope your day went well."

"It did. I will be working with Dr. Godwin."

A cloud comes over Thorne's face. "Godwin?"

"Yes, sir."

"I see." He pauses then speaks quickly as if anxious to get the words out. "I am thinking of giving up the invention of weapons. I am not sure if such activity is a fit thing for me to do and I am not certain it is a good example to you." He stops. "In fact, I am not sure about scientific . . ."

"Pardon me, sir. What did you say?"

"Nothing, nothing, my boy, I merely wanted to tell you what I have just said and ask you about your day, and it seems you do not have much to contribute!" His voice is growing harsher, back to the tone Edgar recognizes. "Be on your way." He takes a few steps backward and leans against the bookcase again, knocking a volume onto the floor. He picks it up. Edgar can see Charles Dickens's name on the spine. He takes a deep breath.

"Why, sir, do you have novels on your shelves? I thought you disliked them."

Thorne takes a moment to respond and when he does his voice is softer again. "I find some of these books quite . . . curious. The Jekyll and Hyde story, for example, contains some interesting ideas." He straightens up and puts his shoulders back. "They are all nonsense, of course, simply fantasies, but one needs to know about them, I suppose. You must be on your way! It is getting late." He points in the direction of the door.

But Edgar is emboldened by his adoptive father's apparent moment of weakness—so he stares over at the body on the table, although he can't quite bring himself to ask what it is.

"It is getting late," repeats Thorne, more emphatically.

Edgar has had enough. He needs to know. He strides toward the body.

"Brim!" shouts Thorne and follows him.

The body is indeed moving. The shoulders below the severed neck are quivering! Edgar can feel a slight breeze and notices a small fan, powered by electricity it seems, blowing on the corpse. But it isn't a corpse. Edgar can see now that it is merely a model, made of some sort of plaster, with organs and blood vessels drawn onto the surface or glued to it, some sticking out, and a fake head removed from the trunk, fake neck bones and arteries evident.

"What is this?" asks Edgar.

"A human model made of plaster of paris, if you must know. I add and take away parts as I experiment. It is drying. Some of the loose bits flutter a little in the wind."

"What are your experiments about?"

"Oh, nothing in particular. I have ideas sometimes that . . ."

"What ideas?"

Thorne doesn't say anything for a moment, as if lost in thought. Then he finds his voice again. "My ideas are none of your business. Scientists do not need to explain themselves, especially to children. You were about to leave."

Edgar makes for the door quickly. When he gets there, he turns and sees that Thorne has followed him. They both reach for the knob at the same time and for an instant their hands touch. They both pull back.

"You know, Brim," says Thorne, "you are, legally, my son. And I wish you all the best in . . . in this new occupation. I have followed you and your life with more interest than you might think." He stiffens again. "Good evening, Brim!"

Edgar falls asleep too quickly that night.

In his dream, he is on a beach in the sunshine walking with Lucy and Tiger on either side of him, holding his hands, both of them smiling at him. But then there is a huge crack of thunder and bolts of lightning, and the girls let go of his hands, and he looks down the beach to the old woman running toward him from a distance. She is *alive*. He is sure of it. She will never let him go.

Edgar comes awake with the next thunderclap and realizes that the cannonading sound in his dream is real . . . and inside the house!

6

The Attack

E dgar sits bolt upright in the bed. Someone has kicked in the
front door with a sound like a gunshot, a blast from one of
Thorne's incredible weapons. And now it is as if a charging
elephant was thundering up the stairs! Edgar hears the thing reach
the first landing, outside Alfred and Annabel's bedroom; he hears
their door open and Annabel crying out for help. She must be
down there alone! He leaps from bed but then can't move, paralyzed with fear.

Now he hears a scream.

"Mother!"

She shrieks again, the way an animal does when brutally
attacked, then there is silence, and then footsteps thudding on the
stairs, but this time coming downward.

They are like the tread of a deer next to the others, which are
now booming upward again, something bumping and banging on
the steps behind.

"Annabel! My LOVE!" Alfred Thorne shouts.

Edgar begins to shake and drops to his knees and crawls back to the bed and scrambles under it. He lifts the floorboard he long ago loosened and reaches for the second-most important thing he hides beneath it. Lear's sword! He takes the big blade into his hands.

The footfalls approach each other on the landing outside Edgar's room, the louder steps arriving first. There's the sound of something—Annabel!—thrown to the floor and rolling up against his bedroom door. Edgar rushes forward and reaches the door but cannot turn the knob. His heart is in his mouth.

The descending steps arrive. "Unhand her, you fiend!" cries Alfred Thorne. And there are several quick steps and a huge crash, the sound of a big body striking the floor. The whole house shakes and Edgar hears a sort of inhuman roar, then several thuds, the dull splat of fists hitting flesh and bones, of a skull being crushed against hard boards, a few groans, a strangled gasp, and then silence.

Edgar presses his face to the door. Something walks across the floor and then it is breathing loudly just inches from his nose. It sounds huge and stinks of refuse. It roars again, like a lion after a kill. Edgar knows this bellow is for him. It has found him—its prime target.

But then there is the shout of other voices, the loudest Beasley's, and many footsteps running up the stairs. Edgar hears the thing hiss and begin to flee. There is an explosion of glass as if something has been thrown through the window at the end of the hall, the thunk of a body landing on the hard footpath two flights down, and then footsteps pounding away into the night.

Edgar puts his shoulder to the door and drives himself into it. It takes a good shove to open it even partway. The voices are nearing.

He feels the weight move from the door, like the body that was lying there is trying to get to its feet. But it falls again a stride away. Edgar tosses the sword back under the bed and pushes through the doorway. The landing is dark, lit only by approaching lanterns coming up the stairs, but he can make out something at his feet.

She isn't moving. He drops to his knees and takes her into his arms but when he does, he can feel her breath on his cheek and then the sensation of her stirring.

"Alfred?" she asks. "Alfred, I love you."

"It's Edgar."

"Where is he? Where is Alfred?"

The butler is now standing across the landing near a wall where a deformed body is lying still. Female servants are crying, their hands over their eyes and mouths. There is blood on the wall and a pool forming on the boards at their feet.

Annabel turns her head toward the light. "Alfred?" she asks.

"You shouldn't look over here, ma'am," says Beasley, moving his lantern away so that it glows upward toward his face, making his protruding brow ghoulish in the dark. "Mr. Thorne, ma'am . . . is dead."

Annabel's scream rockets through the house.

7

Godwin to the Rescue

Annabel couldn't say what it was. She was confined to her bed, speaking very little, only telling the police, and Edgar, that the intruder had seized her by throat and struck her the moment she left her room to investigate. She had seen the face for a second, but its features had vanished from her memory. She had gone semiconscious soon after the blow, aware only briefly of a man—she was certain it was a man, a large one—pulling her by the hair and an arm up the stairs. The next thing she knew she was awakening in Edgar's embrace.

"Alfred saved my life," she sobbed to her son the next day. "He gave his life for me!"

It seemed that it was true.

Thorne's skull had been crushed by a tremendous blow, a series of blows that the police described as being delivered by something "almost inhuman." It had trampled him and crushed his larynx to make sure of its work. The coroner at first believed that many of the injuries were caused by some sort of blunt instrument, but the shape and size of that weapon was more consistent with a fist. The police were searching every inch of London for the villain.

Edgar knew what it was, not *exactly* what it was, but he knew that a monster, *the* monster, had come to Thorne House to kill or at least wound him, to keep him off its trail. Edgar also knew that he had, in essence, been the cause of Alfred Thorne's death. He had, for all intents and purposes, murdered him.

"That is nonsense, my boy!" cried Godwin two days after that, when Edgar finally returned to work at the hospital. Then the good doctor actually took the boy into his arms and embraced him. It was a stiff hug, like something that made sense to do rather than one that was offered based on emotions and true sympathy. It seemed, though, that the intentions were admirable.

But Edgar, of course, hadn't told the surgeon the whole story. He had merely said that he felt the murder was his fault because he had not been able to come to the rescue.

Upon being told that his new apprentice would not be returning to the hospital on his second day of employment and the cause of his absence, Godwin had immediately swung into action, making all the arrangements for Thorne's funeral, encouraging Edgar to stay home with Annabel and comfort her.

Edgar sent a telegram to Kentish Town, telling the others what had happened. He tried to make it unemotional.

```
Thorne killed by intruder. Please be
careful. I will see you when I can.
```

But he imagined the terror his message would invoke.

"My boy, you must get back in the saddle, as it were," said Godwin. "It is the best thing for it. You shall merely do some odd jobs today, but tomorrow, we shall experiment. I delayed the arrival of the new corpse when you could not come. It shall be here in the morning." It seemed a strange thing to ask a bereaved person to do.

Though Edgar is desperate to know if Tiger and the Lears are safe, he feels duty-bound to stay near his widowed mother. He spends that evening sitting in a chair in Annabel and Alfred's room while she dozes off and on, every now and then saying a few words. The laudanum is helping her cope.

"That face!" she cries out twice.

"Describe it," says Edgar quietly the second time. "Do you remember it now?"

"No," she says sleepily. "Yes."

"Yes?"

"It was horrible, a beast. I don't want to say. I can't . . . I don't remember."

When Edgar returns to his room it is almost midnight. But he can't sleep. He knows the hag will come for him tonight.

He decides to go up to the lab. Alfred had rushed from it on the night the intruder had killed him, leaving the door wide open, and the key had been found in his pocket. Edgar had gone upstairs after Annabel had been put to bed, closed the door and locked it as a sign of respect. But he cannot resist the desire to finally explore it without interruption. Perhaps Thorne has hidden the weapons somewhere.

When Edgar enters the lab, he realizes that Thorne had left the huge blind up above fully drawn, so the stars are twinkling down upon him, the full moon making the room's contents clear before he even turns on a light. The tables are still bare, so Edgar searches in the closets and behind desks, desperate to find something he can use now that he is the last line of defense at Thorne House.

He eventually locates what he is looking for but their appearance makes his heart sink. There are many of them, a dozen or more—rifles and small cannons and handguns and even a deadly looking crossbow with a cartridge of arrows, as if designed to fire multiple times without pause. But each and every weapon has been smashed to bits. Alfred had destroyed them and with them went Edgar's chance of defending himself and Annabel. All he has now is Lear's big knife.

Edgar slumps down in the chair at the desk. It is large and comfortable. He stares up at the stars for a while, imagining Alfred doing the same, wondering what his thoughts were on that last night, just hours after they'd had their abbreviated talk. Alfred had been trying to tell him something, but he hadn't been able to do it.

Edgar opens the upper right-hand drawer of the desk. There's a stack of heavy paper folders inside. He pulls them all out. Each has a different title. WEAPONS. IDEAS. MY WORK. MY LIFE. The last one intrigues him. But then he notices another, at the bottom.

EDGAR BRIM, it says.

8

The Truth about Alfred Thorne

Edgar looks at the first page.

Notes about my SON, it begins.

He is touched by this, and it surprises him. It begins with simple facts: Edgar's birth date and the names of his real parents, Allen and Virginia. Then there is a day-by-day account, page after page, of everything Edgar did from the time he arrived at the Thornes', from funny things he said, to big words he employed, to his acts of kindness. Alfred dwells on what he calls the boy's "anxiety," his nightmares and his sleepwalking, and wishes he could do something about them. He worries about Edgar when he is away at school, even follows him north one time on the train. He curses the bullies who tormented him. He wishes he wasn't so stern in his manner and that he could talk with his son about the novels he is studying at school, novels that he himself is intrigued by. He speaks of his awareness that Allen Brim was fascinated with the idea that the monsters and evil creatures in novels might in some way be real. He wonders if Edgar thinks that too and worries that the boy's nightmares might be a result of that concern. He writes of being in the laboratory the night Edgar and Tiger stole the weapons, of watching them doing it from a hiding place in a closet! He had wanted to go with them, help them, and hates the stiff scientific coldness within him that keeps him from ever extending a hand, offering any sort of closeness, knowing what his son was up to, being by his side when it mattered.

Edgar can't believe it. He turns the final page and notices a sentence scribbled on the other side. *I wish I could tell him that I love him, the way I tell Annabel.*

With shaking hands, Edgar flips through some of the papers in the other folders, the ones about Thorne's weapons, his work and his life. Alfred speaks of a difficult childhood as a draper's assistant in Southwark, of his dissatisfaction with religion and his growing belief in science and the way it made him into "a man" and a "success." He speaks glowingly of Annabel, her beauty, her intelligence and free and open ways, and wishes he was more like her.

His notes about his weapons are much less interesting, filled with diagrams and equations. And the papers about his work in general are similarly dry until he deals with the last few years, where he begins to write of his doubts about science, his emerging interest in art and literature. Thorne wonders if there is more truth in art than science. *I don't really believe in the necessity of proof. It is invisible things that matter. The heart trumps the brain.* He frets that the weapons he has made have done so much harm, killed so many people, that he is growing into a sort of monster, that science has ultimately perverted him. He mentions that having a son has made him think twice about all of it. *Why am I so infernally incapable of speaking my heart to him? Why do I lead him, always, in the wrong direction?* He asks himself another question that gives Edgar pause. *Where is the soul? Might I locate some evidence of it in the body?* Edgar wonders if that comment has something to do with the plaster of paris model Thorne was working on in this lab.

Finally, Thorne repeats something twice, the second time in a bolder hand: *I must tell Edgar how I really feel.* **I must tell Edgar how I really feel.**

Annabel seems well enough in the morning to converse. Edgar knows that drawing anything out of her will be difficult, so he decides not to ask her again about what happened when Alfred was killed, at least at first. He wonders if she might be more forthcoming if they start out by simply speaking about her late husband.

"Tell me about my father, about Alfred," he says.

He is sitting on the side of the bed looking at her. She is snuggled under two down quilts, her head propped up on feather pillows. She actually smiles.

"He had a disease."

"You never told me."

"It's called being a man. He felt the need to be a man at all times. Go out on the streets of this city and you will see about half the population similarly afflicted. He couldn't show his affections to anyone or anything . . . except me." Tears well in her eyes. "He was often himself, his true self, while we were alone, but the rest of the time he pretended, about everything. To others, he acted as though he were constantly strong, always brilliant, forever without fear. But I think he was terrified of many things. He was afraid of losing me, of showing his love for you, of setting aside that world of science up there in that laboratory. Dogs bark when they are afraid and men puff out their chests. Me, I'm afraid of many things, Edgar, I'm not afraid to admit it, but now . . . my greatest fear has come to pass."

She sobs, the tears rolling down her cheeks. Edgar wishes he could hug her, but he thinks it improper at this moment, so he takes her hand. She squeezes his, lifts herself and hugs him tightly.

"I went upstairs and read some of the things he had written in his private books, mother. I know him better now. And I know, too, that he would be contented if I didn't become a doctor. He wrote of his doubts about science toward the end. I believe that, deep down, he wanted me to become something else. So, you see, I am free to do what I want now, with his blessing."

"No you aren't," says Annabel, a little sternly. She pushes him back and looks at him. "We will have no more income now, Edgar. It will be just you and me. Our savings will be gone in a half dozen years. He has set you up well at the London Hospital."

"But—"

"Shush. Listen to me. We have no choice. You have a position now, and as long as you do well this year, you will be admitted to the University of Edinburgh and proceed from there. Two of the most noble and esteemed men in the medical profession will recommend you and guide you, give you characters to any hospital in the kingdom when you are done at school. You cannot have a start like this in any other occupation. Oh, Edgar, you will be a doctor! An admired one, I am sure. You will use science the way it should be used. You will heal people! And you will provide for us. I know Alfred would believe in all of that."

She lies back in the bed. Edgar is stunned and gets up and walks toward the door, but she speaks again.

"You must work hard and do whatever Godwin asks of you."

He had intended to ask her much more. He had wanted her to try again to recall the face of the thing that killed Alfred, and he wanted to tell her about the monster, the revenant some call a vampire, that had been brought to life in Bram Stoker's *Dracula*, that he and Lucy had beheaded at the Royal Lyceum Theatre, and of the beast that had killed Hamish Lear, that was after him and his friends now, and that had, indeed, murdered her husband. He wanted to tell her that he believed that some of the creatures in famous books were real. And most of all, he wanted to warn her that the monster that had recently been here, might very well come back.

But both of them have had enough. He has an important day with Dr. Godwin and his fresh corpse and the very thought of it is making his heart pound. He walks out the door in silence.

9

Working the Corpse

Edgar Brim moves forthrightly along the hallway to the back of the London Hospital, determined not to be afraid. A voice in his head is repeating that there is nothing wrong with experimenting on an animal or even on a human body. It is for good. It will heal people. It will contribute to human knowledge. He must continue on at the hospital, regardless of what is asked of him—he must do it for Annabel. And the creature won't return to Thorne House when he isn't there, he tells himself, and won't pursue him here in this public building, and his friends are together and well-armed. But when he gets to the top of the stairs that lead into the basement, he begins to lose his nerve. Godwin and his fresh corpse are nearing. And once he is alone in the clammy basement hallway, he falters even more. Suddenly, a tough-looking man emerges out of the darkness and Edgar thinks he recognizes him. The man is big and scruffy. His thick head, onto which he is now pulling a soiled woolen cap, is shaved on either side of his temples, his nose looks like it has been broken many times, and a black mustache, narrow like a paint brush and only slightly thicker than the stubble that sprouts about his face, sits above a mouth that is slightly open in a grin. His teeth look like pieces of yellow marbles. He stuffs a fistful of pound notes into a pocket of his greasy pea coat, much too warm an item for this summer day, and looks up. His expression sends a cold sensation through Edgar, not just because of the evil intent that seems to be in it, but because Edgar has seen that look before. For a moment he can't recall where. Then he remembers—at Highgate Cemetery. This is the gravedigger. Something else disturbs Edgar: the man has come out of Godwin's laboratory.

"Good day, sir," says the fellow in a guttural voice.

Edgar doesn't respond.

Godwin is standing next to the operating table in the center of the lab, leaning over it with his back to the entrance. The lights above the table are on and create a startling brightness as if that area of the room were spotlighted, even though the rest of the lab is not particularly dark. Godwin turns when he hears Edgar close the door, and smiles. It is a dazzling expression. That handsome face, with its perfect skin and pearl-white teeth, almost glows. For an instant, in that light, Edgar feels like he can almost look through him, as if he can see his bones, his skull, beneath the skin.

"Ah, Edgar, come here." The great surgeon pats a spot next to him on the metal surface of the operating table. "We have a lovely specimen."

Edgar halts. He feels faint.

"Are you all right?"

"Yes, I'm fine."

"There is nothing to be afraid of, this is an elderly gentleman and as dead as a doornail."

"Wh-where," sputters Edgar, "where did you get him?"

Godwin hesitates. "Well, Edgar, you know, sometimes we have to contravene the law in order to do what is right for humanity. I have to procure the services, at times, of somewhat unsavory people."

"Like that man who was just here?"

"You saw him, did you?"

"Yes, and I have seen him before."

"Oh?" Godwin doesn't look pleased. He picks up a huge scalpel. He fumbles it and it clatters on the metal tray before he retrieves it. It makes Edgar jump. "Excuse me."

The corpse is still hidden behind the surgeon. At the slight angle from which Edgar has approached, all he can see are naked calves and feet, and the very top of the head. It is indeed an older man, a large one, with graying body hair.

"I wish I had a younger specimen, but this will do, for now. Beggars can't be choosers." Godwin offers another one of his strange hollow laughs. "Where did you first see the gentleman who brought us this find?"

"In Highgate Cemetery. I was there for a funeral. He was the gravedigger."

"Well, yes, I believe he does that as well. Graft is his name."

"Where did he get . . . this?" Edgar repeats.

"I believe it was Highgate too, now that you mention it, though he doesn't tell me much and I don't ask many questions."

Edgar remembers the gravedigger's way of examining Lear's grave, the whole area around the plot, as if remembering it for future reference.

71

"Come closer."

The boy doesn't move.

"Come on, it won't bite, though it is still fresh. The fresher the corpse, the more I pay and Graft certainly loves money. This one was buried within the last few days."

Edgar edges forward and as he does, more of the naked body is revealed. He sees a large head like a lion's, a big black and gray-streaked beard . . . and an arm missing at the shoulder socket!

"Oh God!" cries Edgar and staggers. Godwin reaches out and seizes him.

"Now, now, my boy, calm yourself. This is for science, for good. Look at the body. There is nothing evil about it. This is one of God's creatures."

Edgar looks again and sees that the corpse actually has both arms: the body was just twisted slightly sideways and Godwin had been in front of one appendage. The corpse isn't his dear, deceased professor. Edgar steadies himself, holding on to the table. He notices for the first time that there are gutters running along either side of the surface, like troughs. He wonders what they are for.

"Good for you, my boy! Ready?"

Edgar nods.

"There is a lab coat on a hook by the Elephant Man's door and a sink near it. Wash your hands and return."

Edgar takes his time. Godwin smiles indulgently when he comes back.

"Stand right next to me," he says.

Edgar moves up close to the corpse but can barely bring himself to look down at it. The skin appears gray.

"I am rather low on organs. That is why I ordered this specimen. We are going to remove all of his and place them in jars of formaldehyde to preserve them. Later, I shall slice up these innards and examine them with my microscope, something I will treat you to as well. The human body is a marvelous thing. You shall see. There is no use being squeamish about it. That does no good at all. I will crack the breastbone with that large instrument you see closest to you on the tray. Might you hand it to me?"

Edgar sees that several instruments have been added to the tray today. They have been polished so they are gleaming, as if someone took a long time at the job. Most prominent are a couple of saws. He imagines them cutting off a limb, perhaps a big leg bone, but prays he won't have to endure that. At this moment, however, Godwin is referring to a huge pair of pliers with business ends that look as sharp as razors. Edgar picks it up and hands it to the eager surgeon.

"That will be my tool to start with. I shall stick it in near the stomach just below the thorax, penetrate the skin there and cut upward with my clever big scissors in the middle of the rib cage, severing the breastbone from stem to gudgeon, as it were. Your tool shall be this large scalpel." He offers the instrument he had been holding in his other hand to Edgar. "Take it up, please."

Edgar reaches out and grips the largest scalpel he has ever seen.

"Note the mark I have drawn upon his skin." There is a thick black line, straight as an arrow, running from the corpse's throat down toward his nether regions. "You shall cut downward as I make my merry way upward. When we are done we shall have this lovely chap split wide open. We shall then peel back the skin and observe the smorgasbord of delights before us. I shall teach you what each item is and why it is placed where it is, its function as part of the human mechanism. But we need to do this quickly, for I want the organs relatively fresh and into the jars lickety-split. Edgar, you look a little green. Are you sure you are up to our task?"

"Yes, sir." Edgar knows he must do this. He is thinking of Annabel and Alfred, of her descent into poverty if he fails. A doctor cannot turn away.

"Good for you. There will be time afterward to observe the spinal cord and its extraordinary design, and we will take off the head too, crack the skull and remove the brain, God's eternally fascinating gift to humanity. There will be another important removal too, though it would be indelicate to name it." Godwin coughs and looks down. "But that lovely endeavor is still a few hours away. We must concentrate on our first chores. Make sure you stab the scalpel into this gentleman far enough to cut through his epidermis and subcutaneous fat, then slice downward forcefully enough to cut him all the way to the pubis bone, but not violently enough to damage any precious interior gems."

"All right."

"I beg your pardon, I didn't quite hear that."

"I said, all right."

"Splendid. Let us begin."

Godwin has his sharp pliers into the corpse in an instant and is cutting upward through the bone with a cracking sound before Edgar can even begin. But then Edgar thrusts the scalpel in, keeping his eyes open just a little. He begins tearing downward, making sure he is following the black line, before entirely closing his eyes. His fingers are wet now. Next to him, he hears the breast-bone cracking and snapping as Godwin works his way upward, breathing heavily with the effort. It is obviously hard work. Edgar has the easy part.

"Wonderfully done!" exclaims the surgeon. His assistant opens his eyes. There is embalming fluid oozing out of the corpse here and there, a little running down the side of the rubbery flesh and gathering in the gutters on each side of the table. The thick liquid is pink with flecks of red. But there is very little smell. Edgar wonders about those gutters. Why are they there when so little fluid gathers in them? Then he imagines this human being opened and carved up just after it had been killed, before it was infused with fluid. There would be blood everywhere, pools of it, and this unusual table and its gutters would be perfectly designed. But Godwin would never have reason to do anything like that. Edgar looks down at the eviscerated man on the table and tries not to throw up. He tells himself to think of the corpse as merely a suit of skin that this human being inside wore in life, like the skin a snake would shed.

"If you are feeling faint, my boy, then just remember that the human body is more like a machine than anything else, and this machine has merely stopped working. It is like a complicated clock that recently struck its midnight."

Edgar wonders how anyone can think that.

"Its soul," says Godwin and hesitates, "its soul . . . is gone!" He stares off into the distance for a moment and then shakes his head, as if to clear it. "Now get those jars down from the shelf above us and let us commence to harvesting these beautiful organs!"

———

A few hours later, the deed is done. All the innards are in the jars, the head has been removed, the spongy brain taken out and preserved, and Godwin has even peeled off several large squares of skin for further investigation. He works energetically and robotically, without much sign of either repulsion or glee. He is merely getting an important job done. Edgar, on the other hand, has been keeping himself from retching with a great effort of will. As they near the end, he cannot bring himself to even glance at the sordid remains on the table.

"Now, you shall clean up this mess!" exclaims Godwin. He looks down at the fluid and carcass and then at Edgar. "That was just a jest, my boy. Do not worry, I shan't ask you to do more. Graft, of course, will come in and take away what is left here. I pay him another few shillings to do such things. I am not sure what he does with all of this."

Edgar is aware of the rumors that body snatchers sometimes sell human detritus to the London Zoo for the animals to consume. He tries very hard not to imagine it.

At the door, Godwin offers a handshake. But he seems to see the strain still in his assistant's eyes and briefly embraces him again. It is just as awkward as their first hug and equally unexpected, but also, Edgar thinks, a remarkably kind thing to do.

"Thank you, sir."

"Not at all, my boy. I know that was difficult, but you came through with flying colors. Keep bearing in mind that what I learn from this poor gentleman will help many others. Even the skin will be well used. I do not know if you are aware of this, but I have some repute as a skin surgeon as well, or what some folks these days are calling 'plastic' surgery. I actually replaced much of one man's face not long ago. If you could have looked into his eyes and seen the joy when he was able to show his visage to the world for the first time, it would fill your heart with joy and with admiration for the world of scientific medicine. I am sure my work will lead to great advances in the future. Some day we may be able to make entirely new men and women out of ourselves, if needed!"

It had been agreed that Edgar would walk home from the hospital every day too. Thorne had insisted that it was good for him. The first day, it had been getting dark during his journey and the trip had been rather harrowing, through the tough streets of the East End, then into the semi-deserted Old City and on into the West End and home. But today, he is walking in bright sunshine. He tries to convince himself that there is some sun on the horizon in his life too, despite what he had to do today and may have to experience in the future and despite the fear of attack that hangs over him and his loved ones. Perhaps the worst is behind him. But he isn't convinced. The monster has struck at them three times. It obviously knew where they were. Really, why wouldn't it come again? But isn't it after *him* more than the others, as Lear once said? That isn't a helpful thought. He wonders if he should tell Dr. Godwin about all of this and seek that brilliant and kind man's advice and help. He also again wonders if he should go north to Kentish Town to see Tiger and Lucy and Jonathan. But he knows his place remains at home with Annabel. He will see them the minute he has a chance.

———

"How is she?" he asks Beasley as soon as he is in the door. The butler takes his hat and coat.

"She is rallying somewhat, though she has slept a good deal today. She is a brave soul, sir, and has asked that she be given no more laudanum. She also asked if you would go in to her the moment you arrived."

He finds her propped up in bed under the quilts again with an array of pillows behind her head, fingering in one hand the cross on a necklace that Alfred gave her and holding her Bible in the other, though she isn't reading it. Her face brightens slightly when she sees Edgar.

"Come sit with me," she says weakly.

"Are you finding any consolation there?" asks Edgar, nodding at the good book.

"Oh, you know me, my child, I'm not the world's biggest believer. You also know that I hate all these new ideas about the whole thing being true, every word of it, every single line of our Bible. That is impossible. No one has ever truly believed that. I think it is a story, a marvelous one really, with a deep goodness and truth within it. So, I've been reading it a little, just the New Testament, for I abhor all the horror in the Old, all the murder and mayhem and monsters. And it has helped me to be not absolutely hopeless. I still believe in happiness and kindness and that human beings are capable of such things . . . even with what happened to Alfred." She sobs and then gathers herself. "People say there can't be a God when bad things happen, but I know that is childish, actually quite stupid, and I'm trying not to think that way."

"I know my father was a good man despite his rough exterior," says Edgar.

"Thank you for saying that, my son, and for calling him by that name." She smiles. "He didn't care for religion at all, couldn't believe in anything that was simply spiritual. He couldn't entirely detach himself from that need for proof about everything. Proof, proof, proof, such is the quest of a man of science. But he never needed proof of our love. He just knew it existed. Formless as it was, and is, it was more powerful than any of his science. I think he knew that in the end." She looks terribly sad again and glances away, but then she turns back to Edgar. "How was your day?"

He wonders what he should say. "It was fine."

"There's that word again."

"Well, it was a little difficult. We did some work in the laboratory."

"Tell me more."

"Another time."

He wonders if he should ask his next question, and then decides he must.

"Do you feel up to thinking further about what our intruder looked like? It would be very helpful to the police. They, and I, and I'm sure you, would dearly like to see this beast brought to justice."

"Oh, I don't know," she says. "Whoever he is, he has to live with what he did, one way or the other. Hanging him or whatever might be done to him won't really be justice. It will just be another evil."

"But—"

"But, yes, I am up to thinking about what he looked like, in truth, I have been thinking about it a great deal. The parts in the good book that I read gave me some courage. I have actually drawn a picture of the intruder's face. Beasley brought me some colored chalk."

Annabel Thorne is a good amateur artist and portraiture is a particular talent of hers. She often entertained Edgar when he was younger with funny images of animals or characters from stories, making sure there wasn't a single monster among them.

"It's on the bedside table."

When Edgar looks at the drawing his heart begins to pound. Annabel had indeed worked color in. The skin on the face before him is so sallow that it is almost yellow and it seems tight on the bone, stretched over a big, square visage that makes it look like the muscles and arteries beneath it are on the surface. The black eyes are set deep in gray, dun-colored sockets and pearl-white teeth gleam in a horrid expression inside a shriveled mouth held in a tight line by black lips.

"My mind must be playing tricks on me," says Annabel. "He can't have looked like that. I have drawn a monster."

10

Back in the Lab

A
nnabel insists that Edgar not take the drawing to the police. She thinks her picture is just too ridiculous and worries that it might be considered the work of a "hysterical" woman, a word she says men like to use when describing her sex. But Edgar fears that her drawing is accurate and asks if he can have it.

"You may," she says, "as long as you keep it to yourself."

Now that Edgar is the man of the house and Annabel is incapacitated, he can do as he likes at Thorne House. As soon as he leaves her bedroom, he asks Beasley to have a footman take messages to two addresses as fast as possible: one to Kentish Town and the other to Drury Lane. And while he waits for responses he returns to Thorne's laboratory.

He pulls the big blinds back, revealing the early evening sky, and walks around the room, finally seating himself at the table with the plaster corpse. He takes out Annabel's drawing. It gives him the shivers. This is what is after him and his friends. This is what came here and murdered Alfred Thorne. He can't look at it for very long, so he lifts his head and stares into the fake eyes on the fake head of the fake corpse.

"Alfred was looking for your soul," he says quietly to it.

He notices something about the plaster body that he hadn't observed before. The different parts look like they've been made separately and then attached. Edgar sees now that the markings on the plaster's surface are especially detailed near each joint, indicating how the bones and the arteries might functionally connect. There is a stack of medical texts on the table and, strangely, among them is a novel—*Frankenstein* by Mary Shelley. The presence of this story next to the corpse and severed body parts, even though they aren't real, shakes him a little. He remembers his father reciting from that book, its horrible scenes coming down through the heat pipe in Raven House and into his brain. No story ever frightened him as much as it.

He recalls that Vincent Brim had this novel on his desk as well. There was another one too. Edgar goes to Alfred's bookshelf and finds it, the title written in a black Gothic slash on the spine: *The Island of Doctor Moreau*, by H.G. Wells. It has a contemporary cover, sandy with red lettering. There's an island drawn on it, sitting there in a yellow sea, looking black and spooky. Edgar knows all about this author. He is relatively young, once a science teacher people say, who writes stories that are combinations of science and fiction. They are fantastic stories, full of amazing ideas and frightening too. Wells is considered by many to be the most modern and imaginative man in the empire—his *The War of the Worlds*, a story about Martians invading earth, is the talk of London and everywhere else at this very moment, running every month in *Pearson's Magazine*.

Like so many other readers, Edgar can hardly wait to devour each installment to discover what is going to happen next. But this book in his hand, this *Island of Doctor Moreau*, is the one Wells novel Edgar has never been able to face. Too many reviewers have called it gruesome and repulsive, disgusting in a way that no novel has ever been. He remembers that the review in the *Times of London* insisted it should be kept away from young people. But now, sitting in Thorne's laboratory next to the body parts on the table, rattled by the fact that both his uncle and Alfred Thorne had this very same tale at hand, and worried about what he will or won't hear from his friends and little William Shakespeare, he picks it up. At first, he hesitates to open it, a wave of fear passing through his stomach like the butterflies he so often used to feel. Edgar Brim cannot read a book or look at a painting or see a play without feeling as though he were part of it, inside its very textures, on its stage, between its pages. And the great sensation novels are the worst: they take him to worlds that terrify him to his soul. But his father had told him to face those fears. *Do not be afraid.* It is the best advice there is.

He turns to chapter one and begins to read. He enters the story. It starts with a shipwreck, like many other adventure tales, and Edgar becomes a man left alone on a small boat on a vast ocean. He can smell the salt water and feel the waves wafting him up and down, and a sense of hopelessness as he stares at the endless horizon. But when he is rescued by a strange ship and crew, everything gets worse. The story descends into scenes of horror. Edgar is taken to an exotic island where a scientist, a vivisectionist named Dr. Moreau, lives and works. And what he is doing there is evil beyond description.

Lightning flashes through the dark sky above the lab and Edgar starts, then there's thunder, and rain begins to pelt out of the black heavens. The corpse seems to glow in the flicker of the lightning. Edgar walks to Thorne's desk, turns on his lamp and returns to the novel.

His character grows more and more terrified. "*I was convinced now, absolutely assured, that Moreau had been vivisecting a human being.*" But Moreau is doing much more than that. He is *making* human-like beings . . . out of animals. And he is doing so in a building called the House of Pain. From his room next door, Edgar hears the animals cry out in the night as Moreau works upon them.

There is another bang, but this time it comes from five floors down. Edgar leaps to his feet, dropping *The Island of Doctor Moreau* on the desk.

In a second he is running out the door, his heart thudding and his mind in a whirl. The creature has come back! He must save Annabel! He must save himself too, for it has surely come to finish him, to prevent him from ever speaking a word about its existence. It was scaring the others, but does it mean him lethal harm? Moreau's evil face is in Edgar's mind as he races down the first flight and then the second on a winding descent into Thorne House. He stops at Annabel's door. All is quiet, and there is no sign of forced entry, or indeed any evidence that anything out of the ordinary is happening at all. He cracks open the door to hear her softly breathing.

Then a dark figure is rushing up the stairs at him, drenched in rain, clutching something in its hand. It's a towering thing and Beasley is on its tail.

The figure comes to a halt. It is the large boy who was sent out with the messages a few hours earlier.

"Forgive me, sir," pants the butler. "It appears we have startled you."

Edgar catches his breath and tries to look calm.

"Not at all."

"You said you wanted the replies the minute they arrived. Griffin waited at each address for a response, as you said, and then rushed in out of this thunderstorm and I sent him right up to you. I'm afraid he slammed the door a little when he entered. Once I sent him up, I realized he might not present the best figure. Perhaps I should have brought the replies myself?"

"Not to worry," says Edgar, taking the wet papers from the soaked boy, who smiles sheepishly. "You may both go."

They head down the stairs, Beasley chiding Griffin, who is dripping all over the steps.

Edgar waits until they have disappeared and then opens the first letter.

We are well. Received your note saying we must meet immediately. I fear what you will say, since you are in such haste. I agree that it is wise, as you suggest, for us to gather at the Crypto-Anthropology Society at midnight. All my best, Lucy.

He takes up the second.

Have read mysterious missives from both yourself and Miss Lear and shall be delighted to convene an ad hoc meeting of

the esteemed Society at midnight, shall alert the wondrous
Messrs. Sprinkle, Winker and Tightman. It sounds like some
excitement is afoot!

It was signed, with great flourish: *Cordially yours, William*
Shakespeare, Esquire.

When Edgar leaves Thorne House a few hours later, the rain is still coming down hard, as if God isn't pleased about something. Edgar doesn't want to use the family carriage or a cab, doesn't want to leave any trail of where he is going, so he walks, umbrella in hand, a poor refuge from the deluge. He keeps his head down most of the way and doesn't look at the strange people he passes, some of whom come out of the dark to call out with pleas or shouts or taunts—they are like characters in scientific romances who live in fantastic storms.

Big Ben strikes midnight as he is crossing a nearly deserted Trafalgar Square and he rushes the rest of the way. His friends have already arrived, every one looking frazzled. Shakespeare is in his usual spot at the center of the table and they have all left chairs for the three imaginary members.

Thorne's powerful rifle is propped against a wall behind Jonathan, and Edgar can see the pistol bulging in his coat.

Lucy is well turned out, as usual, wearing a dark-blue dress and hat, but the look on her face is even sadder than her colors. She tries to offer Edgar a smile, but the expression she gives him is weak. Hatless Tiger, who looks as though she is still recovering from her injury and has been loaned the plain brown dress she wears, merely nods. Her black eyes don't have their normal sparkle.

Only Jonathan gets to his feet. He strides over to Edgar and takes his hand and thumps him on the shoulder. "Our condolences for your loss, Brim." But that is all even Jon can bring himself to say. He returns quickly to the table and sits.

Shakespeare hasn't taken any notice of Edgar's entry. Instead, he is conversing with the invisible Winker, Tightman and Sprinkle, nodding gravely at things he imagines they are saying. There is a stack of newspapers piled next to his right hand.

"Oh, yes," he says finally, turning to Edgar. "Master Brim, it is so nice that you could grace us with your presence this evening. My colleagues and I have several theories we must put upon the table, well not actually upon the table, one doesn't set theories on tables, but in the air as it were, thrust from our minds and mouths and into the intellectual maelstrom . . . and then we have several news items we shall all want to peruse. But first I shall personally call the meeting to order, say the oath, sing the Queen (solo, mind you) and set things in—"

"This is what it looks like," says Edgar, ignoring Shakespeare. He takes Annabel's drawing out of his pocket and flattens it on the table, pushing it into the center so all can see. Everyone stares at it for a moment. Edgar regards it again too, this time noticing something that he hadn't observed before: Annabel has drawn something on the intruder's neck in faint lines. They look like cuts or perhaps stitches. It is almost as if she is drawing a head that has been attached to the neck.

"Oh, my goodness!" says Shakespeare. "Do you see it, Mr. Winker? Do you have any thoughts, Mr. Tightman? Are you thinking what I'm thinking, Mr. Sprinkle?"

"I don't recognize it," says Tiger. "I still can't recall if my attacker's face was visible."

"It doesn't look like anything well-known," says Lucy, "anything famous."

"That's not a vampire," says Jonathan, "though he is a rather handsome chap."

"No, not a vampire, nothing like that," says Edgar, "but as for it being well-known, I—"

"I have a theory, a possibility, a postulation," says Shakespeare in a frantic interruption. "I tried to tell you this before, back at the Lear home." He starts to his feet and waves his hands in the air, talking fast as usual. "I have been in the deepest of discussions with my colleagues here about it for some time and I shall put it to you all at the conclusion of another sentence or two. What you see before you is the likeness of a very famous monster, indeed."

"Not this again," says Jonathan under his breath.

"What did you say, young man? You not only interrupted me but Mr. Winker was about to add something."

Jonathan jumps to his feet too. "We need to be serious. There is no one in the room but the five of us and I could care less whether or not this creature is famous or was once written up in a novel or any other hogwash like that!"

"Hogwash?" says Shakespeare, looking extremely puzzled.

"All I care about is identifying what it is and where it is and whatever it is capable of, and either finding some way to get out of its path, though as you all know I think that ill-advised . . . or exterminating it as quickly as we can."

Shakespeare looks heartbroken. "Hogwash?" he repeats. "I was simply going to say that I, my esteemed colleagues and I, have a good idea of the identity of this beast that attacked Mr. Tilley—"

"Miss," says Lucy.

"No, it didn't miss, Miss Lucy, not at all. It has now struck twice against us and done so very effectively. But it is my theory, my contention, my sacred supposition, that this very creature has struck many times in the past and you have merely been awakened to its existence." His eyes are on fire. He violently pats the stack beside him. "I bear with me a collection of newspaper articles that I have culled over the years, encircling in red ink the incidents in question, attesting to the activity of the beast which is now in pursuit of you!"

"And it is?" asks Edgar.

"A very beastly beast indeed!"

"And it is?" asks Tiger.

"A villainous, insidious—"

"Stop running your gob and name it before I throttle you!" cries Jonathan.

"Well, if you put it that way, then I shall tell you." The little man pauses.

"Oh for God's sake!" says Jonathan.

"It is Mr. Hyde!"

Jonathan laughs and William Shakespeare glares at him.

"Of Dr. Jekyll and Mr. Hyde infamy from Mr. Stevenson's novel?" asks Lucy.

"The very one."

"And what leads you to this brilliant deduction?" blurts Jon.

"Why, thank you for your compliment, Mr. Lear. That is more like it! I knew you would come round!"

Jonathan throws up his hands.

"I spoke to Mr. Robert Louis Stevenson some time ago whilst conducting the most delicate research on behalf of our Society into his motivations for writing the Hyde novel."

Edgar could have sworn that Shakespeare once admitted that he had never met Stevenson.

"This is nonsense," says Jonathan, still pacing. "Why are we still talking about this sort of thing?"

"Because grandfather, for one," says Lucy in a very quiet voice, "was convinced that the creature he killed on the moors was Grendel from the *Beowulf* story."

"No he wasn't. He wasn't sure."

"But it was a *creature* of some sort, like something from someone's imagination."

"And then," says Tiger, "the thing that first came after us appeared to be almost directly from the pages of *Dracula*."

"But it wasn't, not exactly," says Jon.

"But it made its way into that novel," says Lucy, "because it was the living thing from which the vampire legends came. And from the moment we killed it, something else has pursued us."

"That is the spirit!" cries Shakespeare.

"We cannot discount the possibility," says Edgar, "that this creature also has some sort of presence in some novel or story, because that may be our only lead . . . despite the apparent insanity of the idea."

"Insanity?" says Shakespeare.

"Why do you think it may be Hyde?" asks Lucy.

"Are you really asking him that?" says Jonathan.

"Because of what Mr. Stevenson told me when I spoke to him," replies the little man. "He used to spend much of his time in the South Pacific you know, amongst the natives. But he came back to England every now and then. I read in the papers one day, this is a good five or six years ago, that he was in London visiting his publisher. So I went to that publisher's office and waited for him to appear."

"Did Stevenson tell you what a lunatic you were when he realized why you were there?" asks Jonathan.

"No, he didn't mention that. But I did ask him, point blank, whether, as legend had it, he dreamed up Edward Hyde in a nightmare. 'Might that be inaccurate, apocryphal?' I asked him. 'Might the TRUTH be that you actually knew or heard of someone like this strange creature in real life?' I queried him. Stevenson was a strange-looking one, you know, wore long hair and a mustache and goatee like a Musketeer, and he was so slight, so sickly looking that he appeared to be a walking cadaver, a dead man alive. He looked at me with an expression of horror, as if I had unearthed some terrible secret, as if he were seeing something in his imagination. And then he walked away without saying a word."

"Because he was then certain you were a lunatic," adds Jonathan quietly.

"These stories I have encircled in these newspapers are about beastly attacks that have occurred over the years where people were brutalized at nighttime and the perpetrator was never found. They are so much like the two attacks you have experienced! Sudden aggressive encounters with terrible body blows! And strangulation may be involved. And in the novel, Hyde tramples a child without an ounce of pity! He tramples another man too, crushing his spine, his limbs! Your creature did the same to Thorne!" Shakespeare leaps toward the bookcase behind him and runs his finger along the volumes on a shelf there. "Ah!" He pulls out *The Strange Case of Doctor Jekyll and Mr. Hyde.* The little man turns to the others. "Look at your drawing and listen." He sits, searches the pages, then reads: "He is not easy to describe. There is something wrong with his appearance; something displeasing, something downright detestable . . . he gives a strong feeling of deformity . . . the hand that lay on my knee was corded and hairy." Shakespeare drives his forefinger into his mouth to wet it and flips a few pages to find the next line, which he delivers with great drama. ". . . It wasn't like a man."

He snaps the book shut.

"You have proved nothing," says Jonathan. "That's just a story, like all the others."

"What about the fact that Hyde is a LONDON monster? THE London monster! Who always strikes at night! That is what yours does too! Does it not seem to be living here? Right in the center of the city, ready to attack the lot of you the moment you left the Lyceum Theatre with that vampire's blood on your hands!"

Jon says nothing.

"I tell you that you are seeking something very much like Mr. Hyde!"

During the silence that follows, Edgar's mind is working fast. We are indeed dealing with a brutal London creature with a face like a monster, he thinks, one that prowls at night and delivers thunderous blows and batters his victims, like Mr. Hyde. Despite Shakespeare's lunacy, Edgar wonders if his guess might be a good one. But something doesn't seem quite right about it, though he isn't sure why. And another image from another book keeps coming to Edgar's mind, probably because of that plaster corpse with the mismatched body parts, and perhaps because of his work with Dr. Godwin too. And what about the other book, the one that lies on Vincent Brim's desk, the one Edgar had just read in Alfred Thorne's lab, about the man who made half-human beings out of animals in the House of Pain? Those little stitches on the neck of Annabel's drawing . . .

"There is a second author who is bothering me these days," mutters Shakespeare. "He has ideas about murderous invisible men and time travel into a horrifying future and creatures from outer space, and even a story about someone who makes human-like creatures. Where, in God's name, does he get such ideas?"

"H.G. Wells," says Edgar, startled. It was as if Shakespeare had been reading his mind.

"Indeed!" exclaims the little man.

"We are losing focus again," says Tiger. "Whatever and wherever this thing is and whatever it is planning, we must decide for once and for all whether or not we need to lie low or attack it. I vote we seek it out and destroy it."

"So do I!" exclaims Jonathan, smiling at her. Then he looks toward Edgar and silently mouths, "I told you so."

"I don't know," says Lucy. "I just don't know."

Edgar loves that Lucy always tells the truth. There's no pretense about her when it matters. If she is afraid, she just says so. He knows he rarely has that sort of courage, and that Jonathan never does, nor does Tiger. He wishes he had such clarity. "First, we need to somehow observe it," he says, "and then decide IF we can kill it. We can't be rash."

"And if we can't destroy it?" asks Lucy.

"Let us not worry about that until we track it to its lair!" shouts Shakespeare, leaping to his feet. "Then, brave men and women we are, we shall slay it like Godly knights destroying a dragon!"

"Ah yes," mutters Jonathan, "I can see you on the scene now, your little posterior wiggling up and down . . . as you run away."

"What did he say?" asks Shakespeare.

"First, it killed grandfather," says Lucy, ignoring the little man's question, "then it offered a warning and then it went further. What does that tell us?"

"The Thorne House attack was a warning too," says Edgar.

"How can you say that? It was so much more!" says Jonathan.

"It could have come into my room, but it paused, just after it had brutalized Annabel and murdered Alfred Thorne both within my earshot. It was sending a message again, but this time a more extreme one, and with a chosen audience, a message delivered directly to me."

"Professor Lear said," says Tiger, "that you hated monsters in a different way. You *chose* to hunt them. Perhaps these creatures see you as our leader?"

"Whatever it is and whatever it wants," says Jonathan, "it is escalating things!"

"Let us all think about what we have discussed tonight," says Edgar, "about Mr. Hyde, about the likeness in this drawing, about this Wells fellow and his stories, about the manner of the attacks on us, and let us meet here again tomorrow night with a specific plan of action. Everyone bring an idea. We will choose the best one . . . and do it!"

But Edgar already has an idea. And he has some questions for Dr. Godwin.

11

Godwin

Edgar doesn't mention a word to Annabel about the curious marks on the villain's neck in her drawing when he says good-bye to her in the morning. His mind is fixed on what he is going to say to Dr. Godwin.

But when he gets to the lab he is distracted by the fact that the good surgeon is holding a bunny down by the neck on the operating table.

"Ah, Master Brim, I was waiting for you. We are going to cut off this little one's limbs while it is alive and see how it reacts. I need to see how the bones, the blood vessels and arteries, and the nervous system work under these conditions, during trauma, while life is still in it."

Edgar gulps, but he steps forward.

"The first thing we shall do is tie it down. I have made these little straps that you see fastened to the table. We will place Mr. Rabbit here on his back and tie him so the larger straps are tightened around his shoulders and his hind legs, and the four smaller ones pin him down about a quarter of the way along each appendage. We must cinch them all up so they are extremely tight since he must not move whilst we are severing."

Edgar is frantically trying to think of an excuse for saving the animal or at least getting himself out of the room before the dismembering begins. But he can't think of anything.

"Hold him," says Dr. Godwin.

Edgar puts both hands around the rabbit's thumping little chest and belly, but it squirms loose and is about to leap off the table when Godwin seizes it in an iron grip, almost squishing it into the cold metal surface. It whistles and screams.

"There, there now, little one, do your duty," says Godwin. He offers Edgar one of his smiles. He has many of them, though all seem rather awkward. Still, the surgeon is a remarkable man, never given to anger. Edgar thought he would have shouted at him for nearly letting the bunny loose, but he didn't bat an eye. Godwin takes over, keeping the rabbit pinned with one big hand and strapping it down tightly with the other. He cinches up all the straps. The rabbit squirms and cries out but it can barely move now.

"Hand me one of those saws," says Godwin.

Edgar can't move either. He is thinking of the face on the rabbit in *Alice's Adventures in Wonderland*, the fantastic little animal with the pocket watch who is always late.

"I see," says Godwin. "This is not unexpected either. You are a fine young man and this disturbs you. And so it should, on the surface. But remember what I have been telling you about the needs of humanity, science and medicine. This creature is giving its life to all of that, a noble thing indeed." He pauses. "My boy, I have had children come to me with severed arms and legs from industrial accidents, brave men with exploded limbs from the battlefield. I have done my best for them. But one day I would like to do better. I should like to re-attach limbs. Think of a small child, a little boy, without an arm or a leg, think of me replacing it and the smile on his face for the rest of his life . . . then look at this rabbit."

"Sir, might you just give me a moment. Let me sit down. Perhaps you could sit with me. Let me gather myself and then I will continue."

"An excellent idea from an excellent young man with a good heart."

Edgar smiles a genuine smile.

They sit at Godwin's desk across the room and say nothing for a moment. Finally, Edgar speaks.

"Sir, I think it is certainly an admirable thing that you are aiming to do, to replace human limbs."

"Thank you, Master Brim. I am glad you concur."

"How far do you think you might take it?"

"I am not sure I follow you."

"Perhaps you will be able to replace a limb, but what about a foot, the toes or something even more difficult, the hands and the fingers. Could you replace them so they might function as good as new?"

"A challenging task, for certain, full of intricate work based on many, many hours of experimentation, but I have no doubt about the capacity of the human brain to achieve almost anything."

"Well, sir, in a sense that actually leads to my next question . . . what about the brain, what about replacing it?"

Godwin doesn't answer immediately. "That," he finally says, "is another situation entirely. Then you are entering a sort of forbidden realm. The brain is the seat of the mind and the mind is the seat of everything. You would be . . . you would be making a new human being." A wild look flares in Godwin's eyes for a moment and then subsides. "But that is nonsense, Edgar. We are not talking about replacing the human mind here."

"Would you . . . would you ever think of going that far yourself?"

Godwin pauses again. Then he gets to his feet and strides back toward the table. "This is nonsense! It is mere speculation and hypothesis." He stops suddenly, as amazed at his slight anger as Edgar is. "Pardon me, Master Brim, but I have been accused of considering this sort of thing and it frustrates me." He offers another smile, going a bit overboard this time, a huge toothy grin, which he quickly adjusts. "There are many articles in the newspapers about vivisection that are uninformed and filled with emotion and have no place in a scientific discussion. Our critics sometimes actually bring up this 'making a human being' nonsense, as if I were in favor of such a thing or working away on it secretly somewhere in my laboratory. This organization called the Fabian Society, for example, and sometimes the so-called 'progressive' ladies who call themselves suffragettes, have their say against my experiments as if it were something that it really is not. They are all out of their league. Perhaps the National Anti-Vivisection Society is the worst but there is also the Royal Society for the Prevention of Cruelty to Animals and the English Vegetarian Society. I am sure they are all fine chaps but they simply do not understand. At times, I really believe there are more societies and leagues in England now than there are cats and dogs!" He lets out a bolt of a laugh. "Only God can create human beings, my boy, only God, though I am not a believer, so perhaps I should say: Mother Nature or evolution, as Mr. Darwin and Mr. Huxley did. This fantasy of having faith in something that cannot be proven is absolute insanity and it causes human beings to accept all sorts of fantasies and often be terrible to one another. To me, believing in God is almost like believing in an invisible man, like that silly novel by that fellow, what's his name?"

"H.G. Wells."

"Yes, Wells. I somehow knew you would know of him, since he is so much in fashion these days. He is quite the young fellow with his modern and futuristic ideas. He has had a go at me, you know. Some people claim that one of his books has a terrible villain that he based on me. I have been told that he actually snooped around this hospital and even followed me to my home several times. Do I seem like a villain to you, Edgar, here in my lab attempting to find ways to extend the lives of women and children and gentlemen? Do I look like a villain?"

"Uh, no, sir."

"Now, come here and let us carve up this bunny."

Edgar comes forward.

"Pick up the aforementioned saw as you approach."

Edgar stops at the metal tray. He simply can't go through with this. He needs to find a way to get out of it. And he also needs more information. "Sir, I understand why you are so upset by the criticisms you have received and the insinuation that you are the sort who would experiment with human life, but might I ask you this—do you think anyone, any scientist during any time in history or recently, has ever made the attempt to create a human being . . . a monster?"

Godwin had opened his mouth to answer but when that last word was uttered, he stopped suddenly, his perfect lips still held in a circle.

"A monster?" he finally says. "That is a strange choice of words."

"Would such a creature not be that?"

Godwin nods. "Yes, perhaps it would be. I have no answer to your main question. I have never heard of the thing you suggest actually being attempted and have no desire to speculate. Now, please, pick up that saw and approach."

Edgar picks it up. There is a noise like a thump from across the room and then a sound like something scurrying. It seems to be coming from behind the sealed door of the Elephant Man's room.

There is silence for a moment.

"What was that?" Edgar asks.

"Nothing," says Godwin.

"It was something, sir, and it was coming from behind that door." He points to the closed entrance to the room.

"Bats," says Godwin.

"It didn't sound like wings or like it was in the air; it sounded like something on foot, and it seemed like it knocked something over."

"Rats," says Godwin.

"I don't believe it."

Godwin says nothing for a moment. Then he sighs. "Edgar, you are being daft. Do you think the poor wretch is in there, is that what you think? The Elephant Man himself? You have an extraordinary imagination, though it seems that it is sometimes your enemy. That room has been fitted with a lock since Mr. Merrick's death seven years ago and is no doubt infested with vermin of one sort or another. No one ever goes in there because it is a sort of sacred place, and the hospital officials have no idea what to do with it since no one wants to inhabit it, so they have just left it. Your uncle, Vincent Brim, is actually responsible for it."

"My uncle?"

"Yes, if you must know, he has a key for it. But even he never uses it. Vincent knew Merrick, as did I, an unfortunate chap but a lovely man and a wonder to behold. I found him absolutely fascinating!" Godwin's eyes glow again for a moment, but then he remembers himself. "Now enough of all of this, the saw, please. Let us get on with our duty."

Edgar wants to speak frankly with the great surgeon. He wants to tell him all about his situation—that he knew a man, a great one-armed man who killed a creature from an ancient story, and that he and his friends destroyed a revenant, a living dead man who lived on the blood of human beings, severed its head in a guillotine on the stage of the Royal Lyceum Theatre just weeks ago. He wants to tell him that something supernatural is now after him and his friends, and he is sure it smashed his adoptive father's brains out against a wall in his own home. He yearns to tell Godwin that this is why he is alert to any aberration that might be any-where near him. He wonders if Godwin knows that the very H.G. Wells novel he just mentioned tells a tale that explores the idea of making human beings, in a gruesome way, and Edgar fears that this thing in pursuit of him now is even worse, that it is the most frightening monster the human mind has ever created, perhaps made by the hand of man too! But he also wonders if he should admit to the great surgeon that what is upsetting him even more than sawing this poor little animal's arms and legs off while it is still alive, is the fact that you, Dr. Godwin, seem very much like a man—perhaps THE man among all men on earth—who might have the skills to make a monster like the very one in question!

"I . . . I cannot do this, sir."

"Then, my boy, you must put the instrument down. You must take another day or so to steel yourself. I understand. I absolutely understand." He puts his hand on Edgar's shoulder and pats it. "Go home, get some rest, and we shall see you in a few days." His touch is gentle and reassuring.

Edgar walks along the basement hallway greatly puzzled. Godwin is the most skilled surgeon in London, and yet there are those who hate him and the choices he makes within his profession. He seems such a kind and decent person when you know him—a man of smiles and understanding. Perhaps, thinks Edgar, Dr. Godwin is right about animal vivisection and human dissection, perhaps he only does these things to help humanity. Perhaps he is the only one with the courage to do it.

But what if Godwin actually went too far, even just once? Maybe there is some living being made by his hand in existence and perhaps it sometimes gets loose—or someone with a key lets it loose—from wherever he keeps it and it is seen by others and ends up in the newspaper articles Shakespeare investigated. Perhaps Robert Louis Stevenson glimpsed it on a London street and this young genius H.G. Wells noticed it too—such men would pick it out. Maybe Godwin deeply regrets what he did and that is why he is so evasive on the subject.

Perhaps Godwin keeps the creature he made in that room where the Elephant Man once lived?

12

The Key

On his way out of the hospital, Edgar heads toward his uncle's door. There is no one in the silent room. He slips into it.

Edgar surveys everything—the desk, the blackboard, the skeletons, the stacks of papers and the medical texts. Where would the key to the Elephant Man's room be? He cannot believe he is actually thinking about not only stealing it but then using it to get into that unholy holy place down there. But it seems like the only choice he has. He and his friends need to locate and eliminate this beast *before* it strikes again.

He has the terrible feeling that someone is in the room with him, watching what he does. He surveys the space again, every inch of it. The place still appears deserted.

He stands in front of the desk and notices two key chains on two hooks against the wall, on either side of the blackboard. He steps toward the one on his left.

"MASTER BRIM!"

"Yes," says Edgar before he even turns around, ". . . Uncle Vincent."

Vincent Brim has emerged from a door that Edgar has never noticed before; it looks like part of the wall. His uncle is wearing his white lab coat over another dazzling suit with a gold chain slung across the waistcoat that hides his expanding belly, his glistening black mustache and goatee appearing even more well-manicured than usual. He is glaring at his nephew, though his round glass lenses glint in the light, making his eyes only evident in flashes. For an instant Edgar thinks he can see spots of dark blood on one of his hands, but they are simply flecks cast by a shadow.

"What are you doing in here?" Dr. Brim marches toward Edgar, then does a sort of semicircle around him and walks behind his desk and sits at his chair, all the time staring at his nephew. He seems a little uncomfortable that the boy is looking down on him. "SIT!" he blares. Edgar does so instantly. "Why would you come into my—"

"Because I am your relation, Uncle Vincent, family, and I wanted to discuss how things have been going for me in the hospital."

"Oh." Vincent clears his throat. "Please refer to me as Dr. Brim. We have already discussed that. And so . . . so, how *have* things been going here? You are privileged to be working with such a man as Dr. Godwin. He has never asked for an assistant before."

"He is very kind and most obviously greatly respected."

"That he is, unquestionably. Have you been sweeping his room?"

"Actually, he has allowed me to be by his side while experimenting."

"Experimenting! You mean to say that you have been with him during intricate investigations into—"

"No, sir, not that, but I assisted during human organ removal. And he has invited me to observe while he vivisects a rabbit."

"I see. None of that has turned your stomach?"

"I have had troubles with it."

Vincent Brim grins. "I am not surprised. What we do here, my boy, is not for the weak of mind or body. It is a grown-up thing. That is why Dr. Godwin chooses to have me by his side during his most complicated operations."

This fact gives Edgar a bit of a start. He wonders about the nature of those "complicated operations."

"What do you think, sir, of what he does? The vivisecting and the work on the corpses. You know he has critics."

"They are fools. I think it admirable."

"How far would he take it?"

"I don't follow you."

"There are those who have said he would go so far as to play with human life and attempt to adjust it, perhaps replace the human heart with another's . . . or perhaps the brain."

"That would be marvelous!"

Edgar doesn't like his uncle's beaming expression. He wonders about Vincent Brim, holder of the key to that room downstairs, who knows where Thorne House is, has been to it several times. He could easily direct a beast right to the door and tell that creature where everyone sleeps. But that seems to Edgar to be a wild thing to consider, another example of his imagination on the loose. Godwin had told him it is sometimes his enemy.

"I hear, sir, that you are responsible for the Elephant Man's room."

"Where did you hear that?"

"Dr. Godwin."

Vincent hesitates for a moment. "Yes, it is true. I am honored. That freak, half human and half animal, to my mind, was a monument of a specimen."

"Could you show me the room one day, perhaps tomorrow?"

Dr. Brim's face turns red. He glances toward the key chain to his right then back at Edgar. "What a ridiculous and contemptuous idea! No one goes into that room anymore . . . not even me!" Edgar notes the pause in that sentence, the sort of hesitation one takes when not telling the truth. "You need to remove your nose from all of these things that are none of your business. Do not question or even think about the experiments the great Dr. Godwin does, boy, merely aid him when he asks! And do NOT ask me to give you some sort of child's free tour of a place that NO ONE is allowed to see! Do I make that perfectly clear?"

"Yes, sir."

"Good day, Master Brim. It was a pleasure to see you." He glares at his nephew.

Edgar gets up and leaves without saying another word. He waits in the back stairwell and ten minutes later, when Vincent goes out, Edgar darts into his room and back out.

Before Edgar leaves for his midnight rendezvous with his friends, he visits Annabel in her room. He is happy to see her up and dressed, combing out her long blonde hair with a silver brush while she looks at her drawn face in a dressing-table mirror. At least, thinks Edgar, this is some progress. They speak for a while about superficial things and then Edgar brings her around to a more important question.

"You know that father did more than just invent weapons, don't you, mother?"

"I would hope so. He was a bigger man than that. I know he often regretted his role—he said science should be for more than that."

"Yes, but do you think he ever did things that . . . he wasn't sure were right?"

She turns and looks at him, a lock of hair in one hand and the brush in the other. "Whatever do you mean, Edgar?"

"I have come to believe that some scientists wonder if it might be possible to actually make a . . . a human being."

She pauses and then speaks in a clear voice. "The important words you employed in that sentence were *some scientists*. Though Alfred was intellectually curious, I don't believe he would ever have considered such a thing."

"Yes," says Edgar, "I believe you are right. I believe that father was more moral than that."

"Now, your Uncle Vincent is another case entirely. I could believe in a second that he was up to that sort of thing."

When Edgar leaves the house just after eleven o'clock, it is silent. Annabel has gone to bed and the servants are nowhere to be seen. He told Beasley that he was turning in for the night. Now he slips silently through his bedroom door, down the stairs and out the front entrance, closing it behind him as gently as possible. His jaw is set as he walks out of Mayfair and heads toward the West End. He knows what he will say to his friends and what they must do. After this meeting, there will be no turning back.

There's a fog over London of the sort usually found on a winter night. The citizens' demand for better warmth, better everything, keeps adding to this human-enhanced smog.

Crossing Leicester Square at a quickening pace, Edgar hears a ruckus coming from inside a public house. There are still many people walking about in this central London area, a playground for adults, but most are on their way home, since the theaters and the drinking holes are either closing or have been shut for some time. And yet, here is this noise in this pub—violent noise. Edgar pauses. It is several men's voices, some aggressive, others terrified.

"Get out, you beast!"

He hears a grunt, human but barely, then the sound of a cane whizzing through the air and a cry of pain, another whiz and another cry followed by a dull, sickening sound, like bone striking bone, and then silence. As Edgar stands there, not twenty feet away from the pub's front door, loud footsteps approach from the inside, then a big boot comes right through the door, smashing its windows and crushing the thick wooden frame. A man appears, huge, wearing a black cloak, a black bowler hat and black suit, twirling a cane in a big hairy fist. He doesn't see Edgar, who is frozen in place. But then the man seems to sense him and starts to turn. Edgar sees some of the face, wide and grotesque, the lips looking black under the streetlights. Is this *it*? Edgar thinks of Shakespeare's claims about Mr. Hyde. He thinks of Annabel's drawing. The creature looks over his shoulder, just one eye on him. Then it turns and makes off into the night.

At that instant, Edgar remembers something about Mr. Hyde that had slipped his mind, and which makes it impossible that this thing that is after them could be him. "My mind is too flighty. That was just a man." But it hardly seemed like one.

Ten minutes later he is on Drury Lane. He's early. He doesn't bother to knock, just opens the door and slips down the stairs into the inner sanctum of the Crypto-Anthropology Society of the Queen's Empire.

When he enters the room, Shakespeare is alone, sitting at the table with papers and quills arranged for all of the expected guests, including the three phantoms, but he isn't speaking to any of them. He is simply sitting there with a glum expression on his big face, holding his cheeks in his little hands. He starts when he sees Edgar and his usual manic energy seems to overtake him.

"Master Brim! My colleagues and I were just conversing about our plan of action!" *No, you weren't,* thinks Edgar. "We have been awaiting you all with great anticipation!"

Edgar sometimes wonders about this little fellow. How crazy is he, really? Lear is said to have left some of his writings about monsters here in the society's rooms, but Shakespeare has never even mentioned their existence. Perhaps the creatures want those documents; perhaps it's one of the reasons why they are in pursuit and murderous. And why don't these aberrations come after this little man who believes in their existence? Is it just his insanity?

"Shakespeare—" begins Edgar.

"Yes, my knight, my liege, my auburn-haired, pyrotechnically coiffured, perturbation-riddled post-adolescent?" His eyes look wild. "Can I allay any concerns?"

Edgar finds it hard to imagine that lost mind plotting anything. Before he can respond, there is the sound of three sets of footsteps coming down the stairs and Edgar's thoughts turn from William Shakespeare. He is happy to see Tiger looking much better. She is dressed in a pair of trousers and seems her old, unafraid and unusual self. He can tell that the pistol is in her pocket now.

"The cannon is in place at the Lears' home," she says to him matter-of-factly.

"Glad you three retrieved it," he says. "That makes you safer."

"I got it myself, late at night when they were asleep, didn't want to upset them."

Lucy is much more somber tonight, but Jonathan has a spring in his step. He had been carrying Thorne's rifle at his side, trying to disguise its presence when out of doors. Now, he sets it against a wall and begins to pace.

"Here is my plan! It differs somewhat from the others. It is not based on our enemy being any particular creature. It is simply a plan of action, which is what we desperately need."

"I am not so sure, Jon," says Lucy.

"Hear me out. And then do anything other than what I suggest at your peril. We need to all gather at our home in Kentish Town with the doors unlocked and the cannon primed and ready. You need to be with us too, Edgar, so our villain thinks it can kill us all together. We make ourselves enticing, create a situation where this thing feels invited in, and then we tear it apart with Thorne's great weapon, take its head clean off just like we did with the vampire, but this time with an expanding cannonball!"

"What if that doesn't do the trick?" asks Tiger.

"How could it not?"

"If the thing we are after is ghostly, invisible," says Lucy.

"Annabel Thorne saw it."

"She thought she did. She was terrified. No one else alive has actually seen it."

"When it attacked me, I didn't *see* anything," says Tiger.

"It isn't invisible, sis. You read too many books."

"What if it is incredibly fast?" asks Lucy. "Or what if a cannonball won't penetrate it and it just keeps coming?"

"She's right," says Tiger, "we need to know what it is."

"It is Mr. Hyde, I tell you!" exclaims Shakespeare. "You are all light of brain!"

"What is your plan, Tiger?" asks Edgar.

"A more thoughtful version of Jonathan's: do some investigating first and then ambush this thing, know what we are trying to kill so we can finish it."

"And you, Lucy?"

It takes her a moment to answer. "I am not certain, not at all," she finally says. "Perhaps it is best to leave it be, just keep vigilant but do nothing unless it attacks again."

"It has attacked enough," says Jonathan. "We cannot wait anymore. It murdered grandfather and Mr. Thorne, is that not enough? One of us will be next."

"He makes a very good point," says Tiger.

"Then this is what we will do!" says Edgar loudly, rising to his feet. It isn't like him to command their attention like this. Both Lucy and Tiger turn to him with looks of anticipation. His face is flushed, a perfect match for his unruly red hair.

"The valiant Brim has a solution," sneers Jonathan.

"I don't think it is Mr. Hyde," says Edgar.

"But—"

"Be quiet, Shakespeare, and lend me your ears."

The little man looks shocked at first, but then puts his hands behind his ears and pushes them toward Edgar Brim.

"Both Tiger and Annabel said that this creature was a big male, very big. Mr. Hyde was dwarfish. That's clear in the book. It isn't him."

"But—"

"I have a theory about what is after us." He pauses. "I think someone made this creature."

There is silence for a moment.

"I beg your pardon?" says Jonathan, "*Made* it?"

"Annabel Thorne drew a very specific and detailed face. That must mean she truly saw something. And if you look very closely at the drawing—" he pulls it out of his pocket and sets it on the table again— "you can see some barely visible lines done with faint scribbles right at the neck. It looks like they might have gone right across the top of the throat if she had completed them."

Lucy gasps. ". . . As if someone attached and stitched on the head of this beast."

"It," continues Edgar, "appears to be brutish and without morality. It operates by simply breaking into places with sheer force and kills with terrific blows to the head or throat, and sometimes it strangles, and it has a gruesome face like something a 'plastic' surgeon might put together."

"But that doesn't mean that—" begins Jonathan.

"No," says Tiger, "let him finish." She is leaning toward Edgar.

"Thorne had a plaster cast of a human being he was working on in his laboratory. It made me wonder if he was doing what

scientists are being tempted to explore these days, with their occupation in its ascendency. Create life! Thorne was too moral for
that, but others may not be. My Uncle Vincent is intrigued by the
idea; he as much as told me so. And he idolizes Dr. Godwin."

"The vivisectionist," says Lucy.

"With whom I am working at the London Hospital, to whose
side, for some reason, I was recruited. Godwin too is fascinated
by this ungodly possibility, though he denies it. He is a good man,
but I am sure he is tempted on this subject. Perhaps he has already
gone beyond mere temptation? If anyone could do this, that
genius could."

"But are you saying that he—" asks Tiger.

"And this H.G. Wells fellow—" continues Edgar.

"He knows things!" says Shakespeare.

"This H.G. Wells, a science teacher and a man of great imagination and invention, he has a book about a scientist who tries to
make human beings out of animals, ripping them apart, operating
on them, adjusting them! My uncle had two books, two novels, on
his desk when I went in to see him recently. One was the Wells
novel *The Island of Doctor Moreau*, and the other was—"

"*Frankenstein!*" says Lucy, and puts her hands over her mouth.

"Yes," says Edgar.

"A Frankenstein monster is after us, wants to kill us," says Tiger
quietly, her face tightening.

"NO!" shouts Shakespeare. "It lived long ago. NO! No, that
isn't right, it can't be right!"

"It can't be, old man," says Jonathan, "or do you not want it
to be?"

"I'm simply wondering," says Edgar, "if it may be very much like this sort of thing, some creature made by the hand of man and on the loose." He takes a deep breath. "When I was working with Dr. Godwin in his lab, I heard a noise coming from a sealed door in a room connected to his. It sounded like something moving about and it knocked something over. Godwin quickly said it was nothing, and then he said it was bats and then rats. It is the room where the Elephant Man used to live."

"The freak!" shrieks Shakespeare. "He was just a man," he adds quickly, sounding perfectly sane, "an unfortunate human being named Joseph Merrick with a mysterious disease that deformed his body. That is all!"

"What if what we seek is in that room?" asks Jonathan. He picks up the rifle.

"How can we get in?" asks Tiger, rising to her feet.

Edgar produces the key from his pocket.

13

At the Elephant Man's Door

"I tell you, you are wrong," says Shakespeare, shaking his little fist at them as he stands at the door and watches the four of them rush out into the night in a spitting rain. "I am warning you!" It is a strange choice of words.

They don't speak as they walk briskly along the street. Jonathan is hiding the gun by his side as he tries to keep pace with Tiger, who is in the lead, Edgar staying with Lucy behind them. They are down to the bottom of Drury Lane quickly and then move east along The Strand onto Fleet Street toward St. Paul's Cathedral and the Old City.

But Jonathan is impatient. This trip to the East End, even rushing, will take them an hour. He hails a hansom cab and offers to take Tiger's hand to help her up into it. She hesitates for a second, then frowns at him and nimbly hoists herself into a seat. "The London!" she barks to the driver above them. Jonathan sticks his head out the window and shouts back at Edgar and Lucy. "Get the next one! Hurry!"

There are many other cabs on Fleet Street and Edgar whistles for one. A black model approaches, the driver just a dark shadow with a whip up on the box above the cab.

"What if this is the real thing?" asks Lucy.

"What do you mean?"

"You speculated that this creature might be *like* a Frankenstein monster, but Shakespeare insists that everything that pursues us comes from books and we have some evidence that it's true. So, what if this is not simply a wretch that Godwin or someone else recently created? What if it somehow *really is* Frankenstein's monster, the unkillable beast from the novel . . . and it is there tonight, in that room?"

The driver comes into view, an old man with a face like a skeleton.

"Enter," he says.

"Then we will have to face it," says Edgar. "The London Hospital!" he shouts upward. He helps Lucy in, follows her, and the skeletal driver snaps his whip and they are off.

By the time they reach the East End the streets are quieter, though that isn't unusual for this dangerous area. The few pedestrians are either desperately poor or appear to be up to no good. Most of the faces, even those on the frightened-looking street children, look haggard. There are no police officers in sight. It is the perfect habitat and hunting ground for a monster.

Jonathan and Tiger are waiting for them at the hospital doors, standing close to each other but saying nothing. The rifle is on its butt on the ground, held tightly to Jonathan's side. They head into the nearly empty reception room, and Edgar gets them past the desk by nodding at the nurse behind it and then ushers them through the hall to the back of the hospital. They pass just a handful of people and then descend the stairs into the basement.

There doesn't appear to be anyone in the hall, at least as far as they can see, and the lights are out in Godwin's room.

"We didn't bring a lantern!" grumbles Tiger.

"Then we'll just have to turn on the lights," says Jonathan.

"I don't think that is wise," whispers Lucy.

"Wise or not, we have to do it, sis."

But when Edgar puts his hand on the doorknob of Godwin's laboratory, they hear a sound coming from near the stone staircase behind them. They all turn. Something seems to be emerging into the light over there! They slip away from the door and farther down the hallway into darkness. The thing appears to be in a doorway, one that Edgar has never noticed since it seems to be in the wall in the pitch-black beside the staircase and always behind him whenever he walks down the steps and heads toward the laboratory.

They see the dim lights of the East End neighborhood behind the hospital for a moment, outlining the door frame, a big square figure grunting like a beast as it fills that entrance and then the door closes and all is dark there again. The beast sighs, grunts once more and begins to advance toward them. Lucy gasps and Edgar puts his arm around her, gently placing his hand over her mouth.

The beast stops. It drops something with a thud to the stone floor. They can see what it is now—a huge dirty sack with something in it. It's the size of a body, but not a large one, perhaps that of a teenage boy or a woman. The beast steps forward and looks down the hallway toward them. Edgar can see its face. He tightens his hand over Lucy's mouth as he feels her shiver.

It's Graft.

"Anybody there?" he asks in his low, guttural voice. They can see his thick head now, covered in sweat, blood on it, his crushed nose, the black brush mustache and the yellow, pegged teeth. His chest is the width of a gorilla's.

He unfastens a small lantern from his belt and shines it in their direction. They slip farther back into the hallway and find a few crates against a wall and get behind them. But they are barely hidden. The light flashes into the darkness.

"Anyone? Dr. Godwin?"

They try not to breathe as the light passes near them and surveys the crates.

Graft grunts and turns back to his big sack, seizes it with one hand and drags it along the stone floor like a Neanderthal toting a woman by the hair. He opens the lab door and goes inside. The lights come on.

"That's the gravedigger from Highgate!" says Lucy. "We should go."

"No," says Edgar, "he won't be long."

"How do you know?" asks Tiger. "What's he doing?"

Edgar doesn't want to say, but there is no use in hiding it. "He has a body for Dr. Godwin to dissect, likely a fresh one."

Lucy doesn't utter a sound.

They wait for a good ten minutes, hearing Graft banging and rattling inside the laboratory as he struggles with the body, hoisting it onto Godwin's operating table. Finally, he emerges, looks both ways and leaves by the back door under the stairs.

"Let's go in," says Jonathan.

"But that body is in there," says Lucy.

"Yes, it is," says Tiger as she takes the lead.

Inside, Edgar doesn't hesitate to turn on the lights.

"We have to do this fast," he says and points them in the direction of the door to the Elephant Man's room. They move smartly toward it, but then Lucy lets out a scream, which she covers immediately.

"Oh, my God!"

The dirty, bloody sack is on the operating table, open, exposing a dead woman from the waist up, her blond hair clotted and wet, her face turned toward them and her mouth caught in a frozen grimace, almost like a smile. The eyes have somehow opened and they seem to be staring at the four intruders, though rotated up in their sockets.

"We need to concentrate on the door," says Tiger forthrightly. "Give me the key, Edgar. Though I would wager I could unlock this without it."

He hands it to her and she advances quickly toward her target. Sometimes he almost doesn't like her bravery. He takes Lucy's hand.

But then the laboratory door creaks open behind them and as they turn, they see Dr. Godwin closing it behind him.

14

What H.G. Wells Knew

Jonathan holds the rifle behind him but keeps a grip on it right near the trigger. Tiger pulls the key out of the lock and slips it into her trousers pocket, as smooth as the thief she once was.

"Edgar?"

"Uh, yes, yes, sir, it's me."

Godwin walks toward them. "And . . . and you have friends with you?"

"I . . . sir . . . I . . ."

"He is very proud that he is working with you, Dr. Godwin," says Lucy, stepping in front of the others, "and he wanted to show us the laboratory. That is, he *told* us that he wanted to, but shouldn't, but we were so excited about the possibility of coming here that we persuaded him. I cannot believe that I am in your famous laboratory. I hope you don't mind."

Godwin glances at Edgar, then at the others, and seems to cast his eyes down to where Jonathan is hiding the rifle in the dim light, and only then appears to notice that these intruders are standing at the Elephant Man's door.

"I see," he says. "What a lovely idea, despite the remarkably late hour. I do not mind in the least. Come over here, Miss . . ."

"Lear. Miss Lucy Lear."

"Come with me." He takes her by the hand. "I have something fascinating to show you." He guides her toward the half-naked corpse on the table. Edgar freezes, but Lucy doesn't. She goes with the great surgeon with a smile fixed on her face. Godwin stops when Lucy is near the head, which is tilted toward her, its white eyeballs milky.

The good doctor beckons to the others. "Are the rest of you not going to observe this remarkable specimen? How many people ever get to see another human being shortly after it dies? It is utterly riveting. There is much to learn. Master Brim can attest to that. Learn, learn, learn—that is what life is all about. Progress!"

Tiger moves toward the table, staring at the corpse without the least sign of repulsion, as if she can hardly wait to be near it. Edgar follows slowly. But Jonathan stays behind.

"It looks a bit crowded over there," says Jon loudly, then silently mouths, "I need to hide the gun," at Edgar and heads toward the laboratory door. "Enjoy!" he says.

"Would you like to touch it?" asks Godwin, moving Lucy's hand up toward the corpse. "The skin has a different texture in death. Go ahead."

Tiger steps in front of Lucy and reaches out and takes the body's whole face in her hands. "Interesting," she says, smiling at Godwin.

Edgar can see that this body is very different from the first one he encountered. He remembers the red stains on the sack Graft was carrying and considers the gutters on the table, wide enough to gather great pools of blood. This woman's flesh doesn't look gray like the skin on the other corpse. It doesn't seem as tight or stiff either.

"Why are you really here?" asks the great surgeon suddenly.

Edgar can swear he hears the rifle cock over by the door. "It is as we said, sir, they wanted to see the lab, and I was so proud that I was working with you that I could not resist."

"So it was vanity, simple human pride? That is known as a sin, you know."

"Yes, sir."

"There is another reason though, isn't there?"

"Uh, no, sir."

"Come now. Were I a young man such as yourself and I knew that a very famous freak's room could be mine to observe I would not be able to resist. Am I not correct?"

Edgar doesn't know what to say.

"Yes, sir," says Lucy, "you are correct, sir. But we saw that the door was well and truly locked."

"Yes," says Godwin, "and you do not have a key, do you, Edgar?"

"Uh, no, sir." He is so glad that Tiger has it. Godwin wouldn't guess that he would give it to her, a young woman, and put her in charge.

"We were just about to leave when you arrived, sir," says Tiger.

Godwin looks her up and down, taking in her trousers and her manly blouse. "You are an interesting one, young lady. I suppose we must all accept that the roles of women are changing. But I trust that Edgar's friends are good people." He gives Tiger's shoulder a light pat. "I hope to see you again, my dear."

"Thank you, sir," says Edgar. "I will be here first thing in the morning, ready to help with . . ." He glances at the pink corpse. "With that."

"Indeed you will be," says Godwin. "Although, I need to prepare the body first in the morning, keeping half the blood, with just some fluid—and you are up so late tonight, so if you arrive at noon, then that will be fine. We shall commence at that time."

The three friends walk toward the door. Jonathan has already slipped out into the hallway, the gun hidden by his side.

"It is unusual for me to be here at this hour, you know," says Godwin. "You were fortunate to encounter me. I knew we had a fresh body arriving. I am usually home by five o'clock or shortly thereafter, already in bed by this hour. But if your friends would like to be here about six in the evening tomorrow, I will show you all the insides of the Elephant Man's room. I will get the key from your uncle, Edgar."

"That sounds exciting, sir, thank you."

"Not at all. Good evening. My regards to your large friend in the hall too, rather bashful, he is."

"Thank you," says Edgar again.

"And Master Brim?"

"Yes, sir?"

"You do not need to sneak about here you know; I am an open-minded fellow. You do not need to hide things from me. If there is something that you would like to do or see or anything that is bothering you, please tell me. Worries can be eliminated when they are shared. If you are in any sort of need, I might be able to help you."

———

As Edgar walks up the stone steps from the basement with his friends, he tells himself that it really shouldn't matter how long a corpse is dead. Dead is dead. Godwin is doing this for science, he reassures himself, for the betterment of man.

"I keep wondering if I should tell Godwin about our situation," says Edgar once they get to the ground floor. "He is a brilliant man. He might be an invaluable ally."

"He could have been very angry with us," says Lucy.

"He never is," says Edgar. "He is always even tempered and kind. I find it difficult to suspect him of anything truly evil, though I wonder if he may be protecting someone, or someone's secret."

"He delighted in showing us the corpse," mutters Tiger.

"Hard to blame him," says Jonathan. "He had to punish us a little. I'm sorry I had to miss it!"

Edgar leads them up to the second floor and slips into his uncle's room and deposits the key back onto the hook so it will be there for Godwin to find tomorrow, then they head out into the night.

"I have to be honest, Edgar," says Tiger, who has been quiet for a long while. "I don't trust Godwin—"

"But he's the only adult who might really help us now," says Lucy. "Otherwise, we are completely on our own."

Tiger keeps speaking as if Lucy hasn't said anything. "I can take the measure of people, I had to on the streets, and I have my doubts about him. I not only don't want to take him into our confidence, I'm not sure we should go back into that lab with him."

"But we have to," says Jonathan, "whether we trust him or not. Anyway, he's an esteemed surgeon with an admirable reputation.

I doubt we have anything to fear from him. We can't allow the sight of a corpse to disturb us."

"I agree with Jon," mutters Lucy.

"I'm not disturbed by a corpse," says Tiger, "trust me."

Outside, the rain is still spitting down. The street is even more deserted now.

"I don't want to waste time," says Edgar as they stop for a moment, waiting for two cabs to appear, "so I'm thinking we should find this H.G. Wells fellow and speak to him in the morning. He seems to know a great deal about vivisection and perhaps even about making human beings. Maybe he knows something about human-animal hybrids too, like the ones in his novel. Perhaps he's seen one. And, Tiger, you might be right to think we shouldn't go back to Godwin's lab at night. He told me that Wells may have modeled a character after him. I think it's Doctor Moreau."

That night, alone in his room at Thorne House, Annabel fast asleep not far below, Edgar squirms under his bed, lifts the loose floorboard and gets out the most important item hidden there, a black leather journal:

THE PRIVATE THOUGHTS OF ALLEN BRIM
With love to Virginia and Edgar

He turns to the entry about *Frankenstein*, passing quickly over the paragraphs concerning Mary Shelley's life until he comes to the account of how she created her infamous story while half-dreaming in her bed in a spooky house on Lake Geneva in

Switzerland. It was during the nearly sun-less summer of 1816, just days after she took up a ghost-story challenge with her poet-husband and his friends, one of whom wrote *The Vampyre*. There are entries that frighten him: a passage without a source about Mary actually seeing a "hideous phantasm of a man" being brought to life by the "working of some powerful engine"! *Where could she have seen that?* he wonders. And there is another note about her glimpsing a big, bizarre-looking man in the woods not far from where she was living. But there isn't much Edgar can sink his teeth into in Allen Brim's notes, no clues that might connect Mary's fictional creation to what may be in pursuit of him and his friends in this London summer of 1897. Even if it were true that some real creature inspired Frankenstein's monster, thinks Edgar, that was long ago.

But could Godwin have somehow been inspired to attempt a hideous scientific trial by such stories?

"Stop it," Edgar says to himself. "Percy Godwin is a scientist and likely never so much as glances at fiction, probably finds it frivolous. You are making all this up. And Godwin expressly denied any interest when the subject of a Frankenstein experiment was raised; he was disgusted by it."

As he drifts to sleep, worrying that the hag will be with him in the morning, he thinks of the other novel upstairs in the lab, that H.G. Wells tome, and the scientist in it who does forbidden things very much like Victor Frankenstein . . . a doctor.

The four friends meet on Waterloo Bridge early the next morning, the rising sun casting the Parliament Buildings and that part of

London in a lovely glow. Lucy is dressed up for her meeting with the famous young author, in a pin-striped black dress and hat. The others are as usual. They take the early South Western Railway train to Worcester Park, where Wells lives. Edgar had seen an interview with him in *Pearson's Magazine*, complete with an illustration of his house on a street called The Avenue.

They are facing each other in four seats and say little as the train rattles along. But when they are well out of the city, just past Wimbledon, Lucy speaks up.

"When you are with Dr. Godwin in his laboratory, Edgar, do you ever talk about personal matters?"

"What do you mean?"

"Do you ever tell him about your guardians and where you live?"

"I suppose I have. Why?"

"So, if there is something in the Elephant Man's room, some creature, and it can hear just like you and I, and it is listening when you are there with Dr. Godwin, then it may have learned exactly where you live."

When they get out at Worcester Park, they soon find The Avenue and in minutes are walking along it, all a little nervous, not sure what they will say to this great young man whose strange books and ideas are electrifying England and the world.

It is a leafy street, wide and lined with big trees and nice houses, not mansions for the rich, but most certainly not homes for the poor either. They find the Wells property. It sits back a bit from the street, made of red brick and large, almost like two homes, two stories on one half and three on the other with a peaked roof on that part reaching into the sky.

"I'm guessing he writes up there in the top room," says Jonathan, "where he's closer to Mars."

As they turn toward the front door, two people emerge from around the side of the house, a man and a woman: she small and somewhat plain looking, wearing a long dress hiked up to her calves and sporting a hat tipped back a little on her head; he also small, in a tweed suit and cloth cap. They come to a halt on their lawn while upon a new-fangled tandem bicycle they had begun to tentatively ride, their feet on the ground on either side, he at the front muttering instructions and she behind trying to do as he bids. They don't so much as notice the four strangers on their front walkway.

"Jane," says the man, "you must never hesitate when upon a bicycle, remember that; you hesitated yesterday and that was unquestionably the cause of our crash."

"Yes, Bertie," she says, "though your sudden change of speed was not what one might consider of assistance during our dilemma."

It's Wells. Edgar is sure of it. He's seen his face in the papers many times. But he can hardly believe it. Not just because he is suddenly in the presence of greatness but because this slight man, with the thick, straight dark hair parted on the side and the walrus mustache, is so unimpressive. He is not only small but looks rather unhealthy, like someone who is recovering from an illness, and appears somewhat short on muscle. And he speaks in a slightly high-pitched working-class accent that one would never associate with a man of letters or of such bold and forceful ideas.

"Mr. Wells?" calls Tiger.

"Who asks?" he says without even looking at them, staring down at the pedals on the bicycle as he tries to coordinate them and his wife.

"I am Miss Tilley."

Wells looks over at her and does a double take. He scans her up and down, the gaze of a male examining a female of interest. She is wearing her trousers again. He lingers a bit over her lower half.

"And I am Miss Lucy Lear."

Wells turns to Lucy and his smile grows a little.

"Indeed," he says. "You are not a traditionally beautiful young woman, my dear, nose a little long, your skin a little pale, interesting red hair, copper I'd guess, but you have a certain presence, shall we say. It is always good and exciting to tell the truth." He offers her a little bow.

"I am Jonathan Lear."

"And I'm Edgar Brim."

Jon strides toward the couple and reaches out to take Wells's hand. The great man is still looking at Lucy and Tiger. Then he returns his attention to the bicycle pedals, leaving Jonathan standing there with his arm outstretched.

"What would you like? I do not autograph books for strangers. Mrs. Jane Wells and I were just going out on a bicycling expedition. If your mission was to say hello, then you have had it. Good day."

"We want to ask you about Dr. Percy Godwin," says Edgar quickly.

Wells stops what he is doing. "Godwin?" His voice grows a bit shrill. "He is a scoundrel!"

"Is he the model for Dr. Moreau?" asks Tiger.

Wells pauses for a moment and looks to be gathering himself before he answers. "*The Island of Doctor Moreau* is a fiction, my dear," he finally says. "That is the first thing you must know. But if I indeed in any way based that scum of a character—he who took the noble enterprise of science and ran with it until it was a bastard child of Satan—upon anyone, the aforementioned Godwin would be . . ." He pauses. "Perhaps he was in the back of my mind, shall we say." He grins mischievously.

"Why are you so harsh about him?" asks Edgar.

"Why are you asking?"

"I know him. I work with him."

"Then I pity you."

"Why, sir?"

"Because he is a vivisectionist with a large brain and no heart. A human being, and humanity itself, must have both, you see. Vivisection may not be the worst of things, there are arguments that can be put forth in its favor. Godwin, however, is what is presented in our society as a leader of men, but he is a wanker."

"Bertie, language," says Jane.

"Mr. Wells, do you believe a scientist will ever make a new sort of human being, like Dr. Moreau did in your book?"

"What a question! You are a rather intense lad, you are. I like it!"

"Well, do you believe that could happen?"

"Woe to us if it ever occurs."

"What if it already has?"

Wells seems a bit taken aback by that. The bold, talkative personality he has been projecting appears to waver for a moment.

He climbs off the bicycle, leaving his diminutive wife to hold up the whole contraption. She struggles with it. "I . . ." He clears his throat. "I doubt that."

"But you don't entirely discount it?" asks Lucy.

"How about the invisible man," asks Jonathan, "was he real? Or at least based on someone?"

Wells smiles. "Such questions!" He puts his hands on his hips and sighs. "I do not discount any possibility. There are many truths. And one indeed finds truth in novels."

"Dr. Godwin has invited us to visit him today, alone in his laboratory," says Tiger, "and during our visit he will take us into a room that has been locked for seven years. It used to belong to the Elephant Man. Do you think we should go?"

"I wouldn't. You might find it sealed up again with you on the wrong side."

"Are you being serious?" asks Edgar.

"Somewhat."

"I will be honest with you," says Edgar, "since you have taken the time to speak with us. I sometimes believe that some of the villains, the monsters, in some fiction are based on real things, real aberrations. We believe we have encountered at least two."

Wells looks at him intensely with his penetrating blue eyes. "Fascinating," he says. "What did you say your name was?"

"Edgar Brim."

"That could work," says Wells quietly to himself.

"I beg your pardon?"

"Nothing. You were going to say more?" Wells steps closer to him.

"I am worried that there is now in London a creature that has been made by a human being. I wonder, at times, if it has been concocted by Dr. Godwin himself. I am here to ask you if you think that could have happened."

Wells steps even closer to the four of them, who are lined up listening intently. He takes Lucy's hand and then Tiger's. He is not much taller than the latter. He looks back and forth between the two of them. "Science, my lovelies, is a two-edged sword. It can do marvelous things and it can do great evil."

"That doesn't answer my question," says Edgar.

Wells has been glowing at the girls and Edgar's voice almost startles him. "Yes," he finally says, "I believe that science might one day put a new heart into a man and perhaps even a new brain, make a new man entirely. As to whether or not it has been done already, if I have observed one, if I have secret information about some villain who created one . . . you must know that I would not tell you. That would spoil everything. But I will put on record that I have suspicions, deep ones."

Lucy puts her hand to her mouth.

"And Dr. Godwin," says Edgar, "would he do it?"

"Let us just say that if anyone has," says Wells, "it would be him!" He looks into the distance and then seems to come to. "Jane, we have a bicycle expedition to perform. Let us drive off into the future!" He turns and seizes his part of the tandem, mounts and begins to pedal, almost knocking his wife down. They pull away, Jane looking at the four visitors and rolling her eyes at her husband.

"I wouldn't keep that appointment with Godwin," shouts Wells as they head onto The Avenue. "He is the real world's chief candidate to be the Lord of the House of Pain. Stay away from him!"

On the way back on the train they speak of H.G. Wells but Godwin is really the one on their mind.

"Wells is an interesting man," says Tiger.

"Amazing eyes," says Lucy, "and he's quite the talker, with awfully stimulating ideas. Charming."

"That wasn't my impression," says Jonathan, a bit peevishly. "I thought he was rather timid. It didn't seem to me that he had any real reason to be so frightened of Dr. Godwin. He just doesn't like him."

"He warned us," replies Lucy. "Shouldn't a warning from someone like him mean something?"

"Wells obviously has an overly stimulated imagination, sis, as do you, at times."

"And you, at times, have none."

"Well," says Edgar, "should we do it?"

15

The Cold Room

Edgar leaves the others behind at Waterloo Station and makes his way by underground railway to the London Hospital. They will meet him there at six o'clock, since they finally all agreed to go into the Elephant Man's room with Godwin, though Lucy expressed reservations.

The great surgeon is hard at work when Edgar arrives. He has the body out of the sack and cleaned and prepared and all the instruments ready. Edgar sees, with a shudder, that the woman's face has already been removed, and the ears and nose have been sliced off. Despite this, and despite Wells and Tiger's opinions, Edgar tries not to treat Godwin any differently.

But the experimenter seems to be presenting a different sort of personality than at any time before. He isn't happy or excited or angry. He seems almost completely emotionless. He doesn't say a word to Edgar, merely nods at him and motions toward a scalpel and saw. Edgar knows he cannot refuse today. It is as if Godwin has him exactly where he wants him.

The carving instruments are handed over and the operation

begins. It is long and gruesome and Godwin seems to take his time with every part of the procedure. The poor woman's body is disemboweled and disassembled. There is embalming fluid everywhere, freshly injected and mixed with blood. And when all the organs are removed, they use the saw to take off her four limbs and her head, keeping the brain inside the skull this time. Godwin still says very little, and nothing directly about what he is doing. When he does speak he talks about his feelings concerning the rights of women and how some of their organizations have attacked his experiments. But he speaks dispassionately even of that, working on the woman beneath him, praising women's sense of smell and hearing. At the end, he is insistent that each of the corpse's appendages is immediately placed in ice. Edgar wonders what will be done with them, since they can't be kept cold here for very long. It is almost six o'clock by the time they are done.

"Well, Edgar," says Godwin before the hour has even struck, "perhaps your friends are not coming this evening. Perhaps you and I should simply enter the Elephant Man's room alone?" There is a strange expression on his face.

Edgar unconsciously steps back from him, not sure what to say.

Godwin lets out a loud laugh, as if he were imitating how someone might respond when playing a practical joke.

"I am not being serious," he says. "I am playing a little with your emotions again. I hope you do not mind."

"Not at all, sir," says Edgar, but he's sure Godwin saw him go pale.

"I am so sorry for upsetting you. I did not think my joke would have quite that extreme effect, and that is frankly a little disappointing. Edgar, I sense that you have your doubts about me. I sense that, given what I do and the criticisms that are sometimes offered about my work by unthinking people, that you are, well, almost wary of me, deep down. Though that saddens me, I find it understandable. But I would like you to set that aside, comprehend that I am your friend and confide in me." He pauses for a moment. "Something beyond these little operations is bothering you, isn't it? You are afraid of something. Please, share it with me. I would like to help you." He puts a hand on Edgar's shoulder and grips him warmly.

The door opens and Lucy and Tiger enter.

Godwin takes his hand off Edgar. "We will speak more of this later," he says quietly, then regards the others. "Where is the young gentleman?"

Tiger's eyes shift from Edgar back to the surgeon. "He, uh, he was held up at home. He is coming later. It is so good to see you again, Dr. Godwin, and so kind of you to show us this historic room." She goes to him and takes his arm, almost turning him toward her as she does. Edgar steps toward Lucy, embraces her and whispers in her ear.

"Why isn't Jon here?"

"He's coming in twenty minutes or so with the gun. He thought that was the safest thing to do. He insisted."

There is nothing Edgar can do about it.

"Well," says Godwin, "that is unfortunate. I am in a rush. We shall do this quickly and if your friend does not arrive shortly, he will miss the tour! But I will be happy to show him another time. Let us commence!"

Godwin goes to his desk and picks a lantern off it, lights it and motions for them to follow him to the locked room. He knocks some dust off the door frame and around the keyhole. It seems to Edgar that there are remnants of cobwebs there too, but he also wonders if this is a trick. Is Godwin trying to make it look like the door hasn't been used for a long while?

"As you can see," says the surgeon, "no one has been in here for some time."

"I don't think that's true," whispers Tiger into Edgar's ear as she stands close to him and several strides behind the others. "This lock looks like it has been used recently."

Godwin sets the lantern on the floor, slides the key into the lock and opens the door smoothly. The three of them stand still, no one offering to move before their guide. "Come, come," he says gently, waving them forward. They can see that it is dark inside. Lucy moves first, her skirts rustling over the entrance, and then Edgar goes in and then Tiger. It smells dusty and moldy inside. But the most shocking thing is how cold it is. So much so that it is a wonder they can't see their breath.

"I have a weapon," Tiger whispers to Edgar. He cannot tell what it is. It is obviously well hidden on her person. But he knows that whatever it is, she is capable of using it with deadly force.

The door slams behind them, leaving the three of them inside in darkness. The sound echoes. Something seems to move in the shadows behind them, scurrying along the floor and Lucy gasps, but before they can turn around, the door opens abruptly again, shedding the dim light from the laboratory into the room. Godwin stands in the entrance, bearing the lantern.

"I hope you found that amusing," he says. "As Master Brim knows, I am something of a practical joker at times, a 'kidder' as the

Americans say. And besides, you three are so very serious, so suspicious of me—I hope you are not listening to the opinions of fools. I thought I might see if I could scare the wits out of you, but just for a moment. I thought it might help put you at ease. Was that all right?"

"Very humorous, sir," says Lucy, shivering.

"Thank you, my dear." He walks past them into the room. "Now, I am afraid that we will not be able to see everything very clearly in here, since there never was electric light in this room. Mr. Merrick got by on gas lamps and candlelight. He was quite happy with that." Godwin grins. "Ah, I can see him now."

He holds the lantern up and casts light around the room. A few rats sneak in and out of hiding places. They see shadows and dim objects—a desk, a table, lamps, some chairs, a small bed with the covers and pillows still on it—but it is difficult to get a good sense of their surroundings. They appear to be in a single room. Edgar can't even tell how much dust is on the furniture or if there is much at all. The lantern light flashes past clothing hanging from a hook—a black cloak and a canvas sack with two eye holes.

"There was no water closet here. Mr. Merrick used the facilities upstairs, a several-times-daily operation which necessitated his being seen in the hallways, but which he claimed he was not averse to doing, though with his deformed skeleton, he struggled to climb the stairs. He was quite contented here, and Dr. Treves was not just his doctor, but his good friend. It warms the heart. Take a quick look. We cannot linger."

Godwin walks around the room and the other three follow. From what they can tell, it all seems very much like a gentleman's apartment indeed, but Edgar thinks he sees things that surely wouldn't have been here when Merrick was in residence—a hammer, a crow bar and a couple of wooden boxes the size of coffins. He thinks of the stories of vampires living in caskets and especially of Count Dracula in his resting place in his castle in the Carpathian Mountains in eastern Europe, and also of the young woman in the crypt in Highgate Cemetery in that same novel. But Godwin barely shines the lantern in the direction of the boxes.

They could be anything, thinks Edgar.

Before the three friends can inspect any object more closely, Godwin ushers them out of the room and back into the warmth of the lab. They were not inside for more than two minutes.

"I am sorry but I cannot stay any longer. I shall drop the key with Vincent Brim on my way out and perhaps he can give Jonathan his tour of the room."

"We can wait for Jon here," says Tiger.

"No. You have already had your time in that room and I prefer that you three not be alone in my laboratory."

"Then we will wait for him in Dr. Brim's office."

"That isn't desirable either. I recall Jonathan Lear as a powerful, strapping specimen of a lad. I am sure he can find his way here, have his little tour and meet you all at home or wherever you might next make his acquaintance."

Godwin presses a button on the wall. "Dr. Brim and I have direct communication between our rooms. He shall be here shortly. I will show you out."

Edgar can't think of an excuse to stay behind, not one that Godwin would accept, so he and the girls walk out of the lab with the surgeon and make their way up the stairs. Before they reach the top, they encounter Vincent Brim coming down. Edgar introduces him to the girls. He grips the rims of his circular spectacles as he examines them, taking each of their hands to his lips and kissing them.

"Enchanted," he says.

Godwin hands him the key and explains about Jonathan, and Dr. Brim nods. When Edgar glances back as they depart, his uncle is looking over his shoulder at them.

Dr. Godwin sees them right to the front door and out it. In fact, he walks with them down the front steps to a cab, which has been ordered for him. He stands beside it and shakes their hands and watches them walk away.

"The Midland Grand Hotel," Edgar hears Godwin tell the driver behind him.

Edgar and the girls come to a halt as soon as the surgeon is out of sight.

"I hate to say this, but I don't like the look of your uncle either," says Tiger.

"That's quite all right. As always, you are very perceptive," says Edgar.

Lucy looks worried. "I think we should go back. I don't want Jon to be alone in there. He'll have to conceal the rifle from everyone. What if they see it?"

"We shouldn't disobey Godwin. He told us to go home."

"Yes, he did, didn't he?" says Tiger. "That's interesting in itself. Let's go back."

But as they pass by the matron in the receiving room, she spots them and calls out to Edgar.

"Master Brim!"

They walk over.

"I just received a note from Dr. Brim saying that you are not to return to the hospital tonight. I was to tell you that your day is over."

She keeps an eye on them as they go out the front door. They cross wide Whitechapel Road and stand against a lamppost, almost in front of the two-story shop where the Elephant Man was found, exhibited by a small-time showman. They gaze across at the brown hospital.

"Why would your uncle say that?" asks Tiger.

"Because he is an officious sod and he likes to tell me what to do and he hates the fact that the great Godwin has taken me into his confidence. He's just exerting his ridiculous authority."

"Well, we can wait for Jonathan here," says Lucy. "He should be along at any moment."

But he isn't. Nearly half an hour passes.

"Not to worry," says Edgar, squeezing Lucy's hand. "I believe I told him about the rear entrance to the hospital. He may have entered that way. That would make sense, given that he is carrying the rifle."

They walk down narrow Turner Street on the west side of the building and go around to the back. The hospital is U-shaped and there is a garden there, where patients are being pushed in wheelchairs on the footpaths. They find the door where Jonathan would most likely enter.

But he doesn't come. And neither does he leave. They wait for more than an hour. If they wait much longer, the sun will begin to set.

"This doesn't make any sense," says Lucy. "Where is he?"

"Let's go home," says Tiger. "We'll stay together, Lu. He probably went in the back way, had his tour, and then went out the front."

"That's likely what happened," says Edgar, his voice low.

They walk back around to the front and Tiger hails a hansom cab and the girls head northwest to Kentish Town. Edgar trudges home, his head down, deep in thought.

The next morning, as he rushes out the front door on his way back to the hospital to be at Godwin's side for their eight o'clock starting time, Beasley stops him and hands him a telegram.

```
JONATHAN DIDN'T COME HOME LAST NIGHT.
TERRIFIED!
LUCY.
```

16

The Noises on the Other Side

Godwin seems to be in a good mood when Edgar reaches him that morning, or at least what passes for happiness with the great scientist. He says there are no "challenges" this morning, just paperwork to be done and cleaning up around the lab. He hands Edgar a broom and a cloth and goes to his desk.

Edgar can't concentrate. He wants to rush off to be with Lucy and Tiger. But he also knows that he may be in the very place where Jonathan disappeared, and his best course of action is to investigate and do it now. He cleans up near the Elephant Man's door and doesn't hear a sound and can't think of a reason to ask Godwin if he can go in there again. Edgar is wary about saying much to him. Given the events of the past day and the warnings of H.G. Wells, he is now deeply worried about taking him into his confidence in any way.

But he has to.

"Sir," he finally says. "Might I speak frankly with you?"

"Of course, my boy, finally, what is on your mind?"

"My friend, Jonathan, the one who was coming later to see the Elephant Man's room, has disappeared."

"That's an awfully dramatic word. Whatever do you mean by that?"

"He didn't come home last night. He's never done that before."

"He isn't a drinker, is he? He could pass for an adult. Have you inquired at a public house he might frequent?"

"He doesn't go to such places, sir, ever. He would have gone straight home from here, there is no question."

"Well, that isn't good, isn't good indeed."

In the silence that follows, Edgar, who has made sure he is standing as close to the Elephant Man's room as possible without arousing suspicion, again listens intently for any sound coming from it—a sigh, a distant groan, anything. But there is nothing. He unconsciously slides his eyes in the direction of its door, and when he looks back at Godwin, the great surgeon is examining him.

"Well," says Godwin finally, "it was your uncle who was meeting Jonathan here last night. So, you must visit him immediately and make inquiries. Off you go! I am sure he will have an explanation for you. Your friend likely told him something that will set aside your fears. Fear, you know, is an irrational thing. We must always be rational, my boy."

Edgar finds Vincent Brim in his room upstairs with the door open, sitting behind his desk, contemplating something, drumming his fingers on the surface of the two sensation novels. Edgar knocks gently but there is no response. He enters and examines the room as he walks forward, seeing if he can spot the place where his uncle came out of the wall. But he can't and wonders if he imagined it. Vincent doesn't notice him until he is right in front of him, and then looks up, startled.

"Sir, did my friend, Jonathan Lear, meet you here last night?"

"Why are you sneaking up on me?"

"I knocked."

"You did?"

"Is something worrying you, sir?"

"No, why would it be?"

"You seem upset."

"I am no such thing. I am a busy man with many concerns. What do you want?"

"Did my friend Jonathan Lear meet you here last night?" he repeats.

Vincent hesitates before he answers. "Yes, he did. Why do you ask?"

"He has disappeared."

"That is not my problem."

"Did you show him the Elephant Man's room?"

"Yes, I gave him a quick look, much against my inclinations. It is not a showroom, you know."

"Did he seem out of sorts? Did he say where he was going after? Did you notice in which direction he went when he left? Was there anyone suspicious loitering about in the area?"

"Calm yourself, Edgar. Once I showed him the room, I sent him on his way. It was growing dark outside. This is the East End and there are many scurrilous characters about. I did not see him once he exited via the back door. He may have met with misfortune, who knows? Though, it is more likely he has run off to get away from such friends as you, who pester people with questions that have nothing to do with them. Are you accusing me of something?"

"No, sir, though I find it curious that you ask."

There is silence for a moment. Vincent looks a little concerned and then his face grows red.

"Leave me, boy."

Edgar still doesn't know what to think of his uncle. Perhaps he just dislikes him because of the old squabbles with his dear father. Vincent Brim is probably just an unpleasant man, no more than that. He is a scientist, a doctor without much of a soul. That doesn't make him a monster or a murderer. Still, Edgar leaves the room wondering if he should notify the police. He trudges back down the stairs to the laboratory.

"Any luck?" asks Dr. Godwin as soon as he re-appears. The surgeon must have heard the door open, since his back is turned to the boy. He is leaning over the table adjusting his instruments. Edgar can see a big, gleaming knife in his hand.

"No, sir, my uncle showed Jonathan the room and then they parted."

"And Vincent didn't notice anything suspicious after that?"

"What do you mean?"

"Oh, anyone about who might do your friend harm?"

"He didn't note anyone. You went straight home . . . didn't you, sir?"

Godwin doesn't say anything. Then he turns with the knife in his hand. "Why ever do you ask?"

"Because I am desperate to know of anyone who might have seen my friend."

"Well," says Godwin, "you saw me leave in my cab, did you not?"

"Yes, sir, I was simply clutching at straws."

"I see."

It looks as if the door to the Elephant Man's room is very slightly ajar. Edgar takes a few steps toward it.

"What are you doing?" asks Godwin, coming toward him with the knife.

"Did you just go in there?"

"No, Mr. Sherlock Holmes, I did not. Why in the world would I do that? Did I not tell you that I never go in there, except to show it to young folk who ask silly questions about it? I believe it is time for you to return to your duties."

It is difficult for Edgar to concentrate. He sweeps the floor and cleans nearly every glass and beaker in the room. He wishes Godwin would leave so he can test the door to the Elephant Man's apartment. But the surgeon, who usually has business elsewhere during the day, stays in the lab until it is time to depart, not even leaving for lunch, which he has a nurse bring for the two of them. She smiles at the big, handsome man and touches his hand as she gives him their food.

At closing time, Godwin sees Edgar to the lab door.

"Sir, I am thinking about notifying the police."

"You must do as you see fit. Shall I have the pleasure of your company tomorrow?"

"Yes, sir."

"I must tell you that I will have another corpse then. It has been a most fruitful week. This is a young man, large and muscular, extremely fresh." He stares at Edgar. "I am thinking of another female after that, a young one, of teen years. In fact, I'd like two of them, the second female a bit more muscular, and then another young man too."

Godwin puts his hand on Edgar's shoulder again and this time grips him hard, his fingers reaching his neck.

Edgar is shaking when he leaves. He ascends to the ground floor and heads toward the front of the hospital. Then he spots his uncle coming toward him. They pass without a word, but Vincent's eyes slide in his direction. Then Edgar feels a hand seize his arm from behind.

"There is one thing I should tell you," says Dr. Brim quietly. He looks up and down the hall. "I saw Dr. Godwin late last night as I was leaving the hospital. He had returned here for some reason, in a carriage, and he was driving away again from the back door. He passed right by me. I could see that he had something lying on the back seat—it was about six feet long and in a sack."

17

A Particular Body

Edgar leaves the hospital scared and confused. He wonders why his uncle told him that. It seemed calculated. Vincent Brim and Percy Godwin are colleagues and friends. He tries to remember what Alfred Thorne said about getting him the apprenticeship here at this hospital. His uncle maintains he didn't ask for him, but was that true? Did Dr. Godwin request that he be invited?

"Did they bring me here for a purpose," he says out loud, "to be observed . . . or worse?"

He turns on his heels and re-enters the hospital. There is a candlestick telephone at the reception counter. He asks to use it.

"This is a valuable apparatus," says the matron, glaring at him. "It is for the use of the sick and the poorish who need our assistance, and for the great men who administer their God-given skills to those who are brought to us. It is not for just any sort who might walk in here and want to speak upon it. You have exactly one minute."

Edgar telephones Annabel. The Thornes have one communication device in the house, in the drawing room.

"The Thorne residence," intones Beasley.

"It is Edgar. Might I speak to Mrs. Thorne? Tell her it is an emergency!"

Annabel is on the other end in a moment. She is still not entirely used to this recently installed device and shouts into it.

"Yes? Yes, Edgar. This is your mother Annabel Thorne speaking."

"Mother," says Edgar, trying not to meet the matron's eyes. She is already frowning at him.

"Yes, Edgar Brim? Yes, this is your mother Annabel Thorne speaking."

"Mother, why did father decide to have me apprentice at the London Hospital? It was a most unusual thing. Did my uncle ask for me?"

There is a long pause.

"I shall answer now."

"Please do."

"Someone high up in the hospital suggested that you might want to be there. Your father never told me who it was."

Edgar's heart thumps. The matron wrenches the receiver from his hand and slams it down on the switch hook. But Edgar barely cares. He is instantly out the front door and heading toward Kentish Town.

Lucy and Tiger are standing on the front step of the house when he arrives, not saying anything, Lucy ashen and Tiger alert, glancing up and down the street, her hand inside her pocket where she keeps her pistol. When they notice him, Lucy brightens for an instant and smiles in that way that always makes him feel warm inside and Tiger nods in the manner that gives him confidence.

"She is doing fine," says Tiger, straightening up, hands on her hips.

Edgar doesn't respond.

"It isn't me we need to be worried about," says Lucy, her voice shaky.

Edgar still hasn't said a word.

"Why are you so quiet?" asks Lucy, and when he doesn't answer immediately, her pale face grows paler. "Do you have word of Jonathan?"

"No."

"Then why do you look like this?"

"Because my head is full of suspicions. Someone high up in the hospital apparently asked that I be given my position there." He pauses. "And Godwin was seen on the street behind the hospital last night with something large in a sack lying on the back seat of his carriage."

"Oh God!" cries Lucy, putting her hand over her mouth.

"It could have been anything," says Tiger.

"Godwin told me," says Edgar, "that he was going straight home."

"So, how do you know he came back?"

"My uncle said he did. It was curious. He offered the information without my asking."

"Maybe it isn't true," says Lucy, pulling her hand from her mouth.

"Maybe. I was away from Godwin's lab for a while during the day, and I could swear that when I returned, the door to the Elephant Man's room was ajar."

"You and I are going back there, Edgar, right now!" says Tiger. She takes him by the arm.

"No we're not." He shakes her off. "The two of us can't be seen sneaking in there. You've already been shown the lab and the Elephant Man's room, so it wouldn't make sense for you to be back in the basement of the hospital. But my presence wouldn't arouse suspicion, if I do this right. I need to go alone. And I'll go at night."

The girls don't say anything for a moment.

"Take this," says Tiger finally, reaching into her pocket for the pistol.

"No, I want you to have it," says Edgar. *Do not be afraid*, he reminds himself.

"You'll be completely unarmed," says Lucy. "The demon may indeed want to kill you more than any of us. It may be waiting to get you alone. Maybe you are the only one he *really* wants to murder."

"I'll go back to Thorne House first. I'll be armed after that."

"But not until you get there," says Tiger. "I'll make sure you're safe."

"What do you mean?"

"I'll come with you to Thorne House."

"No you won't. You need to stay here with Lucy."

"No she doesn't," says Lucy firmly. "I have the biggest weapon we've got just inside this door."

"If you leave without me," says Tiger, "I'll just follow you." She steps closer to him again and their hands touch.

Edgar hesitates, seeing the determination in Tiger's eyes. "All right," he finally says, "we'll go as far as Thorne House together, but then you must come back here quickly. This is where you are needed. Kill anything that comes. Lucy, stay inside with the cannon readied and turn off the lights. I'll return as soon as I can."

"I didn't tell Lucy everything," he says as they walk quickly in the direction of Mayfair.

"What do you mean?"

"Godwin said he would have a fresh young body to experiment on tomorrow, a very fresh one, a young man."

"That might be a coincidence. Why would he warn you? It's your uncle who concerns me. He knows all about you: exactly where you live and everyone in your house. And now he seems to be trying to cast suspicion on Godwin. He has the key to the Elephant Man's room. Perhaps he is letting whatever is usually in there, out?"

"I need to get into that room, free Jonathan if he's there. That's first."

"And then we have to do something about both your uncle and Godwin."

"Do something?"

Tiger doesn't respond. He knows she is capable of almost anything—she grew up on her own on the streets. Murdering someone, if necessary, wouldn't be something she'd hesitate to do. When they reach Camden Town at the bottom of Kentish Town Road she hails a cab, and Edgar tells the driver where to drop him and then to take Tiger right back. As the carriage clops and rattles through the streets, they sit close together, not saying anything but aware of each other's thoughts. Tiger keeps her eyes on the streets, ready to act. When they reach Thorne House and he begins to get out, she suddenly leans toward him and kisses him firmly on the mouth and then gives him a gentle shove that sends him toward the street. "Be careful," she says.

Edgar watches the cab leave, heading back north. Lucy would have behaved very differently, he thinks—she would have given him a gentler kiss, on the cheek, perhaps a warm embrace. Tiger sticks her head out of the window and nods at him, wearing that confident expression, the very same one she often gave him back on the playing fields of the College on the Moors when they faced the bullies together.

Edgar pivots and heads toward the door and his thoughts return to his mission. He tries to imagine if it is really possible that Dr. Godwin has made a human being, a monstrous one that he cannot fully control, or if his uncle is the villain and unleashing the creature on them. Then he realizes something else—he and his three friends have been separated—they are each now on their own.

When Tiger's cab goes around the corner she turns and slides open the little window behind her head and looks up at the driver. "I've changed my mind," she tells him. "Take me to the London Hospital."

Edgar enters Thorne House quietly and slips upstairs, avoiding Annabel. She is good at seeing inside him, understanding how he truly feels. She will spot his uneasiness and perhaps get things out of him and try to prevent him from returning to the hospital. He cannot tell her the situation he is in. He doubts she would believe it anyway, and if she did, she would want somehow to be involved.

There's something else he doesn't want her to see or know.

After he finishes the meal that Beasley secretly brings up to him in the lab, he sneaks downstairs and into his room. He reaches under the bed, lifts the floorboard, and takes out Lear's gleaming sword. He touches the blade and feels its razor-sharp edge. Then he plucks the long black frock coat Annabel bought him for his graduation out of his closet, slices the lining open and inserts the big weapon into it. He also retrieves the pick-lock instrument Tiger made for him and slips it into a pocket.

Then he waits until it is dark and sneaks out into the streets.

Tiger waits patiently in the alcove of a building on narrow Turner Street on the west side of the hospital, positioned so she can see Edgar approach either the front entrance on Whitechapel Road or the rear via Stepney Way.

"Come on," she says impatiently several times. But she doesn't leave her post, nor does she bother to even lean against the wall; she stands tall and alert. She worries about Lucy, by herself at the Lear home, but can't let Edgar do this alone. She can't leave him, not Edgar Brim. She will watch him go into the hospital and make sure he comes out. Her hand stays on the pistol in her pocket. It has been dark for a while when she sees him approaching, rushing along Stepney Way, eyes intent on his job.

Edgar enters through the back door. All the lights are out in the basement, something he's never seen before. He moves in the dark, feeling his way along the wall until he comes to the laboratory door. It is locked. He's never seen that before either. He takes out Tiger's pick-lock tool. This won't be easy in the dark, but the lock actually proves a simple one, though when he opens the door it creaks. He stands dead still. No one comes. He closes the door behind him and locks it again from the inside. This time he won't chance turning on lights. The lab is like a maze and filled with breakable glass and acids and potions. He cannot make a mistake. He thinks again of where everything is situated and begins to walk slowly between tables, moving gingerly. Then his hand touches something made of glass and knocks it forward. He reaches out in the darkness and somehow catches it. It takes him a while to recover, standing there with his heart pounding, clutching a big beaker.

Finally, he finds what he is seeking—Godwin's lantern on his desk. He lights it and a dim glow illuminates the few feet around him. He makes for the Elephant Man's door. It is locked now. He takes out the pick tool and soon discovers that this entrance is easy to unlock too.

The door doesn't make a sound. Though he is loath to close it behind him, he pulls it shut, so it might look sealed from the other side. Then he turns to the cold interior, casting the lantern's beam around the room. Nothing comes rushing at him out of the darkness, though it feels as if something is lurking, so he keeps his back to the door and continues to use the beam to investigate his surroundings from there.

"Is there anyone in here?" he asks, terrified that there might be a response. None comes and he relaxes a little, though shivering in the cold. He can move around. He pushes himself off the door, wishing he had time to pause over the bed, the writing desk and the table, to think about what it was like when the Elephant Man lived here, but he has to look for specific things, the most important of which is Jonathan himself . . . or his body. There's still no sound in the room.

"Jonathan?"

He flashes the beam higher, across the walls, and sees someone staring back at him! The face is grotesque. *It's the Elephant Man.*

Edgar takes a step backward and stifles a gasp. But it isn't really Joseph Merrick and Edgar feels like knocking the lantern into the side of his head to make himself think straight. What he has encountered is a painting, an accomplished portrait in oil that appears to have been done before Merrick died, he looks so life-like. The deformed head, bulging in several directions, with wisps of greasy dark hair combed over on top, features two handsome eyes looking out, asking to be respected and loved.

Edgar moves even slower now, wondering if somewhere in the far reaches or corners of this room he might find bodies hanging from meat hooks in the nearly freezing temperature.

Then he remembers the two boxes on the floor, the ones the size and shape of coffins. He casts the beam toward the corner where he had seen them, almost hoping they aren't there now. But there they are against a wall, looking out of place in the room. He shines the light directly on them and steps in their direction. Then his heart misses a beat.

One of them is open!

He steps over and slides the cover fully back and looks inside. It is streaked with dark stains, some of which look like gobs of red jelly, which he can't bring himself to touch. But at least the box is empty. The other one is shut with four metal clasps fastened on one side. *Do not be afraid.* He bends down and with a shaking hand, snaps the clasps open and stands back, feeling for his sword. But nothing happens, nothing moves. He lifts the lid slightly and peers in. There's silence, no movement. He gets down on his knees and pulls the lid open farther. He shines the light inside and almost vomits. There are several human organs in there, packed in ice, and a leg made up of two different parts, an old man's gray-haired thigh bolted to a young woman's smooth calf with screws. He slams the box shut. He wants to *flee*.

But for a moment, he can't get up. He can feel the hag standing over him, pressing down on his shoulders, her vile breath wafting across his ear toward his mouth. His heart starts to pound so hard that he thinks he will die. He isn't sure where he wants to run, just away. *Do not be afraid*, he tells himself again. His father's face comes to his mind. He knows he has to fight back. He has to get up and *do something* about all of this, just as Tiger said. He needs to find Jonathan dead or alive, find out what is after them, kill Godwin's creature if he has made one, and kill his own uncle if he is unleashing it!

He struggles to his feet and takes a step but immediately stumbles over a smaller box. There are several more. He shines his light on them.

They are filled with blocks of ice.

"Body parts are being preserved in this room," he whispers to himself, "experimental parts." He tries to be calm and figure this out. "Why do that? Why not just use them in the lab?" He thinks about it for another moment and it quickly comes to him. "The hospital is too risky for the most evil of operations. They are being moved somewhere else!" But something still doesn't make sense.

"Why not just take the parts with you every time you leave? Why keep them here?"

He hears a noise on the other side of the door and douses his lantern and listens.

Someone is unlocking the entrance to the lab out there. Edgar is glad he secured it after he entered. He hears the door open and then sees a line of light appear at the bottom of the Elephant Man's door. Someone is grunting as if carrying something heavy.

Graft!

The gruesome gravedigger walks across the lab lugging or carrying a weight until he stops at about where Edgar figures the operating table is. Then he hears Graft grunt even louder.

"Let's get you up 'ere, dear," Edgar hears him say and there is a bang as if the weight was dropped on the table. Then there's a very different sound, like a little cry, like someone who is semiconscious, struggling to awaken. It sounds like a female.

"Get in 'ere, my dear, it shan't be long until we get you where you is goin'. 'Ide you inside this, we can. You 'ave an appointment with the surgeon, you do! Let's give you a shot for your trip."

Edgar imagines a needle going into the body, drugging it more thoroughly. He hears rustling and then another sound. With his heart in his mouth, he realizes what this new noise is—the ties being bound on one of Graft's body sacks, the ones used to transport corpses.

Edgar steals quietly toward the door and pulls the sword from his frock coat. He hears Graft grunting again, likely lifting the sack. Then he hears the hideous man's heavy footsteps heading toward the outer door. Edgar opens his own door a crack. He sees Graft dragging something along the floor toward the laboratory entrance, then pausing to turn out the light. The second he does that, Edgar leaps through the doorway and comes after him, weapon out and ready. But he can barely find his way in the dark and by the time he gets to the entrance and then into the hallway Graft is gone. Edgar runs toward the hidden door under the stairs, pulls it open and goes out into the moonlit night. He spots Graft at the end of the back lawn, loading the sack into a carriage. Edgar runs after him, resisting the urge to shout. But he slips and falls on something: a patch of hair, as if torn from a scalp, dark blond like Jonathan's, caked with dried blood. When Edgar looks up, Graft's carriage is careening down the street. In seconds, he is long gone.

Edgar sits on the ground, Lear's sword in hand, not sure what to do. Part of him wants to pursue and murder Graft and another wants to flee again, fly away from all of this, run back to Thorne House and get into his bed or under it and try to forget everything. But Jonathan has been attacked, may be dead or still out there somewhere, worse than murdered: disemboweled, his limbs or his brain or his face being used to make some sort of human creature. And Tiger and Lucy are on their own too, or . . . who is in the body bag that Graft put into the carriage? And where is he going with it?

Tiger observes the short, thick-set man leaving the hospital from the rear in a hurry in his loaded conveyance. From where she is standing, she cannot see the back door of the building.

Edgar has no hope of catching Graft. He rushes back into the hospital and up to the first floor and down the hall to his uncle's office, his face flushed red, anger replacing fear. He is suspicious that his slimy relative is still here, up to no good. He needs answers, *now*! He brandishes the sword, unconcerned about who might see him. But he encounters no one in the hall and when he gets to Vincent Brim's room the door is locked and the lights are out.

"He never locks his door!" says Edgar. "Where is he?" He thinks again of Graft's carriage heading out into the night. "Is he going to my uncle's home? He is the one with the key to the cold room!" He takes in his breath. "Godwin's collaborator," he says with a nod, "or worse." Edgar knows where Vincent Brim lives.

But he also knows he should fly to Lucy and Tiger first, make sure they are alive and well. He shoves the big blade back into his coat and rushes through the hospital to the front door and out onto Whitechapel Road. He doesn't care anything about the scur- rilous people he sees now. If any man threatens him, he'll drive Lear's blade right through him! He screams for a hansom cab. But there are none, so he begins to run, west on Whitechapel Road back toward the city. Finally, he spots a cab up ahead, moving away. He sprints toward it.

Tiger goes into the hospital by the back door. The lights are out in the downstairs lab and there is no sign of Edgar inside. Her heart pounding, she races through the building and out the front door onto a nearly deserted Whitechapel Road. She spots Edgar in the distance, running after a cab, the only one in sight.

Edgar seizes the hansom from behind and leaps up onto it. The driver stares at him and then cocks his whip in a threatening way.

"Off! Off, boy!"

But Edgar reaches around and opens the passenger door and sticks his hand in and pulls out a well-dressed, red-faced drunken gentleman from the cab by the collar and deposits him on the street. There's a shabbily dressed woman with him, the top of her dress open. Edgar growls at her and she leaps out the other side of the carriage onto the cobblestones and runs away. The driver's whip comes snapping down from above and cuts through Edgar's coat at the shoulder, drawing blood.

"Now, wait a minute," slurs the gentleman as he staggers to his feet. Edgar pulls out his huge knife and jabs it toward him. "I was just leaving!" cries the man, "please have my cab, sir!" He turns away, tripping and landing on his face on the pavement. When Edgar looks up at the driver again, he has pulled back his whip and looks scared.

"Please don't 'urt me," he says. "I shall do as you say. You ain't the Ripper, is you?"

"Kentish Town!" shouts Edgar. "Sixty-six Progress Street! As fast as this nag will go!"

The driver lays his whip into the horse and the poor animal almost sprints through the London streets in the early morning, making good time through and past the Old City along the nearly empty streets and then north beyond Regent's Park to Kentish Town. Edgar gets the driver to drop him at the corner of Progress and Mansfield and runs as hard as he can to the Lear home.

The door is wide open. There is no sign of Lucy or Tiger.

18

Monster Maker

E dgar frantically searches the house. There is little evidence of a disturbance. The loaded cannon sits there facing the front door, as if it hasn't been so much as touched. There are no bullet holes in the wall, nothing. Then he sees little drops of red on the floor, as if from blood, a few strands of hair, copper colored, but none black.

"Whatever came here didn't have much trouble," he mutters. "It surprised Lucy and took her." He looks around, thinking the villain broke in just after he left, before Tiger got back. "It was watching the house!" He goes out the front door but halts on the step, unsure what to do, feeling absolutely impotent. "Where's Tiger?" he asks himself. Then his stomach nearly turns. "Where, dear God, are the other two?" They are abducted or dead or dying or being tortured and he is standing here unable to do anything about it.

Think!

He wonders if he should indeed go to Vincent Brim's house in Kensington and extract information from his uncle at swordpoint. He starts to run along Progress Street back toward Mansfield and then onto Highgate Road. There aren't any cabs to be seen and he doubts there will be any for some distance at this hour. He runs harder and reaches Kentish Town Road and then plunges downward and southward toward central London, the air getting colder, as if a storm is brewing. A lone cab passes heading north and he thinks, for an instant, that he sees Tiger sitting inside. But that's impossible. She must be moving the other way, or deep in the city, frantically searching for Lucy.

He imagines Vincent Brim's luxurious home, the private lab that might be in it, just like Alfred had in his house, and what might be going on there. Edgar had been in his uncle's house once. He can't recall the exact address, but he thinks he may be able to find the street, and if he can, he knows he will recognize the house. He imagines what he will do if the painted Carmilla tells him his uncle is not at home—he will take her by the hair, her fake powdered white face terrified, and hold Lear's razor-sharp blade to her throat until she tells him where his uncle is. But he thinks about how far away Kensington is and imagines all that could happen before he gets there. Then a memory comes to him. He stops.

He sees an image of Dr. Godwin the other night climbing into the hansom cab.

"I have a wonderful imagination," Edgar says out loud, breathing hard, reassuring himself. "Everything in life is bright and intense for me. I remember everything." Now he hears Godwin's voice calling out an address to the driver.

"The Midland Grand Hotel!" he had shouted.

That isn't far from here! Just keep south a little, then a little east. It is right near the St. Pancras Railway Station, almost built into it.

He turns onto Camden Road and races down it, not noticing anyone or anything in the foggy gas-lit night. Before long, he's on Pancras Road and can see the hotel and the station in the distance.

It's an ominous looking building made of red brick and huge, like Dracula's castle looming above the London streets. Black turrets rise into the sky along its roof, a clock tower at one end, another tower at the other. It is nine stories high, and the towers are the height of nearly fifty men, the tallest occupied building in the metropolis.

"Godwin must live there!"

Edgar runs up the hard steps under the red and blue arches, and past the uniformed doorman through the front door. He stops inside, stunned by the elegance of his surroundings. Everything is blue and red—the carpets, the grand winding staircase, even the glittering chandeliers. He feels a big hand grip his arm from behind. He turns to see a doorman with a broad, lined face and a vein-filled nose under a smart red and blue captain's cap.

"Might I help you, young man?" The fellow's eyes slide down to the rip on the shoulder of Edgar's frock coat, a line of blood evident where the whip had creased him.

"I . . . I'm here to see Dr. Godwin."

"Is that so?"

Edgar realizes that he has come to a dead end. This man will never let him see the esteemed surgeon, let alone tell him where he is. And the only clue Edgar has, the only shred he can hang onto as his friends go to grisly deaths, is the possibility that Graft has been bringing his specimens here in sacks, and that somehow, something can be done about it before the night is out. Or maybe he can still fly to Vincent Brim—he could easily break in there, overpower the old servants. No, it is Godwin he must pursue, the great surgeon himself! Edgar has his sword, which he can feel in his frock coat, easily accessible to his right hand. He could take it out now and demand to know where Godwin is.

But then another plan comes to him.

He tries to look calm and reaches under his outer coat to the breast pocket of his suit coat. Godwin had given him several of his personal cards so Edgar might run whatever errands were needed. *Doctor Percy Godwin, Chief Surgeon, The London Hospital.*

He produces the card and hands it to the doorman, who looks at it with some surprise.

"Dr. Godwin asked me to visit him tonight."

"At this hour?"

"Yes, it is an emergency. I am to take a note from him to a Dr. Vincent Brim at the hospital, who is performing a most delicate surgery tonight."

"Dr. Brim? I've heard of him. He has been here."

"He has? Tonight?"

The man gives him a puzzled look. "Not that I know of," he says. "You may go up."

"Up? I don't know where Dr. Godwin's room is."

"Top occupied floor, seven up. Seven hundred and seventy seven is his. Good evening, sir."

Edgar doesn't bother with the new electric elevators. He takes the stairs one step at a time until he is out of view and then takes three and four at each leap until he reaches the seventh floor, completely out of breath. The hallways are decorated in blue and red too and pillars are carved into the walls at each end, a sort of Far Eastern décor. The door to the apartment at 777 is wide and wooden. Edgar stands in front of it for a few moments wondering what in the world he will do and say when Godwin appears. Then he realizes that what he observes after the door opens will help. If the surgeon is just out of bed and confused by Edgar's appearance, Edgar will tell him everything, all of his concerns, his worries, what he saw Graft doing, of Jonathan's bloody hair, Lucy's disappearance, of his suspicions of his uncle . . . but if Godwin comes to the door fully dressed, as if he is at work upon something . . . Edgar will take up his sword!

He bangs on the door. He bangs again. No answer.

"Godwin!" he hears himself shout. "GODWIN!"

A door opens down the hallway and a man steps out into the corridor in his dressing gown. He stares at Edgar, who returns his look with a glare. The man disappears back into his room.

Edgar won't wait any longer. He can't. He takes out his sword, holds the thick blade high above his head and drives it through the door just above the lock. The door shudders and splinters. He reaches in and turns the knob from the inside and opens and closes the door quickly, stepping into the apartment. There's no sound in the vestibule. He looks along it into the living room and sees the lamps on Euston Road through the tall windows on the far wall, casting dim light into the whole space. He sees chairs, sofas, an ottoman, a writing desk and table. He moves toward them.

"Godwin!"

But there still isn't a sound. He turns left in the living room and into a dark tight hall that leads toward a doorway that he can barely see. It must be the bedroom. The blade ready in his hand, he advances toward the door.

When he is almost there, Edgar puts his back to the wall outside the room and listens for a response to his footsteps, for any sound at all. But there is just the distant hoof-claps and shouts in the London streets outside. He slides into the room. There seems to be something on the bed.

"Godwin?"

Nothing.

Edgar advances, blade pointed toward the thing in the covers. He touches it with the sword and then smacks it—still nothing. It's just a lump in an unmade bed. Godwin, after all, is a bachelor.

Edgar searches the other rooms in the apartment and finds them empty. He heads back toward the outer door, unsure what to do next. He steps out into the hallway and gently closes the door behind him, only aware of the sound of his breath. Something tells him to look down. There's mud on the floor, just tiny bits but evident when you look closely.

"That could be from my own shoes," he tells himself.

But the mud goes in a trail in the opposite direction from which he had come. Edgar follows it, walking past a window that looks out over London, and discovers that this trail leads toward a door at the far end of the hall. He goes through it and finds a staircase. There is more dirt evident on the steps that go upward. Edgar climbs. When he reaches the next floor he sees another window and when he looks out he can not only view the London streets but the roof of the Midland Grand Hotel, dark and ominous in the foggy night. But the stairs keep going upward and so does the mud. He puts his head against the window and gazes straight up the exterior wall and realizes that only the clock tower is above him. Godwin, or someone, must have come up here, either with muddy boots or dragging something with mud on it. Some of the dirt looks clotted and red. Edgar swallows and walks up the next flight, then another, his blade in hand. At the top of the last one, he encounters a big black door. When he tries the knob, it turns. He steps inside and releases the door behind him. It shuts with a bang, as if on a spring.

It is a remarkable room, about forty feet across, round and with a spectacular cone-shaped ceiling. It smells of chloroform and animals. A crash of lightning sounds the instant Edgar enters and he looks up to the roof to see a large open window and something thrust into it—a long steel pole. He follows the pole down to the floor and sees Godwin standing at its base, smiling at him. Gaslights and rows of kerosene lamps give the room an eerie glow, as if lighted that way for effect. There are a half dozen tables against the walls and a bigger one right next to the celebrated surgeon. Much brighter lights illuminate it in a dazzling spotlight. There's a body on it, strapped down, struggling.

Lucy.

Edgar takes a step toward Godwin with his sword but it is immediately struck from his hand with great force from behind. Graft picks up the weapon with a thick hand and shoves Edgar toward the surgeon.

"Lovely to receive you!" says the good doctor. "I see you listened carefully when I uttered my address. Well done! Perfect!"

"You wanted me to come here?"

"Why, yes, my boy. I made the scientific calculation that you would be drawn into my lair if I played my cards correctly. I believe that is the expression. There is humor in that way of putting it, is there not?" He looks at Edgar questioningly and lets out a laugh, then stops it. "Perhaps not, but still, it is indeed lovely to see you."

"What are you doing?"

Edgar can see Lucy clearer now. Her mouth is gagged and she has turned her head and is staring at Edgar with her eyes wide. The corpse sack is under her on the steel table and he can see that her dress is nearly ripped off and her hair is disheveled and her shoes are gone; she is bruised and there are little dabs of blood on her. She had fought back. Godwin has a big scalpel out.

"Oh this?" he says, pointing down at Lucy. "I am happily in possession of a very healthy and still living young woman, almost seventeen. Fresh, fresh, fresh!"

"But . . . that's Lucy." Edgar can feel tears coming to his eyes.

"Yes, I know," says Godwin. "Isn't it marvelous? This has all worked out so well. I have been thinking for some time that I needed a young woman and man simultaneously to make my experiment work effectively." He nods toward another table. Edgar turns and sees Jonathan lying there, almost motionless, only his chest moving gently up and down. His face is battered, his hair matted with blood. Edgar turns to Graft and sees blood on him too, a nasty bruise on his protruding brow, a rip in a clotted ear. Jon had indeed fought back.

"This has been a trying night and day, Edgar, so I would appreciate it if you didn't create a fuss. Graft and I have had to bribe the hotel employee who operates the back-door lift, twice! Two fresh bodies had to be got up here in sacks. Normally, we simply have parts delivered via the hotel butcher's ice-and-meat lorry. Graft is a good friend of his, you know, beautiful man. Twice a week, Mondays and Thursdays, organs and limbs and skin on ice arrive in the back kitchen and find their way up here! One can't have such things brought in past the front doorman, you know."

There's another sound in the room, a sort of animal groan. It is coming from a darkened area. Edgar thinks he can see the outline of the panther trying to get to its feet in a cage, but its head doesn't look like a panther's anymore.

"Where is the monster?" asks Edgar.

"I beg your pardon?"

"Where is the monster you've made? Do you know that it has escaped several times and attacked people? It killed my friend Professor Lear. It killed my adoptive father."

"Oh dear, I suppose that was awfully upsetting for you. But I know nothing of a Godwin-made monster of which you speak."

"You are lying."

"No. No, I'm not. I have not, unfortunately, ever created a human being."

"Then who has?"

"That is a very good question, my boy. One I have been exploring all my life."

"My uncle, Vincent Brim, does he work with you? There IS a monster, I tell you! It must be *him* who made it! You are in this together!"

"Him? Vincent Brim? What an absolutely absurd idea. He has not the brains or the intestinal fortitude to do such a thing. He is an inferior sort. I would place him low on the eugenic scale of humanity. Deep down, he is too soft. He does not have the brain capacity or the necessary morality to do what you suggest."

"And you do?"

"Why, yes, I do. Thank you for saying that. I believe that was a compliment."

"I beg you to let my friends go, sir."

"Why on earth would I do that? I have searched all my life for a situation like this. What we have here is a confluence of opportunities for me. You see, I have come to the conclusion that I must eliminate all four of you and I also need healthy young people to make my creature. And here we are!" He holds out his hands to Edgar and sweeps them in the direction of Jonathan and Lucy.

"Why," stammers Edgar, "why are you saying you *must* eliminate us?"

"I know, it is unfortunate, and I take no pleasure in it. Pleasure is an interesting concept for me. I am not sure about it, still. The ladies at the hospital and even some in the streets, many of whom throw themselves at me, seem to be in pursuit of pleasure when they interact with me—after all I am blessed with a strapping big body and I have taken great care to adjust myself and make myself as handsome as possible—but personally I have not experienced the same interest in the opposite gender or even my own." He looks sad for a moment. "I am trying, though."

"What do you mean . . . you have made yourself as handsome as possible?"

"Facial surgery, my boy! I have used advanced techniques on myself, exclusively on myself, and transformed my face. This is the way of the future! Do you like it? No, you probably aren't moved by it. You are a male who appears to be heterosexual. Perhaps I should ask your friend Lucy here?" He looks down at her. "Do you find me attractive, young lady?" He gives her a particularly dazzling smile. Her eyes bulge and she struggles with the straps. "Oh," he says, "I forgot. She is muzzled. How silly of me!" He attempts another laugh and then looks at Edgar for approval.

"There is another one of us!" shouts Edgar.

Graft drops the big blade and seizes him from behind.

"Not for long, my young assistant of the remarkable red hair. You are quite a striking lad, I think—I can calculate why your two young ladies are intrigued by you—and you are sensitive and humane in the extreme and females appreciate that. I would have much to learn from you. But alas, you indeed must be eliminated. Strap him to the third table, Graft."

The wide, hairy man instantly has Edgar in a hold that goes across his chest and under his shoulders, paralyzing his arms and making him feel like he is being gripped by a huge vise. He tries to struggle.

"Is this funny?" asks Godwin. "I am never sure."

Graft lifts Edgar right off his feet and smashes him onto a table, then climbs on top of him and pins his chest with his knees. As Edgar thrashes about, he sees the hag's face on Graft's and it multiplies his terror. He freezes for a moment and as he does, he is tied down to the table. The straps cut into his wrists and ankles. Another holds him tightly at the waist. Graft picks up Lear's sword and sets it on the table next to Edgar, tantalizingly close.

"Is this funny in *any* way, Graft?" asks Godwin. "Or is it sad? Or frightening? What is it?"

"It is a money maker, sir, that's what it is."

"Indeed. You are correct. For you, it is most certainly that, and for me it is a scientific accomplishment! A bonanza!"

"You won't get away with this!" shouts Edgar. He hears Lucy sobbing. "Our friend will come after you. Tiger is indestructible." He imagines her out in the city somewhere, searching for them.

"I believe what you are now exhibiting is pride," says Godwin. "No one, no human being is indestructible, as you say, Master Brim. I find a statement such as that from you rather disappointing, very unscientific. This Tiger thing, that hermaphrodite friend of yours, is quite easy to destroy and of interest for use in these experiments as well. We shall have her! One just needs the sufficient amount of masculine brawn to bring her to heel. Graft, you know where she lives, though she may have wandered up to this other one's address." He nods down at Lucy. "Find Miss Tilley and bring her back here!"

"That will cost you more, sir, you know that."

"Yes, of course."

"Fifty quid, agreed?"

"Why, certainly, my good man. I promise."

"You is good on your promises, sir." He walks over to the table where Jonathan is tied down, picks up Thorne's rifle, which had been leaning against a wall in darkness behind the table, and goes out the door.

"What an imbecile," says Godwin after he leaves. "Of course I am good on my promises. If you do something like he shall now do for me, I pay you. It is a simple equation. I suppose, in a sense that makes me a moral man, doesn't it, Edgar?"

"It must be you who made the monster. It MUST be! Why are you denying it?"

"Because I do not tell lies. That is indeed immoral. I have made no monster, not yet."

"Then what murdered Professor Lear? What murdered Alfred Thorne? I have seen a drawing of its face, a monstrous face!"

"That sounds like a judgment of someone's appearance that is not pleasant. It is beneath you, Master Brim."

"You should let us go. We could work together to find this creature. We would help you. We could capture it together, and then you could examine it, learn how it was made."

"I have no need to capture it."

"What do you mean?"

"Because the so-called *monster* of which you speak—and that truly is a terrible thing to say about him—is in this very room."

Godwin steps toward the table and stands over Edgar. He reaches up and turns on the bright lights above. As he does, his head is in profile and Edgar can see that the light is shining right through the side of his face.

"I am the monster," says Godwin.

II

The Creature

Where there is knowledge, it will pass away.

∞

1 Corinthians 13:8

19

The House of Pain

Tiger is finally entering the Lear home on Progress Street, in Kentish Town, and discovering, to her horror, that it appears to be empty. After Edgar had vanished in his hurrying cab, she'd had trouble hailing a ride. She'd had no idea where he was going. Then the horse on her hansom had gone lame and she had had to travel the last few miles on foot. She curses herself for taking so long to get here, for leaving Lucy alone. The cannon sits pointing toward the front door, unused. She takes the pistol out of her pocket and puts both hands on it, a finger on the trigger as she searches the rooms, hoping to find something. She points the barrel head high.

"Bloody freak," she whispers, "come to me."

But she discovers nothing. She walks through the living room and spots the bits of blood on the floor. Lucy put up a fight, she thinks. She nods and almost smiles.

Tiger paces for a long while, her speed picking up, unsure what to do. She needs to find Lucy, find Edgar, find Jon . . . find Godwin.

She almost stumbles over two books that must have been knocked to the floor during the struggle. She bends down and picks them up. They are both hers, volumes she had brought with her from home when she knew she would be staying at the Lears'. The first is *A Vindication of the Rights of Woman*. She has been thinking more about the fight for equality lately and this is an important tract, written by Mary Shelley's mother, Mary Wollstonecraft, perhaps the first book ever written on this subject. But Tiger turns to the other book, Mary Shelley's own, *Frankenstein; or, The Modern Prometheus*. Maybe this novel can somehow tell her something. Tiger loves that it was a nineteen-year-old woman who wrote it. The story seems to her to be about many things, not just about making a monster, but about how men have such egos that they believe they are like gods. But she bought this book because of Edgar. She wants to understand him, this sensitive boy. More importantly, this book has been scaring the life out of her and she's loved that sensation. It makes her feel alive.

She opens it and sees something she hasn't noticed before. It's the dedication at the front. Mary Shelley has dedicated her famous novel to her father. Tiger reads his name, Mary's maiden name.

GODWIN.

Then she hears a thud at the front door.

Back at the lab, Edgar is staring up at the great surgeon.

"Your face!" he cries, unable to stop himself.

"Ah, the light has caught it just right. Intriguing, isn't it?"

"What's . . . what's wrong with you?"

"You see, my boy, I have another face."

"What do you mean?"

"I have reconstructed my visage so that it is much more acceptable to the human eye. I shall turn my head about for you now and see if you can see it any clearer." He turns his head slightly, back and forth. There is something visible underneath again . . . like another face. It almost seems as though the visage beneath is much like the one that Annabel drew!

"Do you get it now?" asks Godwin.

"You! It was you!"

"Yes, I had to pay a few visits."

"But how . . . you removed your face?"

Godwin laughs out loud. "I believe *that* is indeed humor! No, I cannot remove my face. I am beginning to think your brain may be inferior. That is not good. Perhaps I will not use the sponge in your skull. Perhaps it should be the girl's. The human female brain is smaller, you know, but is so wonderfully connected. Thus, the fairer sex can do many things at once, not a masculine specialty. The male brain, on the other hand, has severe divisions, thus males focus well, not always a feminine strength. I really should slice up your brains and put them together. That would be best! But, Edgar, you must show me that you can think better than this! I do not *remove* my face! It is much cleverer than that. I will show you."

Godwin walks over to a shelf with several rows of big jars by the door. He takes something out of one of them.

"I keep this face in this jar in order to wear it when needed. It is an exact replica of my original, or the one that was given to me. It is made of human skin. Quite exquisite, took me years to construct. I thought it would work well when eliminating your friend Lear and entering Miss Tilley's home and Thorne House. It had the correct dramatic effect, put everyone in the right frame of mind. Fear, my boy, is such a useless and yet powerful and debilitating thing. And human beings are *so* susceptible to it. They are such fools about it." He is holding the face in his left hand. It looks like wet dough, though it has eyes, eyebrows and a hole for a nose and mouth. The skin is yellow and there are rubbery black lips on it, everything remarkably realistic. "Here, try it," he says and slaps the skin down onto Edgar's face. "Humor!" he exclaims. "You are Frankenstein's creature!" He smiles. "Just like me!"

Edgar feels like he may throw up. The thick human skin is moist on his face. He wants to tear it off but his hands are tied. He shivers and shakes his head violently and sends it flying into the air. Godwin catches it with the snap of his hand, a lightning fast reflex.

"Ah, I was given such skills!"

"What did you say?"

"The man who made me gave me such skills!"

Edgar swallows. "The other thing . . ." He stares at the surgeon and can barely get his breath. ". . . about Frankenstein's creature. Why did you say that?"

"Because," says Godwin, striking a pose, "I am not just any monster. I am HIM!"

Tiger leaps to her feet as the front door closes with a slam. Whoever is entering doesn't seem to be concerned about sneaking up on her.

"Edgar?" she says, lowering the gun. "Why are you slamming—"

Graft's wide body appears in the hallway. He has Thorne's rifle in his hand and is raising it toward Tiger. She raises her weapon back at him.

"Just the lass I was looking for," he growls. "You is coming with me."

Tiger pauses. Her heart is pounding.

"Where?" she asks.

"To the Midland Grand Hotel. Lovely accommodations they 'ave there, and you is going to the top floor, the toppermost of the poppermost."

"I'm not going anywhere with you."

"Oh yes you is, my dear. Now put down that gun. Girls shouldn't be playing with things that ain't in their line. Hand it over."

"Say that again."

"Hand over the man's weapon, little girl."

Tiger squeezes the trigger and puts a bullet right through the center of his forehead.

20

Frankenstein's Creature

"You are *him*?" gasps Edgar.

"Yes, I believe I am, though I was not made by the hand of Victor Frankenstein. That book is a fiction, you know, and he is not real, not like I am. He is a mere character. It is a curious thing, this making up of stories that human beings do. Novels are lies, but I have discovered that they can tell great truths."

"You aren't human! No wonder you are doing this!"

"Come, come, such a naïve view of humanity. I have learned, and you should know, that there is no greater evil on this earth than that which is perpetrated by human beings. After all, some horrible man made me! Some evil creature decided he could create a life and then ABANDON IT!" His face grows red.

Edgar struggles with the straps. "What do you mean *some* horrible man?"

Godwin steps away from the table and looks up at the great pole thrust into the hole in the roof. There is another crash of thunder and the flash of lightning. "I do not know who gave me life, though I have done a lengthy study and have my suspects: three in particular, all great scientists from the past who are said to have attempted the re-animation of dead flesh! One of those, a man named Aldini, famously experimented on an executed criminal and made him move his muscles and lift a leg and open an eye with the use of electric current right here in London. Mrs. Shelley would have been an impressionable child at the time. But it may have been one of the other two creators!" He pauses for a moment and then stares off. "I came to consciousness in Germany in a forest near the Swiss border, naked, bloodied and scarred, the soles of my feet ripped to shreds. I had been running away from someone!"

"But that doesn't mean you are a creature made by the hand of man. Maybe you just suffered from some terrible occurrence and it may have been a head injury that caused you not to remember what—"

"It was more than a century ago!" shouts Godwin. "I am a human being with no lineage! No father or mother! No childhood!" Edgar hears Lucy shudder on her table. The handsome surgeon looks at her and then back at Edgar and walks toward him, coming to a sudden halt at the operating table. He stares down at his own body and then moves his arms as if they were foreign objects. "And these were different then." He unbuttons his shirt, exposing his throat. Edgar can see a faint scar running all the way around the muscular neck. Godwin undoes his cuffs and rolls up his sleeves, exposing his powerful arms, his forearms and biceps, all swelling with thick muscle too, admired by the nurses at the London Hospital. He shows Edgar similar faint scars around his wrists. "My hands were put on here, quite intricate work. He must have used the best parts from others." Then he leans down, bringing his face up to within inches of the boy's, and separates the hairs on the top of his own head. Edgar's bulging eyes see another scar encircling the scalp. "This," says Godwin, "is where the fiend opened the skull he gave to me and put in another brain. A good one, mind you, a brilliant one. I often wonder where he found it. One admires his taste . . . and his skill." Godwin presses the top of his head into Edgar's cheek and the boy can feel how flat it is under the carefully combed hair. Edgar again senses that he will retch. Godwin stands back and begins to elegantly fix his collar and pull his sleeves back into place. "I have repaired these scars so they are almost invisible. But alas, I re-drew some for my attacks on Professor Lear, Miss Tilley and Mr. Thorne."

"Why are you doing this to us?" asks Edgar. "If such a horrible thing was done to you, why would you perpetrate such a horror on anyone else?"

"An excellent point, very skillfully put, perhaps your brain will indeed be of significant use." He pauses. "This is why: I am a scientist and a supporter of progress but also a supporter of myself, I'm inwardly prone, as I have learned all human beings are. I must go on living and science must keep progressing. What I am doing this evening is indeed regrettable, in a way. I wish I could spare you and your friends. But the problem is that you know of my existence. I will not be allowed to live if people know what I am. If you think about it, you will understand. So, it is a mere fact that you must be removed, a mere scientific fact. I knew of that revenant you murdered in the Lyceum Theatre, that "vampire," as human beings call it and Bram Stoker characterized it. It is in the interest of such creatures as the revenant and I to be aware of each other's existence, so he and I were searching for evidence of beings such as ourselves. The revenant actually discovered me in my hospital when he was in London. He wrote to me. He said someone was on his trail. I kept abreast of him after that and knew you killed him, was nearby when it happened. I arranged for you to be brought to the hospital to apprentice to keep an eye on you. I queried you about your guardians, your friends and your integrity. The latter worried me. But I thought I might spare you. But you kept asking the wrong questions and sneaking around. So, I put the destruction of all of you into motion. And here you are!" Godwin turns away and paces. "I simply have to kill you, Edgar. I wish I could be sad about it, cry about it, since it seems to me that you and your friends are excellent people, and the girl on this table appears to be lovely, I think . . . I'm not sure. And you and I both lack a father—we are connected in that way. But you see, I cannot cry for you, myself or anyone. I have tried. Let me try once more."

There is near-silence again in the room, though the rain is now pounding down on the roof. Godwin holds his big hands over his face.

"No," he says after a while, "I have no sense of sadness. I don't believe my tear ducts work well, anyway. And I'm not certain that sadness, crying, that sort of weakness, is helpful in this world, which as I say, should be built upon improvement. A real man, a man of resource and industry, does not cry."

Tiger, thinks Edgar. In his paralyzing fear, he had forgotten about her. But at any moment, he fears that the door will be flung open and Graft will appear carrying her limp body in his meaty arms.

"You have read *Frankenstein*, I am sure?" asks Godwin.

Edgar nods.

"Well, who hasn't? It is universally considered a marvelous human creation, though I personally do not understand what is so great about it. It is a mere fiction concerning a situation similar to mine. And fiction is nothing next to science! Some people say they are moved by *Frankenstein*, and it has certain impressive literary elements, yes, but I cannot perceive anything more. The monster is a bit of an emotional wreck, a *sissy* as some say these days. Still, I am honored that it is essentially me within the book's pages. And it really is, you know. She saw me."

"Mary Shelley?"

"Yes, I didn't know that for many years, but I am sure of it now. You see, I actually was near her in Switzerland in 1816 when I was hiding out in the forests near Lake Geneva. That was the year the skies were dark throughout the summer, something to do with a massive volcanic eruption in the Far East." He stops for a moment and seems reflective. "I saw a young woman one day in June in the forest. She was a lady with copper-colored hair and pale skin and an intriguing expression of inquisitiveness and intelligence in her eyes. There was a man with her, blond with a beautiful face and a faraway look in his countenance, and another man with dark hair and intense eyes. There was a second young woman too, who kept staring at the dark-haired man with what I now understand to be love, or lust. I hid in the woods and watched them. Then the extraordinary one with the unique hair drifted off alone picking wildflowers, just the beautiful ones. I had a sudden desire to murder her. I had been killing human beings in those days. I'm not sure why, though it may have come from a hatred of humanity that consumed me for a while before I understood the great opportunities available to me. But when I saw this woman's face clearly I could not take her life. There was something about her. I stood up as she approached, a twig snapped and she looked directly at me. I was perhaps a hundred feet away, somewhat camouflaged amidst the greens and browns of the forest. The look on her face wasn't fear. It was more like fascination. Then I dropped down to hide myself, and when I looked up through the leaves, I could tell that she couldn't see me anymore. But I heard her speak. My senses are extraordinary. 'What was that?' she said to herself. Then she shook her head and laughed, but almost immediately and very quietly said something else, a remarkable thing: 'That might be an idea!'"

"Let us go!" cries Edgar.

"I followed them from a distance. They went back to the place where they were staying: a wonderful house on the lake called the Villa Diodati. It was there, you know, where she began to develop the story for the great novel. It has been some guidance to me in understanding who I am. I even took my name from its dedication. It seemed so appropriate!" Godwin walks over to Lucy and looks down on her. "It took me nearly a century to learn the science of medicine. I had merely been on the run for many years, fleeing from people because I was grotesque: with my size, long black hair, scars and yellow teeth. I have replaced all my teeth, you know, covered them. Do you like them?" He offers his dazzling smile. "I settled into farming in a distant countryside in northern Germany, away from people, and I grew crops and raised chickens and fed myself. I only employed superior breeds. With my prodigious strength, I could do almost anything, and my extraordinary brain allowed me to learn how to read, and I purchased scientific books and devoured them. It became a mission of mine to do what had been done to me. Though the circumstances of my creation had been unfortunate, upon reflection it all seemed awfully clever. Science! The reason for living! I have been employed at many hospitals and have further developed my plastic surgery with each appointment. If I only had feelings, perhaps I wouldn't be doing this tonight!" He turns back to Edgar and almost runs into him. "Can you tell me a jest, a joke? I would like to see if it can make me laugh!"

There is a sound at the door. It opens with a slam. Tiger stands there, holding Thorne's marvelous rifle, the one with the expanding bullets that destroyed three-quarters of the vampire's neck.

"It's him!" shouts Edgar to her. "Godwin is the monster! Kill him!"

Tiger Tilley loves Edgar Brim and trusts him. She doesn't hesitate. She aims and fires at Godwin, right where the skull meets the neck. That's what Lear had said to do with creatures. *Take off the head.*

There's a shuddering recoil as the gun fires, driving the butt back into Tiger's shoulder as the bullet explodes from the barrel and rockets toward Godwin. Edgar feels a thrill go through him, a masculine thrill at the violent action of this weapon, this object moving through space. The shot is perfect! Tiger is extraordinary!

But it doesn't hit its mark.

Godwin darts his head away with superhuman speed and the bullet hits the brick wall behind him and makes a foot-wide hole in it.

Tiger and Edgar and Lucy gasp.

"Good evening, Miss Tilley."

"It won't be for you," she says.

"And yet, you have missed, Miss," says Godwin. "You cannot kill me with that thing. You cannot kill me at all."

"We'll see," says Tiger, advancing toward him, the gun trained on his head again. But suddenly the barrel is in Godwin's hand. Tiger has the reflexes of a cat but her opponent made her look like she was standing still. Lear was right when he said that this one was worse.

"Ah, I now have your weapon," he says, "and I have you too." He reaches out and grips her by the neck, his big hand wrapped almost around it, pinching a nerve and causing her to go limp. Then he lifts her with just one arm and sets her with a crash onto the remaining empty steel table.

"No!" cries Edgar.

"Yes," says Godwin. "And please do not shout. There is no need for that. We must be civil and intelligent about all of this." He straps Tiger to the table and turns the bright lights on above her. He clasps his hands together and hyperextends them backward from the wrists, making all ten fingers crack at once. "Ah! This is a wonderful specimen! Graft did not return, which means she must have eliminated him. That is delightful. She is a strong young female indeed, strong of mind and body. There is room in the future for women like her. All of that attractiveness and femininity is just a waste. Her limbs, her brain, are exceedingly difficult to resist!" He turns to Edgar. "Now!" he says. "I shall make something out of the four of you!"

The panther, whose head has been removed and replaced with another creature's—Edgar can't see it clearly in the shadows—offers a kind of growl, but it cannot get to its feet.

"That beast has a male body and a female head, my boy, from different species! And it survived. I shall get it going before long. My task with the group of you is to see if I can employ the best of the two genders and make you into something even better! I shall use your powerfully well-built young friend's arms and perhaps his legs, take either your brain or this hermaphrodite's and either connect up your male cortex better or divide up hers a little. Which gender's torso to use, ah, that is an excellent question! How much testosterone to employ . . . or any? Now that is indeed a conundrum, for despite its power, testosterone may be the source of all life's problems. Sometimes I even think that is the point of the *Frankenstein* novel." He looks around at the four bodies. "I'm not sure whose pelvic area or hands would be best?" He looks at Lucy. "Now, this beautiful girl, well, beautiful except for her nose—though I could fix that—and rather too pale skin and abnormal colored hair, what could I use of hers in particular? In many ways she is too slight and too weak, but lovely and symmetrical. She is fragile yet incredibly strong. I have observed that she has something none of the rest of you have . . . an obvious soul. How, in God's name, do I get at that? You, Edgar, may have a soul too, of a sort. You have both the masculine and feminine about you. It is quite remarkable."

Bound and gagged, Lucy is crying; Jonathan, battered and bruised, is trying to rouse; and Tiger is groggy. Only Edgar can speak. He tries to keep calm and rational.

"Sir, you seem as though you want a soul for yourself too, you want humanity and you want a sense of humor and human pleasure."

"Yes, very good, that is accurate."

"The human way, the humane approach, would be to release us."

Godwin pauses for a moment, rubbing his chin. "No," he finally says, "I don't see it. The human way is to kill you." He stares up at the long pole that goes through the opening in the ceiling. There is a crack of lightning and then thunder rolls through the sky. "The meteorological report was accurate for tonight. It so often isn't. Have you noted, Edgar, that when these weather people tell us in the papers that it will be fair, it isn't, or when they predict that it will rain, it doesn't! It is most upsetting. But tonight, success! Once I have carved up the four of you and attached you together in a new way, I shall use a jolt from God—not God, no, that is such nonsense—Mother Nature . . . to electrify your reconfigured dead flesh back to life! Galvanize you!"

There is a knock on the door.

21

A Visitor

"A late-night guest?" says Godwin. "Alas, Miss Tilley, you have not locked the door behind you!"

Vincent Brim appears in the entrance.

"Unfortunate," says Godwin.

"Dr. Godwin . . . what, what is the meaning of this?" Vincent Brim surveys the scene, shocked.

The great surgeon sighs. "This is turning into a truly busy night. Now I must eliminate you as well, Dr. Brim. And that is really a waste, since I have no need of your mind or your withering body. I already have several brains here, and souls and youth!"

"I don't understand. What are you doing to them? I've been worrying about our—" His eyes dart back and forth between the restrained young people. "You can't be—"

"He is going to kill us and you," cries Edgar. "Run! Get help!"

Vincent Brim sees the rifle that Godwin had tossed to the floor when he seized Tiger. He hesitates for a second, then picks it up and aims it at the monster.

"It's useless!" shouts Edgar.

Vincent Brim fires. Godwin dodges the bullet as easily as he had the first time and smiles back at his colleague. Vincent fires again and Godwin merely turns his head to save himself.

"Impressive, think you not, Dr. Brim? If we put our minds to it, we could make more perfect people like me, perhaps even better. Well, not *we*, not you and me, just me and whatever I might—"

The gun goes off again and again and again. But Vincent Brim, who has a larger mind than Godwin seems to have imagined, isn't shooting at the great surgeon. He is firing Thorne's remarkable weapon and its exploding bullets at the shelves of combustible liquids and at the lit gas and kerosene lamps that are everywhere. Everything is igniting! In an instant the entire room is on fire, a boiling hell of flames.

There are explosions and human screams and the cries of the panther creature. Vincent races toward Edgar, seizes a scalpel by the side of his table and slices off one of the straps on his hands. Godwin comes striding out of the flames and delivers a blow to the side of Vincent's head that knocks him down as if he had been struck by a sledgehammer. Then Godwin picks up his colleague as if he were a toy and raises him high above his head and throws him across the room. He turns back to Edgar, but the boy has already snatched up Lear's sword, sitting there on the table next to him, and sliced open the other straps, freeing himself in seconds with the razor-sharp blade. Godwin is coming for him though and reaches out through the conflagration. Edgar swings the blade at him and misses but cuts the surgeon's left thumb clean from his hand. Godwin doesn't even wince. Edgar rolls away from him and onto the floor, catching a glimpse of the monster's face as he dives—it seems to be melting.

Edgar rushes through the inferno toward Lucy's table and cuts her loose in five violent slices that may have lacerated her too, and then goes for Tiger. At first he can't find her in the orange and red blaze and black smoke: mind-bending fear is paralyzing his brain. He hears other sounds—the shrieks of the hag running about the room in glee. *Do not be afraid*, he remembers his father saying again and concentrates on where Tiger might be. Finally, he hears her. "Edgar," she is saying in a loud but firm voice. "Edgar, I'm here!" He drops to the floor beneath the worst of the smoke and crawls toward her, reaches up and feels for her body on the table, which is already getting hot. He finds her naked arm, the sleeve of her blouse ripped off by Godwin's rough treatment. Tiger's skin is soft but her bicep is hard and tensed. He wants to stay there with her, holding her, their flesh touching. He has heard that sometimes a slow death can be like this—seductive—you want to expire and just let it be. They could perish here: he and Tiger, friends and more since the moment they met; they could go to heaven with their skin touching. But Edgar wants her to live and wants to live with her, so he darts to his feet and cuts off her straps, releasing her. He wants to save the others too, but he feels Tiger's grip holding him fast. Though she is shorter and slighter than him, she is strong and has him around the waist and is lifting him away in seconds, powering him toward the door, both of them coughing and dizzy. On the way, she seizes the rifle from the floor and keeps moving. She slams the door behind them, they collapse, and for a moment lie together in an embrace. Then Tiger leaps to her feet.

"Jonathan!" she cries out and reaches for the door.

"No! We have to leave! We can't go back in."

It's Edgar's turn to seize Tiger. He grabs her sinewy arms and pulls her down the stairs, but it is Lucy Lear's face that is in his mind. He has never met anyone like her, no one as sweet and perfect. And she is back there in that inferno. He starts to cry as he pulls Tiger with him and hopes his sobs sound like mere emotion from their escape from the fire. It is just the two of them again, he thinks, and for the first time in his life, to his surprise, it doesn't seem like enough.

They pause for a moment when they reach the seventh floor hallway, leaning against a wall, their chests heaving.

"Jonathan," says Tiger softly.

Edgar looks up and his sightline goes straight through a window into the dark stormy sky. From here, he can see the turret that contained the lab. It is engulfed in smoke and huge angry flames. But then a figure appears, climbing up the pole that is thrust through the opening in the ceiling. The creature is huge, nearly black, charred. Somehow it ascends the sizzling pole without releasing it.

The sound of the bells of several London Metropolitan Fire Brigade engines rings in the distance.

"Tiger, look!"

The figure is now at the top of the pole. It swings itself around the tip by gripping it with its muscular arms and then releases it, sending itself flying into the night toward a rooftop. For a moment, they both see its face in its black hair, the plastic skin burned completely off—the face is yellow with black eyes and lips, a monstrous visage!

The door to the hallway slams open and Lucy comes through it, dragging her brother by his arms. His shirt is almost seared from his body and he lies there, groggy, his big chest bare, his face wounded, attempting to get up. Tiger runs to him and pulls him all the way into the hallway. Lucy staggers forward, her dress burned beyond recognition, her arms and legs exposed, those usually white appendages angry red. Edgar embraces her.

"We need to get them out of here," says Tiger, her arms wrapped around Jon's muscular chest as she holds him upright.

They all stumble forward, and by the time they reach the end of the hallway, firemen are rushing past them.

"Stay there, we'll send someone to help you!" shouts one of them.

But they can't be questioned about what has happened here. They disappear through another door and take back stairs downward, Lucy and Jonathan walking better with each flight. They descend all seven floors and leave by a rear door. The rain is pelting down on them, soaking them to the skin. Edgar takes off his coat and wraps it around Lucy who accepts it with a weak smile. Jonathan and Tiger have no outer clothing to offer each other.

"Give me your arm," he says to her, "I can help you walk. You must be spent."

"I am fine," she almost spits and starts walking quickly, at an arm's length from him, the rifle in her hand. "You are the one who is hurt." Indeed, there are awful bruises on Jon's face and blood in his hair.

Edgar looks back toward the hotel and sees something running on a rooftop across the street on a building just a few stories high. But it isn't a man. It is an animal with the body of a panther and the head of some sort of huge, black-faced ape. It leaps down onto a lower building, heading toward the street.

"We have to get far away from here, out of this mess," says Lucy, bringing Edgar's attention back to his friends. The scratches on her face are still red. "We have to fix ourselves up and change our clothing and figure out what to do next."

"We can go to Thorne House. Annabel will be asleep. I will explain everything to her in the morning, somehow."

"No," says Tiger, "Godwin escaped! He is out in the city somewhere. We can't go to Mrs. Thorne's. We can't endanger others."

"Then where?" asks Jonathan.

"Follow me," says Edgar, and in moments, they know where he is leading them.

William Shakespeare answers his door again in the middle of the night fully clothed. This time they don't bother to remark on his appearance or his clear-eyed expression.

"Find us some clothing," says Edgar, "anything will do."

"What has occurred? You appear to have been boating upon the River Styx."

"Much more fun than that," says Jonathan. "We'll explain in a moment."

"Lovely! We shall chat of a daring adventure. I can sense it. I shall light my heartwarming hearth!"

But a fire is already roaring when they reach the main room. Shakespeare has obviously been up in the night. It seems like he often is. He putters down a hallway in search of dry clothing for his visitors. Lucy throws herself into a big, cushioned chair and pulls Edgar's coat tightly around her as if he were hugging her, her teeth chattering loudly, letting little gasps escape from her lips. Edgar sits on the arm of the chair beside her, not sure what to do or say. The other two stay on their feet, acting as though the situation is just a temporary irritation. But Edgar can see the horror in their eyes.

They hear Shakespeare in another room, whistling "God Save the Queen" and opening and slamming drawers.

"This one? Well, yes, Mr. Sprinkle, bring it forth!"

"That one! Are you but a lump of foul deformity, Mr. Tightman, a young lady cannot wear that!"

"Mr. Winker, that is not a manly enough color for the likes of Master Lear, have you not glimpsed his masculine physique!"

In the other room, the four friends say nothing for a while. Then Jon breaks the silence.

"I'm sorry about your uncle, Edgar."

Edgar hadn't given Vincent Brim a thought since they'd escaped and it immediately shames him. His uncle, incinerated in the turret lab at the top of the Midland Grand Hotel, had not only saved them but given his life for them. "A human being couldn't do more than that," whispers Edgar. There had been goodness deep within his uncle that Edgar had never tried to glimpse.

"Ah! Here we are!" exclaims little Shakespeare re-entering the room at top speed carrying a load of clothing piled so high that it nearly reaches the ceiling. It has rendered him incapable of seeing where he is going and he slams into the table and all the clothes fly across it, as if laid out for them to choose from—a series of chiffon dresses and bright red military coats and other extravagances that look like costumes from seventeenth-century plays. "I do desire we be better strangers!" shouts Shakespeare at the table, rubbing his shin.

"Brim," says Jonathan, "I think the pink one would match your eyes."

The clothes are ridiculous, but the four friends are too wet to not take something. Jonathan, Edgar and Tiger pick out scarlet military coats, while Lucy chooses the least outrageous and warmest dress she can uncover. Shakespeare boils some water for them and they retire two at a time to use the washbasin and tub in the little man's living quarters. Then they all change into their new outfits and return to the main room to lay their wet clothes over the fireplace. Lucy somehow keeps her underclothes out of sight, but Tiger spreads out hers in plain view.

Jonathan has cleaned the blood from his hair and dabbed his wounds a little, but his face still looks bruised. He doesn't seem to care. "We must go after him," he says, the second they have seated themselves at the table, sipping the tea the little man has made for them.

"Him?" asks Shakespeare. "Who is this enigmatic *him* whom we must pursue!"

Edgar gives their host a quick account of their terrible adventure.

"We have to go now," says Jon, the instant his colleague is done.

"No, no, no," says Shakespeare, "leave him be! He has no heart, no soul, he would kill you all without a thought, and now he is desperate!"

"That isn't an option for us. We have unleashed him. It is our responsibility to destroy him."

"But how do we kill something like that?" asks Tiger. "You saw what he could do."

"I think he will be afraid at first," says Lucy. "I think he will flee. He will not be able to return to his work at the hospital, since not only do we know what he is, but his hideous face is exposed. He said it took years to build that handsome countenance."

"Then we must chase him!" says Tiger.

"I actually feel a little sorry for him." Lucy drops her head.

"Sorry for him, sis! Have you lost your senses? He was about to kill us all, experiment on us!"

"But he can't feel anything. That is the worst thing I can imagine. And he didn't choose to be what he is."

Edgar puts his hand on hers. "We cannot let him do evil to others. He is indeed desperate. I agree that he will flee, find someplace where he can recover, fix himself, but who knows what he will do while on his way. Everyone who sees him clearly will think him bizarre, an aberration, and he will feel the need to destroy anyone who can do anything about it."

"So the question is: where will he go?" says Tiger.

"Well, what does the creature do in the novel?" asks Shakespeare.

"That's ridiculous, why would—" says Jonathan.

"No," says Tiger, "I think Mr. Shakespeare may have something there. Godwin appears to take some pride in the fact that he is essentially in such a famous book. He seems to have a fixation with it. And he took his name from its pages too."

"In the novel, the creature goes northward," says Edgar. "He ends up in the distant reaches of Scotland. Then he goes farther north to the arctic and flees on the ice. That's how the story opens: with a ship's captain writing home to his sister about a creature he and his crew see that looks like a phantom on the ice floes, driving a dogsled north toward the Pole, and then they see its creator, Victor Frankenstein." Edgar can feel the cold arctic winds as he speaks and see the hideous monster before him on the ice.

"So, you think he's headed toward the North Pole," smiles Jonathan, "perhaps to talk things over with Father Christmas . . . Santa Claus?"

No one speaks for a while.

"Somewhere way up there would be perfect," says Edgar. "It's remote, it's sparsely populated. He could set up there and word wouldn't spread to London. He could rebuild himself."

"And kill anyone who interrupts, unobserved," says Tiger.

"Let's track him," says Jonathan.

"We'll need money." At the mention of that word, their little host leaps to his feet and starts to walk away.

"Shakespeare!" says Edgar.

Shakespeare grinds to a halt, sighs and walks back toward his safe, hidden behind a painting of the witches' scene in *Macbeth*. "Foot licker," he says under his breath.

"We can't chase him dressed this way," says Lucy.

"Why not?" asks Shakespeare, stopping in his tracks and looking hurt. "They are simply lovely on all of you!"

"Let's go together to Kentish Town, safety in numbers," says Edgar. "We'll get better clothes there, and some food. You all have clothing in the house and I can wear some of Jonathan's."

———

Half an hour later they are at the Lear home and properly clothed in thicker trousers and dresses, and carrying heavy coats, food, and other clothes in sacks. Jonathan takes up the rifle, getting a hold of it when Tiger sets it down for a moment. He reloads it with their four remaining bullets, and as they leave the house he conceals it at his side, partially in the folds of his coat. He also slips a notebook into his sack. Edgar wonders what in the world Jon would ever do with such a thing.

"Should we bring the cannon?" asks Lucy.

"It would slow us down," says Tiger.

"Too bad," mutters Jonathan.

They head southeast to the London Hospital in two galloping cabs, sure that Godwin, despite his exposed appearance, will go there to gather up whatever he might have to take with him—operating tools and chemicals. He likely has clothing there too.

One day, thinks Edgar, *we may still unleash that cannon.*

The sky is pitch black as they slip around to the rear entrance of the hospital. Someone is coming out at the very moment they arrive—they duck behind a bush. He is tall and thick, wearing a long black cloak, and has the Elephant Man's hood over his face. He carries several sacks.

"Sensational!" whispers Jonathan.

Edgar sees something move on top of the hospital. It has the body of a panther and the head of an ape and it watches Godwin as he leaves. Edgar doesn't say anything.

Godwin hurries out onto the rear lawn and then heads west along narrow back streets, and the friends follow, keeping well behind. As they rush down Old Castle and Goulston streets, where the Ripper struck and one could believe still lurks, they hear screams from upper stories and the sounds of violence, but they keep pursuing Godwin, who maintains a steady, aggressive pace and never looks back.

"If he would just stay still for a moment, I could get a shot at him," says Tiger. Her eyes are lit with excitement. She has kept the pistol.

At wide Bishopsgate Street, Godwin enters a nearly deserted Liverpool Street Railway Station and darts along under its glass ceiling to look at the train departure times on the wall. His followers stay in a doorway, waiting. In seconds, Godwin shakes his head angrily and goes out, back into the streets, heading northwest, keeping to the narrow roads again.

He resurfaces from the tighter streets up on Euston Road and makes for the big railway station on that artery. They can hear his operating tools jingling inside his sacks.

"I know what he's after," says Edgar. "It's our old school train."

And indeed it is. With his monstrous face still inside the Elephant Man's hood, causing people to stare, Godwin gets himself a ticket on the first early morning express for northern Scotland and so do Edgar and his friends, keeping an entire train car behind. The locomotive powers out of London heading for Edinburgh. All but Tiger fall asleep.

When they reach the Scottish capital, she rouses them and they change for Inverness and there observe Godwin from a distance as he hides himself on a bench in the shadows in the station for hours. Edgar buys some paper, a stamp and a pen from a little station shop and posts a note to Annabel, telling her he has been sent to Scotland on urgent hospital business, wondering if she will believe it. Then they watch their monster, still hooded, board the Far North Line to steam farther north. They follow and move out onto the moors. It has been dark for a long while by then but they know what is outside their windows—a bleak and misty world; and they all remember what happened when they were last here— the bloody words carved into Driver's chest, the presence of the vampire. The College on the Moors is nearing. What occurred in that place brought them to where they are now. They hold their breath when the conductor calls out "Altnabraec Station," but not a single passenger rises and the train zooms on through the night.

"I really thought he would get out there," says Jonathan, looking relieved.

"No," says Edgar, staring straight ahead, "we are in *Frankenstein.*"

22

North

The train gets to Thurso, a small town on the North Sea on the northern Scottish coast, just before dawn. It is the end of the line. Jonathan leaps to his feet.

"No," says Edgar, "we need to stay put. He will see us at this little station. I know where he's going."

"There he is!" says Lucy, gazing through the window. Godwin is moving along the platform toward them. They duck down and wait. There were only a few passengers on this train and because it is so early in the morning, the great surgeon can walk about hoodless without much notice, simply keeping the cloak and its big collar partially pulled up over his head. The locomotive's engine has stopped and it is quiet outside. Their window is cracked open a little. They can hear footsteps approach and pause. Then they see a shadow stretch across their seats and the floor. They have the sense that the monster has come up close to the glass and is peering in. None of them breathe. Then the shadow fades away.

They wait a good ten minutes before they disembark from the train. Though it is a late June day, the air is cool here in northern Scotland.

"Where are we going?" asks Jonathan.

"To the docks," says Tiger.

They make their way through town and then spot Godwin down by the water, his cloak now almost completely covering his face, speaking to a man near a large boat. Gulls are squawking up above. The man is staring at what he can see of his tall inquisitor's visage, shaking his head. But then Godwin pulls something from his pocket—a wad of money—and the man becomes more interested. Finally, the fellow takes the banknotes and Godwin throws his sacks into the boat and gets in.

"After him!" says Jonathan.

Edgar shakes his head. "He'd see us coming. We'll have to follow in another boat."

"But we'll lose him."

"I doubt that. Not where he is going."

There's an island—several of them—far out on the horizon on the North Sea.

"The Orkneys," whispers Lucy.

Fifteen minutes later, they make their own agreement with another distinguished man of the sea—thirty English pounds' worth—and get into his rickety wooden boat. He's a grizzled old fellow wearing a dirty sleeveless shirt in the cool air, a blue felt cap and a filthy rag around his neck. His Scottish accent is so thick that they can barely understand him. They make their way slowly along the coast and then out into the open water. The old man pumps two of the oars and Jonathan, Edgar and Tiger take turns with the others. The boat looks rotten in places and even has holes up near the gunwales.

"She's as calm as glass today," says their captain. But it isn't true, at least for them. The man happily sings and whistles a song about a long lost "lass" on the Highlands for most of the three harrowing hours it takes to cross, the waves growing and growing, eventually nearly as high as a fully grown man. When they become particularly steep, their captain switches to a mournful tale of Mother Nature taking another loved one to his death upon the high seas. But no matter how much the waters lash the boat, he doesn't seem concerned. Lucy sinks down into the stern, wrapped in the warm coat she has brought, her eyes closed. There is no sign of Godwin and his vessel.

"We may be goners," says the sailor as they approach the Orkney shore, though he shouts it with a smile. "You can't fight Davy Jones! If it is time for you to go, then it is time, that's me motto!" There is a strange glee in his eyes.

There don't appear to be any docks. The sailor, insisting that Jon now man the other oars, heads for a series of black rocks, the boat bouncing up and down like a rubber ball in the waves, which are now angrier than they have been at any point in the crossing. Tiger sits stone-faced, gripping her seat, her mouth set in a slit, telling Lucy that all will be fine. Edgar holds on to the edge of the boat, trying not to retch, reminding himself that fear is never helpful.

They encounter the rough shoreline at high speed, just after the old man insists it is a good place to land. He stands up in the boat and seizes one of the rocks.

"Now each of you just step out, the lasses first."

But Tiger won't go until last. She helps Lucy disembark, then Edgar goes, and then Jonathan, who reaches back for Tiger. But she won't take his hand. Each of the first three had fallen in the water when they got out but were able to cling to the rocks and struggle to land. But the waves seem even higher as Tiger, left in a boat with little ballast, tries to get out. She tosses her coat and sack to the others, but before she can take a step a spray of water hits the side of the vessel and the sailor loses his footing and the boat rocks out into the North Sea, a good twenty feet from shore.

"You'll have to jump for it, sir!" says the sailor to Tiger.

"No!" cries Lucy.

Tiger pauses, looks toward Edgar, and then leaps into the sea. She goes under the waves and disappears.

"Tiger!" cries Edgar.

She resurfaces, her face white but determined, and swims hard until she can reach for a rock jutting out from the shore. She grips it and pulls herself up, then staggers toward them on land. There's blood oozing from a tear in her trousers near her knee.

"I'm fine," she says.

The boat vanishes out into the waves and in the distance they can hear the sailor singing. "Mother Nature," he croons, "must be feared."

When they have found their legs on land, they turn to see that they are in a wilderness, on the edge of a brown field with no buildings in sight, a pattern of rock fences crisscrossing in the distance. They see sheep grazing on the spotty grass.

"There!" says Lucy, pointing.

Far away, not much more than a dot five fields from them, they see something moving. It isn't an animal, though it barely seems a man.

"Godwin!"

He appears to be traveling at a brisk pace, as if he knows where he is going. They follow and pursue him for more than an hour, stopping to eat some of the food—bread, cold mutton—they brought with them, always making sure they are at least a mile behind him.

They pass stone farmhouses and spot a few distant citizens, but Godwin keeps far away from people and buildings, and the four friends are thankful for that. The land continues brown and desolate and full of rocks, though small trees and stretches of green intrude here and there.

They keep going north and then reach a shore where a channel of the North Sea separates them from another island. Godwin leaps into the cold water and swims. He powers through the waves like a shark, his bags wrapped around him as if they were an inconsequential albatross on his neck.

"At some point he will stop," says Tiger, "and then we will take him."

Or he will take us, thinks Edgar.

Tiger starts removing her clothes.

Jonathan gawks at her.

"What are you doing?" asks Edgar, startled as her strong, smooth limbs come fully into view in the cool Orkney Island air while she strips down to her few undergarments.

"I'm going after him."

"It's nearly half a mile across!"

"Yes, and if we wait to find some sort of boat, then we may lose him. And we'd have to explain what we are doing in order to rent anything."

They have been toting two large sacks, one of which Tiger has insisted she carry most of the way. She stuffs her boots and clothes into it. Edgar has the other sack. Jonathan grabs it from him and starts removing his own clothes, shoving them into it. He bares his chest and takes down his trousers. His powerful legs are chiseled like a Greek statue's. Tiger, who was about to enter the water, pauses for a moment.

"Let's go!" shouts Jon, taking her by the hand.

"Better to do this individually," she says as she shakes him off and dives into the water. The waves aren't nearly as high as they were on the crossing from the Scottish mainland, but the water here is far from flat. Tiger goes under the waves and then surfaces, her head pointed toward the land to the north.

Jonathan ties his sack to his back and then realizes he has the rifle as well. He hesitates and looks at Lucy.

"You can't swim with that too," she says.

He gazes out toward Tiger, grabs the gun's strap and slips it over his shoulder and dives into the water. It takes him a while to surface but he comes up before long and starts swimming after the girl he so admires, struggling with the heavy weapon and bag on his back.

"Well," says Edgar, turning to Lucy, "I guess we have no choice. Are you ready for this?"

"I think so," she says. "Stay close to me. You know, women float better." She smiles at him and turns her back to take off her coat and brown dress, down to a light, white shift that goes to about mid-thigh. Edgar turns away. It occurs to him that Lucy often seems afraid of challenges, yet she never shirks them. It is remarkable.

She has been carrying a smaller sack, which she's dropped on the ground. Edgar takes off his clothes and puts them into it and stands waiting for her, his slim chest bared. She turns to him, her head down, but then looks up at him.

"I'm ready," she says.

He puts her shoes and outer clothes into the sack and ties it around his back.

"Take my hand," she says. They go into the water together.

Lucy turns out to be a better swimmer. She finishes second in the marathon across the water, Edgar is third, and then they turn to see Jonathan, all thick muscle and a heavy sack and a big rifle, struggling just three-quarters of the way across. Then he goes under.

"JONATHAN!" sobs Lucy. Tiger's face goes white.

But he comes back up, almost as if in response to his sister's cry. They can see him set his mouth and work harder despite his failing strength. Minutes later, Tiger leaps into the water and helps him across the last ten feet and up onto shore. He pushes her away as he staggers to his feet.

"I am fine!" he shouts.

Tiger looks at him in admiration. They all struggle back into their wet clothes, shivering in the early evening air.

"Let's keep going," says Jon. "We can't lose him."

But they can't locate Godwin anywhere in the distance, at least for a while. An hour of fast walking brings him into sight. Beyond him they can see a town.

"Kirkwall," says Edgar.

"Dear God, don't let him go in there," says Tiger.

"He won't," says Lucy. "He can't."

Godwin steers wide of the town and they follow him for another half hour to another shoreline where he heads northwest along its rocky surface. Crouched down on a barren hill above, they observe him. The sun is getting lower in the sky.

"Where is he going?" asks Jonathan.

"I believe we have a last swim to accomplish," says Edgar. As he looks out over the cold, gray water, he thinks about the famous novel to which Percy Godwin is connected and, against his will, finds himself slipping back into it as if he were lying in his bed long ago listening to his father unknowingly unfold the horrific tale for him from the floor above. Edgar becomes Victor Frankenstein and leaves his loving family home for a German university town where his interest in science and thirst for knowledge grows dangerously exciting. He visits gravesites and steals dead bodies and makes a human being in the attic of his apartment! He is immediately devastated by what he has done and flees, but his monster pursues him, kills his brother in the woods near the family's home, educates itself and comes after him again. Edgar agrees to an evil contract, promising the creature that he will make a female partner for it so it will leave him be and seclude itself from humanity. Edgar makes his way from Switzerland through England to the Orkney Islands to its most northern isle, bearing body parts and chemicals to attempt the gruesome operation in a secluded place. But he knows he cannot really do this horrific act. And so the wretch, who repulses him to his very core, takes revenge . . . and murders Edgar's bride on their wedding night!

Edgar shakes his head and tries to leave the story. He looks at Lucy and Tiger, thinks of the danger they are all in, drawn way up here to this barren place with this creature. But the story keeps chasing him and he fades back into the novel, rushing into the marital bedroom on a stormy night to find his beloved Elizabeth strangled, bloodied and beaten in their bed. Her face looks like Lucy's! He howls in anger and, blind with his own vengeance, chases the monster farther north into the arctic.

Down below them, Godwin is gazing toward a northern shore and dives in.

"We have to pursue him," says Tiger, "like in the book."

"This may be a trap," says Lucy softly. "There are no authorities here, no police, almost no one at all where he is going. He will have us alone in a near wilderness."

"Yes he will," says Edgar. Then he turns to the others. "Are you ready?"

It takes less time to cross this stretch since the surface of the sheltered channel isn't as rough. But when they reach shore, it is immediately evident that this island is more desolate than the others and just a few hills rise gently. They put on their wet clothes again, shivering more this time as the temperature has begun to drop sharply, and stand on the rocks and look out over the terrain at a rough road hewn into the ground leading into the center of the island. There are wagon tracks on it.

"There are people here," says Lucy.

"Of course," says Tiger, "he needs a new face."

Edgar climbs up onto a big rock. Though it is getting darker, he can see almost all the way across the island, a brown-and-white, almost sepia-toned setting. It looks to be just a few miles long and less than that across. He spots the dim outlines of rock fences and a few sod barns and houses. Gulls swoop about and crows caw in the distance; the water hits the rocks around them in sprays. Godwin is on the road, already far away. But he is walking slower.

"I think this is his destination."

"If that's true," says Lucy, "then he'll search for somewhere to set up, maybe an abandoned building."

"We kill him here," says Tiger.

"An excellent idea," says Jonathan, "but first, what about our accommodations for the evening? Shall we book an elegant room in the Orkney Ritz . . . or do we get to experience the great outdoors on this glorious night in these southern climes?"

Their cold mutton and loaves of bread are soaked and inedible, so they throw them into the sea and let their stomachs go without that evening. They will have to somehow get food in the morning. Before they lie down they run around to dry out. It turns into a game of tag and they are all surprised by their laughter. But Tiger stops before the others and snaps off dry branches from nearby low-lying bushes and uses another of her seemingly unending skills to start a fire. They take off their partially dried outer clothes and hang them on little stakes, made from other branches driven into the hard ground. Then they huddle close to the flames, both to stay warm and to hide the light.

"He could come at us out of this darkness," says Lucy, looking around at what is now utter blackness.

"No worries," says Jonathan, "if our esteemed surgeon does happen to pop by, I will be waiting for him with this." He pats the rifle he holds in his lap. "I shall delay until I can see the yellow of his lovely eyes, and then I'll offer him an exploding bullet, up close and personal, and blow his bulb to smithereens."

But he doesn't say it with much conviction. And none of the others bother to respond. When it's time to sleep, they know they need to lie close to each other but there is an argument about the arrangements. Jonathan makes a tactical error.

"Ladies in the middle," he says. "Brim and I will protect you two from the outside. I'll need to face toward the interior of the island, rifle at the ready."

"I don't need protection," says Tiger before he is even finished speaking. "I would say that you, Mr. Lear, have the least acute senses, so your arrangement makes little sense. I should be on the outside, Edgar and I."

"Fine," says Lucy, "then I'll go between Edgar and you."

Tiger hesitates. "I'm not sure—"

"Makes perfect sense," says Edgar.

"I thought the order," says Jonathan, "could be me, then Tiger, then Lucy, and then Edgar."

Tiger obviously doesn't like either choice. "All right," she finally says, "I'll sleep on my own and I'll keep the pistol." She lies down quickly, stiff on the hard ground.

"But . . ." says Jonathan.

Edgar whispers into Jon's ear. "I would cut my losses, if I were you."

But they don't sleep well—not helped by the fact that the sun comes up early on the Orkneys in mid-summer—and they all rise feeling tired and sore, Tiger surprised to find herself almost right beside Jon, who hasn't moved at all.

They walk along the rough road in the direction Godwin went, spotting a few bedraggled sheep and wishing they could shoot them for food. But they think better of it—they need their few remaining bullets anyway. Finally, they spot someone, out in a yard near a sod farmhouse and barn. He is a young man, a big fellow, carrying two pails, which he drops in a crash when he sees them. Strangers on foot must be a nearly miraculous sight.

They approach cautiously.

"Good morning," says Edgar.

The man's response is likely a similar greeting, but his voice is so low and the accent so thick that they aren't certain. It sounds a bit like a grunt. But they hear the words he adds.

"Where did you come from?"

"We are from England," says Tiger.

He eyes her suspiciously and they aren't sure if it is because of her unusual attire or simply the fact that they are all foreigners.

"We are here for some sight-seeing and walking," says Lucy,

stepping in front of the others and giving him a pleasing smile. "A gentleman was kind enough to convey us over on a boat."

The man looks doubtfully at their unkempt clothing. "When is you going back?" he asks.

"Well, we thought we might stay a night or two. Is there any place where we can put up?"

"No."

"Nowhere at all?"

The man hesitates. Edgar notices that he is strikingly hand-some, that his features actually bear some resemblance to the good looks that Godwin manufactured on his prosthetic face. He is almost as big as the surgeon too, and well proportioned. Edgar realizes with a chill that this man's countenance and body parts would be perfect materials for the surgeon's grisly task.

"Well," says the young fellow, "there is a few abandoned huts on this island. If you keeps walking along this road and then bears left when you gets near the water, you will see one in particular. Matter of fact, you can almost see it from here, land's so flat about these parts."

"Thank you," says Lucy. "You are very kind to offer informa-tion to travelers."

"Have you seen anyone else?" asks Jonathan suddenly, moving up close to his sister. The young man takes a step back and plants his feet.

"I sees me neighbors regular-like."

"No, I mean another stranger, a big one, unusual looking, in a black cloak."

"There been no other foreigners about. I have me chores to do."

They walk farther along the road, which is nothing more than a horse path in places, and the wet soil and pebbles stick to their boots. The shack the young man referred to appears within minutes in the distance. They don't see Godwin, but they move more cautiously. They come to a slight inclination in the land and can see the shoreline and the air smells saltier. The shack is below them and still at least a cricket field away.

Then a figure comes out of the little building and looks about. All four friends instantly drop to the ground.

It's Godwin.

He is bareheaded: no Elephant Man's hood and with the collar of his cloak down; they can see his pale yellow face, the watery eyes and black lips. He turns toward them and pauses, his hideous countenance looking their way for a long while. It doesn't seem that he sees them. Then he turns toward the water and gazes out over it. The four young people remain glued to the ground watching him through the low, brown grass. He takes a few steps toward the shack, then turns toward them again and begins to walk in their direction. They squirm backward. But he stops after a few hundred yards and returns to the shack. When he reaches it, he has to wrench the door open. It closes with a bang behind him. Then they hear another thud like some sort of lock or board being snapped into place.

"That was close," says Edgar.

"Perhaps he needed to pee?" says Jonathan.

"Not sure there is indoor plumbing in there."

"We must finish him while he's inside that hut and can't see us approach," says Tiger.

222

"Let's do it now," adds Jonathan, gripping the rifle in both hands. The others nod.

They move along the ground like snakes and it takes them a long time to get near the shack. All along the way, they hear a pounding sound coming from the little wooden building. They slow as they near it and when they are right next to it, Tiger reaches for the rifle. But Jonathan snatches it back from her. He wants to be the one who kills the creature. He tries to smile at her, but she won't look at him.

Now they realize what the pounding is—Godwin has been boarding up the windows. Their only chance had been to look through a window and take direct aim, drilling a shot or several shots into the back of the wretch's skull before he can react to the sound of the gun. But now, with the entrance locked as well, who-ever takes the shot will have to do so blind.

Jonathan gets to his feet, but Edgar pulls him down. They strug-gle for a moment in silence, but Tiger puts both hands on Jon's shoulders and grips him hard, pinching the thick trapezius muscle there and making him grimace. Then she takes him by the arm and leads him away. He goes with her and the others follow, slith-ering along on the ground back toward their little hill.

"I could have destroyed him in a second!" says Jon in a loud whisper.

"You'd have had no idea where to aim!" says Tiger.

"And if you'd missed," adds Edgar, "and the odds are anyone would have, even if all four of our remaining bullets were used, Godwin would have then come after us while we were defenseless and killed us all."

"He's right," says Lucy.

Jonathan grumbles but keeps moving.

When they reach the little elevation, they get to their feet but almost instantly hear the shack door open a couple hundred yards behind them and then close with a smack. They drop to the ground as if they were all shot and then squirm around and look toward their enemy. He is coming in their direction again, this time at a fast pace. They get to their feet and run down the far side of their little hill, keeping low, not sure when they will come into his view.

"We can't outrun him!" says Lucy, her face white.

There is a group of bushes not far away, like a little island on the island. They make for it and get behind it.

"We don't stand a chance," says Lucy. "We have to reason with him."

"That isn't possible," says Jonathan. "I'll kill him, no matter what."

Tiger wrenches the gun from him. "He'll see you the moment you stand up, but I'll have an extra second because I'm smaller and he'll take more chances with me too, may even go easy on me." She grins. "I can wait until the last moment, until he is right upon me. I'm the one who can blast him from up close. I'll fix him."

"You'll never get close enough," says Lucy.

"You're right, but I would," says Jon.

"Be quiet," says Edgar, "just be quiet." He is terrified but can't bring himself to say it.

"I'm terrified," says Lucy, "take my hand." Edgar reaches out for her. His own hand is shaking. He is surprised to feel that hers is warm and steady. The hag should be here now, sitting on his chest, but Lucy's grip makes him feel stronger.

They all turn over onto their stomachs and look through the branches of the bushes toward Godwin. He has stopped suddenly and is gazing about. From where he is now, he can see for miles. The few farms and the metallic blue sea are the only other things in sight. But Godwin can't spot his four observers, not clearly. He stands for a while surveying everything thoroughly. Finally, he slaps himself in the head, as if to try to knock some sense into his brain. They hear one of his bursts of attempted laughter as he turns and walks away.

Lucy lets out a sigh.

They all twist onto their backs and stare up at the sky for a while, which is a slightly lighter hue than the water, sparsely decorated with wisps of white.

"If we can't come up close to him to kill him and we can't do it from far away, then what can we do?" says Jonathan.

"We need different terrain, different circumstances," says Edgar. "We simply can't kill him here."

"Well, then," says Jonathan, "perhaps I should pay a friendly call on him and ask him to step out with me to some more convenient place so that I might blow his head off?" He turns back onto his stomach.

"We have to flush him out, make him go somewhere else," says Tiger. "I have an idea."

23

Deal with the Devil

Tiger's idea will put her in mortal danger.

"When it gets dark I will steal down to the shack and push a note through a crack in the door telling him that we were here in the Orkneys, that we tracked him and know where he is, and that we have left the islands to tell the authorities who he is and what he has been doing. We'll simply follow him when he flees. He'll have his guard down too."

"Good idea, but I'll do it," says Jonathan. "It should be me, in case the note bearer is discovered. I'll have the rifle. Let's have your pen and some of that paper you bought at the train station, Edgar." He gets to his feet. But Tiger doesn't.

"It's best it's a female," she says. "You would be too loud, too obvious."

"Then I should do it," says Lucy. "I'm the smallest."

Edgar doesn't like anything about these ideas.

"Your plans are too dangerous. He will hear you, any of you, and kill you. And if whoever takes the note survives, he won't flee. He'll come after us! He'll wonder why we've warned him.

Why would we do that? He will know we are either still here or have just left and he will be on us almost immediately. There are no authorities of any real consequence until you get to the mainland."

"But—" say Jonathan and Tiger at the same time. They don't continue, however, because they know he is right.

"Thank you for destroying our last hope, old chap," says Jon. "Now we have zero options. You have always been such a charming fellow."

"There is another way," says Edgar.

Lucy doesn't like the look on his face. "What are you talking about?"

"I'll go down to the shack."

"No," says Tiger, "why would that be any better?"

"Because I won't try to sneak; I'll speak to him."

"No, you won't," says Tiger. "That is not going to happen. And besides, it would be worse. He'd—"

But Edgar interrupts her. "I'm the only one who can do this, and I'll tell you why and exactly what I will do."

He lays out his plan. The others sit stone-faced as he speaks. They know almost immediately that he is presenting them with the only chance they have. Still, they argue about it. Edgar can barely believe he is volunteering for this. But a strange feeling had come over him when Tiger and the others offered to go. It was terrible fear, yes, but it concerned his friends, *their* well-being, not just himself. A half hour later, after a long argument, they agree to let him go.

Jonathan turns his back on Edgar and sits on the far side of the hill, staring out over the water. Tiger crouches nearer the crest, watching her dear friend walk away, memories of their lives together flooding her mind, making her want to break down in tears. But she holds firm. Edgar Brim has always been the one for her and now he may be going to his death. She wants to move closer to Jonathan, but she doesn't. Lucy positions herself nearer the shack, closer to Edgar, tears welling in her eyes.

Edgar strides toward the building in broad daylight, the gun loaded and at the ready, already pointing it at the door. When he gets there he turns the butt toward it and pounds hard. There is silence for a moment and then the door opens slowly.

"Ah, Edgar! Lovely to see you! I had the feeling that you might be about. That was an awful thing that your uncle tried to do to me back in London, simply awful. Why would one try to burn another human being alive? There is no need to point that gun at me."

The yellow pallor of the creature's skin is almost translucent and patches are burned to the bone, the eyes are watery and the lips black. There are remnants of rips on his face and big scars like zipper marks around his neck and crisscrossing his skull, now apparent through the wisps of black hair that weren't burned off in the fire. One thumb and the tip of a second finger are severed and the stumps are gray. There is a look in this wretch's eyes that Edgar has never seen before in a human being . . . a sort of wildness.

Edgar has stepped back from the door a bit, somewhere between five and ten feet, to a place where he thinks he might be able to get off a shot, right into a spot directly above the creature's nose.

"You are shaking, my boy. For that, I wish I had feelings, I think. I believe it is something called sympathy, concern for others. I have the sense, however, that I might not thrive with such an emotion.

It might slow down my research. Such sensations are, I would contend, enemies of science and progress. I must eliminate you now. You are in possession of a most dangerous secret! It does not seem an intelligent move on your part to appear here, certainly not scientific. But I know you are not a stupid boy, so I am guessing that you calculated that you could kill me at this distance. Think again, Edgar. I can seize the gun from your hand the instant I see your finger press the trigger. If you back up any farther, I shall simply, as you know, dodge the bullet."

"I am willing to test your abilities."

Godwin lets out a bolt of a laugh. "I believe that is humor, or is it?" Then his face grows grim. "You do not want to play games with me, child."

Edgar lowers the gun.

"That's a good boy. Take your medicine, your death, like a man."

"That is an old-fashioned idea, Godwin. And I'm not planning to die today anyway."

"Oh?"

"I am here to make a deal with you, a rational one; we might even call it a scientific one. You are an intelligent man, so I suggest you listen."

"I am all ears. Well, not exactly, I am numerous different body parts." He lets out a genuine laugh and it startles him. "My God, I think that *was* humor!"

"I came here with the other three. We followed you to this shack."

"And?"

"After we surveyed the situation, we realized that it would be almost impossible to kill you here, and I'm guessing you had some sense that we might be nearby and boarded up the windows in this building because of that."

"You are correct."

"So, the others wanted to leave the islands and tell the authorities about you and what you are trying to do and your exact location. I didn't feel that would work. I felt the authorities would think our story was ridiculous and we were insane. My friends also had the idea that we might leave you a note saying that we were informing on you, so you might at least leave here, thus ensuring our safety. But I said you would not believe that or would just quickly follow and kill us all."

"Well, I must say, Edgar, that in this debate I am on your side. Your reasoning is extremely sound and theirs has holes in it like those in the cheese the Swiss manufacture."

"We argued, long and loudly. We split up."

"I am sorry to hear that. Well, maybe not entirely."

"The other three have gone. They are intent upon telling the authorities. I was left here alone. I wasn't sure what to do. Then I decided I would talk to you. I remembered the times we had together in the operating room, the kindness you showed me when I was repulsed by the dead bodies, the way you helped my adopted family when Mr. Thorne died, and your desire to have human feelings, to care . . . to laugh."

Godwin looks startled. It is as if he were feeling a pain inside that he wasn't used to. "You and I, Edgar, we are both fatherless. Perhaps we—"

"So, I decided to appeal to what might be called your better side, the side you wish you had, but also to your brain, your rational brain. You see, if the authorities do believe the story my friends tell, then your game is up. A well-equipped force will come for you."

"But they won't believe them."

"Can you be sure of that? What are the odds?"

"They are calculable."

"And you know that such odds do not have zeros in them. There is *some* chance, however slim, that by tomorrow morning a group much more lethal than us will be here to destroy a menace and nothing good can come of that for you, even if you escape. You will be exposed, one way or the other—if they simply see you or even if you murder them all. And if you kill me now, you run a risk too. My disappearance might give some credence to the things my friends tell the authorities."

"Why, that is sound reasoning, Edgar, sound indeed! I am proud of you!"

"Thank you, sir. But I will take it another step or two. I believe that I can assure you that you will not be exposed if you do as I say and that what I say will be attractive to you as well."

Godwin smiles. He looks excited and his face turns red, almost as if he were aroused. "I am fascinated. Please go on, immediately!"

"I will tell whatever authorities who might believe my friends that what they are saying is ridiculous. I will discount their statements. Thus, a barely believable claim will sound like utter hogwash."

"I love that word!"

"In exchange, you will leave here, go far away and never return to London. Exiled, yes, in a sense, but alive. Perhaps you can find some place to rehabilitate your appearance and perhaps you can even find yourself a mate, regenerate a dead female body. I promise to say nothing of your existence as long as you do not harm anyone, no living human being. I think that you, sir, as a scientist, have a sense of honor, and that you have respect for a rational, intelligent pact."

Edgar can't tell if Godwin can see that he is shaking even more now.

For a moment, the creature is speechless. He narrows his watery eyes and the seared yellow flesh around the protruding brow wrinkles.

"Well," he finally says, "I believe you have offered a most excellent proposal. I shall pack my bags."

"A wise decision." Edgar turns to go.

"Oh, Mr. Brim," says Godwin, "may I shake your hand? It seems like a fitting thing for two gentlemen to do, to seal an honorable contract."

Edgar hesitates, but then lifts a trembling arm toward him. He sees the creature's big burned hand approaching his, the two gray stumps evident. Edgar realizes his mistake: Godwin will crush his hand, perhaps rip his arm from the socket and then kill him right here while his friends look on. Then this creature will go up the hill and hunt the others down and murder them and remove their appendages, organs and brains.

But the hand is warm and gentle.

"Thank you," says Godwin.

Edgar feels an overpowering guilt. He turns to go up the hill where his friends are hiding, his head down.

"I saw Mrs. Shelley a second time, you know," says Godwin. Edgar stops. "It was in the middle of the night, hours after she had glimpsed me in the forest—I went to that ominous place, the Villa Diodati, where she was staying, and I sneaked up to a window and looked inside. At first, I couldn't find her, so I began moving around the exterior of the house, peering into the other rooms—I saw Lord Byron sleeping and Mr. Shelley and then I found Mary. Her oil lamps were lit with something thrown over them to keep the light dim, as if she were frightened to sleep with them completely out. I watched her as she tossed and turned in bed. I was so fascinated that I leaned forward and pressed my hideous face to the pane. She seemed to notice me and sat up in a start. I ducked down. And when I looked back a few minutes later, she was asleep, though her eyes were moving frantically under her lids."

"It really *is* you," says Edgar softly.

"My friend," says the creature, "I know you offered this pact because it makes sense and I admire that deeply. It is a sound plan. But . . ." He pauses. "Did you at all . . . do it because you felt some compassion for me?"

Edgar looks into Godwin's eyes and thinks they are more watery than before.

"Does it matter, sir?"

"No . . . of course not, I just thought . . . no, of course not." Godwin's voice resumes its old confidence. "Have a good life, Edgar. I wish you the best." He smiles. "I shall fulfill my end of our deal and I know you will fulfill yours. You are, after all, human."

When Edgar reaches the others on the far side of the hill they are surprised by his demeanor. He doesn't seem pleased.

"It worked?" asked Tiger, looking incredulous.

233

"He bought it?" says Lucy. "He's leaving?"

Edgar nods. "As soon as he can."

Jonathan is pacing. "Excellent! We go back to the farmhouse now and buy some food, and then we follow Godwin. He'll likely leave by boat and head farther north. We track him to wherever he goes, probably some godforsaken place where there are no people about . . . some place where he has no shelter, no building like here, no place else to go, absolutely killable. And he won't have any idea that we are following him! He'll be vulnerable. We can wait until he falls asleep, put the business end of the barrel right to his temple and blow the contents of that freakish skull to hell!"

The other two smile. But Edgar doesn't.

"Let's go get him," says Tiger.

24

To the End of the Earth

dgar knows they must do it. It is a simple fact. A pact with a monster is no pact at all. But as they walk together back to the farmhouse, he can't shake a sense of guilt. Lucy notices. The other two are marching out ahead of them, as if they can't move fast enough.

The young farmer is still outside, now pouring a pail of some sort of brown food—smelly gruel, half liquid half solid—into a pen with two scrawny pigs. They snort at him and then squeal when they see the strangers. The young man turns his handsome face toward them and then plants his feet and holds the pail in a tight fist. A woman comes to the door of their hut, hatless and in a dirty dress with a restless naked child in her arms, cooing at it with a toothless mouth.

"We will pay English pounds for whatever food you can spare us," says Tiger to the man, "and we need a boat. We will pay well for it too or for someone to take us somewhere in it."

The farmer waits a while before he answers. "There is two boats on the island. They goes south twice a week."

"North," says Edgar, "we will need something going north."

"There is a whaling boat," says the young man, "goes upwards to the arctic, stops here on Wednesdays to drop off supplies, north end at the dock. I don't keeps much track of time, so I don't knows when that might be."

"Today is Monday," says Lucy.

They are allowed into the two-room hut and notice that the walls are not plastered and the thatched roof is sagging. They choose two crude loaves of bread, a few lumps of cold ham, some hard biscuits and a half-dozen wizened apples, and pay the woman handsomely for them.

They sleep under the stars again, this time on the far side of their little hill where they can see Godwin's shack. At the crack of dawn they follow him as he walks around the coast in the dim light, carrying his large sacks, in search of something. When he finds it, he steals it and within moments he has rowed one of the island's two boats out of sight toward the arctic, his strength monstrous. The waves are growing high around him.

"He has stolen some poor man's only vessel," says Lucy, "and we just stood here and watched him do it."

"It is better that the man has his boat taken," says Tiger, "than his life."

Twenty-four hours later, the whaling craft appears at the docks on the north end of the island, a small Norwegian steamer with two smokestacks and masts, and a rugged-looking crew of some half-dozen men, who appear to speak a multitude of languages. The sailors' eyes linger on Lucy and Tiger, transfixed by the former and unsure about the latter. Edgar shudders at their appearance and some of the words they use, but he knows he and his friends must interact with these men and get aboard this ship and pursue and kill the monster or risk his return and the horrible things he would visit upon them. He finds it difficult to believe that Godwin will let them live with his secret tucked away in their minds, no matter what he has promised. So, Edgar convinces the captain to take him and his friends northward, a substantial quantity of Shakespeare's English pounds his most persuasive argument.

"Where exactly are you going?" asks the captain in surprisingly good English. "Where shall we set you down?" Though his crew are lightly dressed in the warm weather, some bare-chested and others in dirty cotton shirtsleeves, this slightly stooped and aging man with white whiskers, creased skin like dark leather and fingers as thick as sausages, wears blue wool trousers, a double-breasted pea-coat and a captain's hat.

"North," says Tiger.

"North is a long way and not an exact destination, sir, ma'am."

"Well, where do *you* go from here?" she asks him.

"We will be touring about. We are the remnants of the last great whaling crews around these parts, so we have the sea to ourselves much of the time and go where we want." It seems the captain likes to talk. In fact, he is a bit of a speech maker. "There was a day when expeditions would be gone for years at a time, but we are just out for short stretches and then come home to our families, those of us that have them. If we get one whale or two then we is happy. We always stop at Spitsbergen Island up at the gate to the arctic near the top of the world and we sometimes use some of the abandoned whaling huts there on a night or two. We search the waters for the dark giants of the sea that give us the oil and the bones and flesh to help us make it through another year. We slaughter them right on the boat, our own factory ship this is, *The Little Walton*, our moving whale laboratory. We'll spend but a week up there this time and return by the same route."

"Spitsbergen Island?" asks Edgar. "That's a long way, isn't it? Do you encounter any other places before that?"

"Well, there's the Shetlands. We'll be there by this afternoon."

"They are inhabited, are they not?"

"Why, yes, of course, many folks have lived there for as long as can be remembered. Is that not what you want? Why would you seek out a barren place?"

"I will add another ten pounds to your pocket if you never ask me that again."

"All right," the captain finally says.

"And there is no one on Spitsbergen, for certain?"

"Not a soul, not permanently, though I've heard some talk of building a rough hotel for hardy tourists. There seems to be a growing interest in that sort of thing. Explorers on their way to find the Northwest Passage have used it as a launching place too, but there is nothing but rock and ice up there most of the time, that and the animals and mountains beset with glaciers. It is godforsaken. Once we pass the Shetlands, we enter the vast Norwegian Sea and leave human civilization behind."

"Set us down at Spitsbergen."

"Whatever you say, sir."

"And pick us up when you are ready to return home."

The captain pauses again. "All right," he says.

The ship smells not just of these filthy men's bodies and clothes but of urine and whale and blood. There are red stains everywhere on the deck. Hoists and mammoth hooks for lifting the ship's gargantuan catches and holding them while they are butchered, tower above. The many death instruments and sharp blades—knives and swords and axes, even spade shovels—are fastened to the gunwales and bottoms of the masts. At the bow sits a giant harpoon pointing the way north.

"It is called an *explosive harpoon*," the captain tells Edgar with evident pride, "and it can be shot like a cannon at a surfacing whale. You see, it is long and iron and barbed and attached to stacked coils of thick rope nearly half the width of a man's waist."

Edgar imagines what firing this weapon must be like—there would be a bang, then a hiss through the air and then a strike that drives the evil instrument deep within the majestic whale's flesh, penetrating through the blubber, severing organs and blood vessels, fracturing bones, even the spine. Does the whale shudder and cry out? When they haul it in and lay it down or hang it up, they must peel its body open and carve it into parts. Such is a feat of humanity in the late nineteenth century.

Edgar wonders, for a second, if Godwin could dodge that harpoon.

They settle down for the night in the open air again, huddled together on the deck, wrapped in their heavy coats, Jonathan keeping the gun near him. Every last member of the crew had eyed the weapon throughout the day.

The four friends have trouble sleeping again, and not just because the sun is only down for a couple of hours. They toss and turn on the hard wooden surface, every one of them dreaming of monsters.

In the morning there is still no horizon in sight. They eat the brown beans and black potatoes the crew offers them and say little. Jonathan keeps trying to position himself between the girls and the men, blocking their views. But Tiger often steps past him and goes to the bow and looks out over the waters, sometimes examining the huge black harpoon.

When bedtime nears again, they sit close together talking.

"How do we know they will pick us up again after they set us down at Spitsbergen?" asks Jonathan.

"We don't," says Tiger.

"Maybe we could tell them that we'll pay them more if we return safely?" says Lucy.

"Why would they be motivated by that?" replies Jon. "They can simply kill us and take our money any time, dump our bodies anywhere here, the farther north, the better."

They look out over the endless salt water under the endless sunlight in silence—at first, no one has an answer for that.

"I suppose," says Edgar finally, "we are just going to have to trust to their humanity, their sense of honor." But he doesn't like the sound of that word the second it leaves his mouth. He remembers it coming from the black lips of Percy Godwin.

———

They sail north for three more days, the sun never setting. At night there is an eerie glow in the sky. During the days the water is so calm it feels as though they are drifting quietly and smoothly through a dream. They hear the men whispering; they suppose they are talking about them, of money, of the two girls. There is no sign of a creature rowing a boat upon the vast sea.

Edgar wakes in the middle of one night and watches Lucy sleeping peacefully by his side. He was dreaming of being Victor Frankenstein and of the monster he had created killing his beloved, who again had Lucy's face. He wonders why it is her and not Tiger. Lying still so as not to wake the others, he turns his head toward Tiger and realizes that Jonathan is sitting up, gazing at her as he quietly writes in his notebook, which he had dried in the ocean air. In the morning, Edgar sneaks a look. It is a poem about a fearless young woman, extraordinarily well done.

"I will not ask you what you are doing or seeking in this place," says the captain to Edgar near the end of the third day as he joins him, appearing out of thin air like a ghost and leaning over the railing beside him, "but I will tell you that I have learned that contentedness is the greatest gift God can give you. When I was a young fellow I sailed with men who sought the fabled passages through the arctic to the Orient. They came over these very waters and many died during those attempts. Why do human beings need to do such things? Be contented, my boy, let it be. I wish we could let these poor whales be. But we must pursue." He spits down into the water. "People are always in pursuit of something." He pauses for a while before he speaks again, and when he does, his voice is low. "My men wonder if your mission here is evil."

Just as he says this there is a shout of "land!" from the mast above them.

It takes five hours to get to the distant shore. As they near, they see a rocky terrain and mountains, great ranges of them, white aprons draping their sides. There isn't a single tree or even a bush. *Grim* is the word that comes to Edgar's mind; everything is grim and gray. He has never seen so much gray. But there is a magnificent silence too, and everyone on board stares at Spitsbergen with a kind of awe. It is as if they were looking at heaven . . . or hell.

25

Prey after Prey

"Where do we look for him?" whispers Jon.

"He could be anywhere on this island. It looks vast—it could be a hundred miles long and just as many across," adds Lucy. "What have we done?"

They have no idea exactly where they should be set down so they take the captain's advice and stay with the boat as it sails up the western coast to the first large fjord, where there is some shelter from the winds and the land is somewhat more hospitable near the water and one might at least be able to stay outdoors for a few nights. They see stretches of green tundra.

"Spitsbergen is a mythic place," the captain pronounces. "It is said there are creatures here unknown to the rest of the world. They say there are deep lakes up there in the mountains, so deep they go to the center of the earth and that prehistoric monsters live in their waters. The sea here beneath this boat is awfully deep too. I've heard tell it goes all the way to hell."

They move along the southern coast of the fjord and drift inland for nearly an hour. Then Lucy spots something.

"There!" she cries out.

It's a rowboat, pulled a good fifty feet onto the pebbles and rocks.

"That is unusual," says the captain, standing beside Edgar. "Whoever rowed that vessel is likely long dead, not worth even searching for."

"Let us off here," says Edgar.

The ship's small boat is lowered and they get into it, Jonathan making sure that it is he and not the eager crew members who help Lucy in. Tiger, of course, refuses any aid. A big hairy sailor, one who had watched her with greedy looks throughout the trip, follows behind the four of them, the captain's choice to row them ashore. They all sit silently on the wooden benches.

"You know about the regular wildlife here, do you?" shouts the old captain from above, as they begin to pull away.

"What wildlife?" asks Jonathan.

"There are reindeer and arctic fox, and, of course, the bears."

"Bears?"

"Polar bears, the most dangerous bruin known to man. But you have a rifle. Make sure your first shot counts and save your bullets because you may encounter many of them in the week you will be here. Them and who knows what else!"

The four friends are well aware that the weapon in Jonathan's hands has all of four bullets remaining.

"What is that?" cries the sailor up in the crow's nest. He is pointing across the island.

They all turn and see a figure in the distance, walking in the opposite direction, climbing toward the bottom of the glacier on the nearest mountain.

"It can't be human," shouts the sailor.

"It's an ape, for sure," says another man, "a sasquatch, a Yeti! I hear tell there is some of them here."

"Seen mermaids, seen giant squid bigger than whales, but never seen one of these!" shouts the sailor in the mast.

"If it comes near us, we'll kill it!" yells a crew member near the harpoon gun. He gives that weapon a pat. "Drive this into it and haul it in! Put its head on a pole and take it home and sell it for the museums to show. Would fetch a pretty price, it would."

His voice and the laughter that ensues are beginning to fade into the distance as the big sailor rows the boat toward shore. The four friends aren't saying anything, but they are looking at each other, and Jonathan is gripping the rifle so hard that his knuckles are white.

They have no idea what time it is when they land. Their best guess is that it is nearing midnight. It doesn't matter, since the sun is never out of the sky on Spitsbergen in late June. As the whaling ship sails away, its promise of return something they all know they cannot count upon, they gather in a semicircle facing the mountain and the tiny figure that is now climbing it, carrying its sacks. It hadn't appeared to turn to look back at all, which means it doesn't know they are here.

"We need to eat something, get our strength up and then follow it," says Jonathan.

No one responds. They simply get out the food they bought on the Orkneys and eat in silence.

"Just four bullets left, for sure?" asks Edgar.

"Four is enough," says Jonathan. "I'm not going to miss."

"If you do miss, I'll take over," says Tiger.

Jon smiles at her.

Soon they are trudging toward the mountain, their boots first crunching over the stony surface and then sinking slightly into the stretches of spongy green moss. The weather is surprisingly mild and the light is comparable to dawn, although somehow almost artificial, hazy like the glow given off by stage lights or like one might imagine a dim morning in a storybook.

A half hour into their trek, they begin to climb. Since there are no trees they feel exposed and vulnerable, but the figure in the distance never seems to pause, let alone turn around, and they try to keep to the crevices and the areas in the rock where his view of them would be obscured.

Edgar's chest is tight, as if the hag were on his back with her wrinkled arms wrapped around him, in her glory. They are walking into oblivion to face a monster. Up ahead in the distance the rocky surface is covered in snow and ice, a massive glacier. Godwin will be there soon.

But it seems to take forever to reach the snow. They walk for hours in the rocks and eventually have to sleep. There is nothing they can employ to make a fire, so they are obliged to snuggle together again. Though Jonathan and Tiger try to stay awake, they all drift off. When they awaken, they are still alone. They get to their feet and see Godwin, very far away, a black dot on the ocean of ice, still moving.

Lucy looks the other way for a moment, back down the mountain and out toward the gray water, endless and empty. "Shouldn't we still be able to see the whaling ship?"

Jon scans the horizon. "It seems to have vanished awfully fast."

"They're hunting whales," says Edgar quickly. "That means going far out to sea. It could be just around a corner, too, or gone to the other side of the island." But he wonders. He imagines the boat steaming away far out in the waves, that deadly black harpoon pointing the way, locating and butchering their prey and then heading home without so much as a pause at Spitsbergen. He imagines he and his friends starving to death on this desolate place, forced to eat each other until the last one dies . . . if the creature up ahead doesn't kill them first.

"Let's get moving," says Tiger.

Soon their climb becomes steeper, and in another hour they reach the glacier. Not long after that, Godwin vanishes.

26

Monstrous Surprise

They search and then find two sets of footprints in the snow and ice. One belongs to Godwin, the others are even larger, each with the imprint of five long claws.

"A polar bear," says Tiger.

They stop again without a word and sit in a circle in the snow, all of them facing outward and speaking in low voices. There are now two deadly creatures nearby, maybe more.

"We can't go back," says Edgar finally. "It would be almost as dangerous as going forward."

"Maybe we should at least get off the mountain," says Lucy. "Be somewhere closer to the water where we can see him or a bear or whatever the hell else lives here when it comes after us."

Edgar has never heard her use that sort of language.

"Then, Godwin would be able to see us better too," says Jonathan.

"So, really, we're caught. We are in mortal danger whether we go forward or backward."

"Sounds about right to me," says Tiger. "Though, we have one small advantage over the good surgeon right now. He doesn't seem to know we are here. So, I propose we take that advantage, polar bears or not. Let's get moving."

But Lucy has more to say.

"Godwin seems to be almost un-killable. I think he's drawing us here on purpose. Why else would he be trekking way up this mountain? He is so much more capable of living through any hardship than we are. Maybe we won't be able to take him by surprise, maybe we can't kill him no matter what we do? Edgar, you were able to talk to him. He said you had a deal. Why can't we trust him?"

"Because he's a monster," says Jonathan.

"So are we, sometimes. We are monsters for doing this, aren't we, for not keeping our end of the promise? Goodness has to start somewhere, doesn't it? In the Bible, doesn't it say: love your enemies?"

Jonathan smirks, but Edgar wonders if she is right, at least about leaving the mountain, leaving Godwin alone, trusting him. There had been a soft look deep in the monster's eyes for a moment when they made their deal. Edgar feels responsible for bringing them all here.

"We need to go after him," says Tiger firmly, a grim look on her face. "There isn't any other way. I'll go alone if I have to."

"But what if we do kill it?" says Lucy. "We seem to keep conveniently forgetting that we not only have evidence that there are living aberrations in our world but that if you kill one, another will come after you. We can't say it's just Shakespeare's ravings! We know for certain that the vampire, the revenant, whatever it was, pursued grandfather after he killed Grendel."

"It took him a few decades," says Jon.

249

"But it came. And this thing—Percy Godwin—made by the hand of man, admitted that he pursued us after we made our kill in the Lyceum Theatre. Godwin has been even worse, just like grandfather said. So if we kill him . . . what comes next?"

What, thinks Edgar, could possibly be worse?

Jonathan is staring up the mountain. "There's something up there," he says suddenly, lowering his voice to a whisper and flattening himself to the cold ground. They all immediately drop onto their stomachs and look in the direction Jon is gazing. He pulls the rifle into shooting position, resting it on the snow and ice in front of him, and aims it, his finger on the trigger.

A couple hundred yards away, thankfully upwind, something exactly the color of the snow is getting to its feet. Lucy is the only one to gasp, but all four feel the same way inside. They cannot believe the size of the polar bear. It rises onto its hind legs and sniffs the air, an awesome sight. It was this magnificent animal's tracks they had seen following Godwin's. It must have stopped for some reason. Perhaps it was tired, perhaps it sensed that Godwin had stopped and had paused to make a decision, maybe it was feeding on something. But now it is moving again. Its rear end is toward Edgar and his friends as it ambles away, its nose to the ground, smelling the tracks. Then it starts to move faster.

It is hunting Percy Godwin.

They follow, staying a safe distance behind, keeping as low as possible. The bear sticks to Godwin's footprints and is so fixated on his trail that it rarely looks back, though any time it does linger, Edgar and his friends immediately plaster themselves to the snow and ice. Lucy has taken the lead, convincing the others that her size and the light color of her hair won't stand out as much on the white snow as Jon's big body and dark-blond locks or Tiger and her raven-black curls or Edgar with his bright-red, disheveled mop that sometimes looks like flames swirling around on his head.

About half an hour later, the bear seems to suddenly disappear. It is moving up a particularly steep area, and then they see its rump vanish over an outcropping of extraordinarily jagged rocks.

"It might be trying to ambush us," says Jon.

"But staying here just waiting does no good," says Tiger.

They move slower, cautiously climbing the stretch the bear just accomplished, an unusually tough section. It is almost straight up. Edgar is second in line, with Tiger and Jon bringing up the rear, everyone trying to walk silently and saying nothing.

Halfway to the point where the bear disappeared, they meet a little rocky precipice more than ninety degrees vertical and about six feet high. Lucy reaches up and grabs the top of it and tries to pull herself up, but she struggles, her arms shaking. For a second she is dangling there and in danger of falling back down. Edgar figures he has no choice—he puts both hands on her rear end and shoves her upward. He hears her grunt as she feels his strength power her upward and she gets onto her elbows and then, with a heroic effort, pulls herself over the edge of the rock and onto the next section. She gets to her knees and looks down at Edgar and smiles.

But ten minutes later none of them are smiling.

The mountain had flattened a little after that steep part and following another gradual climb of a few hundred yards, a vista had appeared before them: a sort of huge rocky field on the side of the mountain. Above it everything goes straight up and below it everything descends nearly straight down. For several hundred yards in front of them the glacier is a flat snowy surface and behind it they see a lake, almost black but glistening in the surreal arctic sun, its ice thin, the dark water beneath coloring it. And partway toward that lake, they see the polar bear and a hundred feet beyond it, Godwin. The bear is running at him.

He has turned and is facing it.

The four friends drop down to observe, their hearts racing.

They can hear the bear growling, its head thrust out as if it is locked onto its prey, its teeth bared, the claws on its giant paws gripping the ice and powering it forward. Despite Godwin's size it looks much bigger than him.

He isn't running from it. He has set down his sacks and is waiting.

The polar bear leaps at him. But it doesn't knock him down. They come together in a fantastic collision, Godwin upright and strong, his hands around the bear's throat. They both roar while they battle, the animal struggling as Godwin grips its larynx but raking the human creature's shoulders and his back and chest. Though thick lines of dark blood appear where the claws are doing their work, Godwin doesn't falter, in fact, he shoves the bear back and leans over it, tightening his hands on its throat. The bear fights valiantly but then shudders and slumps down, quivering on the snow. Godwin inserts his iron fingers into its mouth, exposing its enormous fangs, and forces its jaws wide open, hyperextending them, snapping the mandible down onto its throat and the top of its jaw over its mane, fracturing it all so loudly that Edgar and his friends can hear the CRACK from hundreds of yards away. The sound echoes over the mountain and the bear falls in a heap at Godwin's feet.

Stunned by this surge of superhuman testosterone, this extraordinary masculine triumph, Jonathan rises to his feet and stares across the snow and ice toward the scene.

Godwin sees him.

"Oh, God!" cries Lucy.

"Run!" shouts Jonathan.

"No," says Tiger quietly, "it won't do any good . . . it'll be worse."

Godwin is staring at them, as if he is stunned by their presence.

"We have to speak with him," says Edgar. "That's our only chance."

"I'll speak to him," says Jonathan, "with this!" He raises the rifle.

Godwin begins to walk toward them, increasing his pace as he comes, soon moving at a terrific speed, his strides long and purposeful. He only slows when he is within ten feet, his eyes on the barrel of the rifle. He halts.

"I am disappointed, Edgar," he says. "This is betrayal and it will be fatal to you and your friends. It is also extremely STUPID!" His voice bellows out and echoes throughout the mountains. One would not have been surprised to see an avalanche begin to descend from the heights above.

Edgar is speechless. Fear has seized him the way it used to when he was a child. As the monster's hideous yellow face glares at him, the hag climbs onto his shoulders. Edgar wants to say something, to fight back, to protect Lucy and his friends by his side, but he is frozen. He can't even summon his father's words, the words he needs—*Do not be afraid.* He is petrified! He can't even run.

Tiger's black eyes are alert. She is quickly considering the things she might do, how she might effectively assault this supernatural creature. She thinks it will go for Edgar first. She must protect him.

Lucy is quivering. She steps forward. "Please," she says to Godwin, "do not harm my friends, for I love them and cannot bear to see them die. Take me."

Godwin turns to her for an instant, shocked by her irrational words, and in that split second, Jonathan hits the ground and rolls and like the crack-shot soldier he one day intends to be, fires a point-blank blast upward from Thorne's extraordinary rifle right toward the place where the great surgeon's skull is attached to the rest of his body. The shot misses, but not by much. The bullet travels on a line just a few inches lower than Jon intended and speeds toward Godwin's chest. The creature's eyes snap toward the barrel, the deadly bullet rocketing his way. He turns in a flash, faster than the human eye can follow and the bullet enters him, ripping through his skin, into his flesh, and through his breastbone, exploding on contact as Thorne ingeniously intended, creasing the edge of Godwin's one-hundred-and-one-year-old heart, placed there by a man who took it from another man. Then the bullet exits through the breastbone three inches farther along the big chest and out through the flesh and skin and thwacks into the ice and snow some twenty yards away. The report echoes in the mountains.

Blood spurts out of the great surgeon and he turns to Jonathan and stares down at him, his eyes bulging.

"You've shot me!"

"Excellent observation," says Jon. "You must be a scientist."

"Now, die," says Tiger quietly.

But he doesn't. Instead, he suddenly seems like a new man. His yellow, burned face flushes.

"I am filled with anger, Edgar!" he cries. "I AM FILLED WITH ANGER!" But he doesn't look angry—he looks excited, as if an experiment is working. "I have a sense of your deceit, a deceit as wicked as anything I might do. And I am moved to action. You are to be eliminated instantly!"

He has Jonathan's rifle in his hands so suddenly that the four friends don't even glimpse it happening, and in another flash he has cracked open the chamber, taken out the last bullets and flung them away. Edgar keeps his eye on one bullet. Godwin pitches the gun far into the snow too. Then the monster turns on them.

"Brim, you were always my primary target. You will be the first to die."

Godwin shoves Lucy aside and swings at him, an awesome swipe of one muscular arm, with his fist intent on contact with Edgar's temple. But at that instant someone else moves with almost the same speed.

Tiger.

She steps in front of her beloved and takes the blow that was intended for him. The bone in Godwin's thick wrist strikes the top of her skull with a sickening sound and her limp body cartwheels into the ice and snow where she lies motionless.

Edgar looks down at her, stunned. He feels sick to his stomach.

Godwin seems even more shocked.

"Why?" he says staring down at Tiger too. "Why would you do such a thing? That wasn't logical; it didn't make any sense! You will die now: your brain has moved inside your skull and collided with the bone that is there for protection, struck it more than once. It is like jelly thrown against a rock. There will be lesions, fatal injuries! This is your second brain trauma of late, you strange female, and you shall not recover!"

Godwin turns back to Edgar. "Well," he says, "all this means is that you will die second."

He raises his arm to Edgar. But now Lucy steps directly in front of him. The motion of Godwin's arm halts and his mouth drops open but he says nothing.

When she sees that the surgeon seems unable to act, Lucy turns to Tiger and drops to the ice near her, sobbing. "Tiger!" she cries. She puts her shaking hand onto her friend's deathly still face, white and beautiful in the frame of her black hair, and caresses it.

"Soul," says Godwin under his breath and an expression of fear comes over him as he stands there with blood oozing from the wound in his chest. A tear drops from a watery yellow eye and he lets it fall into his hand and stares at it. Then he turns and runs away.

Edgar rushes to the gun and pulls it from the snow, then lurches sideways to find the bullet he had kept his eye on. He takes it up and snaps it into the rifle.

"Stay with them!" he shouts at Jonathan. "You've got your pistol. Help her! Protect them!"

"Oh God," he says to himself as he begins to run, "please let Tiger live."

27

Terror on the Ice

After a while, the creature slows and starts to walk, trudging along with his shoulders slouched, moving aimlessly, his footprints describing a winding path in the snow, blood dripping down. He turns his head every now and then to see Edgar behind him. The boy is moving slowly too, his eyes intent on the monster, his face red, brutal revenge on his mind. *Tiger! There is no one like her, no one!* If he can catch this thing, get close enough to it, he won't be satisfied with killing it. He will take its life with an expanding bullet to the brain and then beat the carcass until it is a bloody pulp. Behind him, he can still hear Lucy sobbing in the distance.

When Godwin reaches the lake, its surface a dark gray sheen, he stops and turns to face Edgar.

Do not underestimate this creature for a second, says a voice inside Edgar. *It has no soul. It is a monster. It will kill me without thinking twice.*

"Edgar," shouts Godwin before they are close, "do not come any nearer. I learned something back there. I do not want to eliminate you anymore, but I will if I must. You do not stand a chance against me."

Edgar halts. He looks out over the frozen lake. An idea comes to him.

"You are correct, I don't," he shouts back. "But you are weakening and not just in the body but in that magnificent brain someone gave you. You *must* eliminate me. And I will tell you why: I will expose you. I promise you."

"That is not wise."

"If I get out of here alive and you are still breathing, I will tell everyone and anyone that there is a creature about on this earth, one made by the hand of another man . . . a monster, a FREAK that—"

"Shut up!" cries Godwin. Edgar starts moving toward him. They are now about twenty strides apart. "If you come another step closer, I will be upon you in a flash, my hands around your neck as they were upon Professor Lear and Mr. Thorne. Do NOT tempt me! As I have told you . . . I now prefer to let this be."

Edgar stops. "But I WILL expose you," he repeats. Then he starts walking again, but not directly toward Godwin. Instead, he moves out onto the lake. "I will expose you," he says again, "I will expose you, I will expose you," like a mantra, over his shoulder.

The monster stands still for a few moments as he watches Edgar move across the thin ice of the bottomless lake, filled, thought the ship captain, with prehistoric beasts. Godwin doesn't know what to do. Then he seems to make up his mind. His eyes narrow and he sets his mouth and he runs after Edgar, who is now far away on the hardened water, stepping gingerly.

Five long, thunderous strides onto the ice, the surface collapses beneath Godwin's heavy body and he vanishes with a crash under the frigid lake. The noise is like a cannon going off and

Edgar actually turns toward the top of the glacier to make sure the snow is not cascading in a thundering wall toward him. Then he looks back across the ice and stands still for a moment, waiting to see Godwin surface. But he doesn't. Edgar, whose every step on the thin ice had been made with shaking legs, drops gently onto his stomach and squirms along on the slippery surface toward the spot where the creature went under, the rifle scraping the ice as he grips it with his right hand. When he gets near, he sees that the water beneath him and the thin surface is turning red and then something appears that chills his heart.

Godwin.

He is several body lengths away, under the ice, struggling, his eyes filled with fear, his blood clouding around him, unable to move his arms effectively enough to break a hole so he can survive. The wretch is floating toward Edgar and soon he is directly below him and their eyes meet, in fact, for a moment their eyes are only inches apart. Edgar's lips and the monster's thin black ones, pulled back from his yellow teeth, are almost touching through the ice. They stare at each other for a heartbeat or two and then Godwin begins to struggle again, trying to get back to the opening in the ice. Edgar squirms closer to it and takes the rifle in both hands. In a minute the monster has propelled himself in the right direction and approaches the opening too. But at first he can't get his head to the hole; instead he is clawing at the underside of the ice beside it, one hand splashing in the open water. But slowly, he starts to pull himself sideways and Edgar realizes that in seconds, the surgeon will have both arms in the free water and will be able to haul himself up onto the ice.

Edgar trains the gun on the opening.

Godwin comes out of the water like a whale breaching the surface, mouth wide open and teeth like baleen, flailing at the rifle so fast that before Edgar can fire, the monster has smacked it hard and sent it spinning in the boy's hands. The wrong end is now facing Godwin. Edgar grips the weapon and drives the butt at his target with all his might, connecting with the huge forehead with a crack. The sound is like a sledgehammer breaking stone and the force of the blow actually knocks Edgar backward, the rifle flies from his grasp and drops into the freezing water and disappears. Godwin's eyes roll up in his head and he sinks under the surface again. All is quiet for a moment, dead silence in the arctic air. Edgar lies still, praying.

But then the beast returns. He comes up from the depths in another mighty thrash, his big frame surging out of the water, blood oozing from his chest and head. In an instant he is lying on the flat surface of the ice. He has the rifle in his hands.

"You are correct, Edgar," he says, his yellow teeth chattering. "I *must* eliminate you."

Edgar runs. Any concern about crashing through the ice has fled in the terror that now seizes him. He sprints with all he has and in fifteen or twenty strides is off the ice. He keeps anticipating the sound of the bullet whizzing through the air. It will be a strange ending: to be killed by the rifle that Alfred Thorne made, the one that destroyed the vampire, the one that was meant to eliminate Percy Godwin.

But no shot comes. Then Edgar realizes that Godwin won't be concerned with firing the rifle at first. He simply will be trying to get his heavy body off the ice without crashing through it again. So, Edgar turns up his speed. He isn't sure where to run.

Certainly not back toward his friends. If he does, Godwin would kill them all. This may be a chance to lead the monster away. But he knows that is likely useless too, for as long as the creature has strength, it will seek out the others once it is done with him and brutally murder any who are still alive. It makes him sob and he tries not to picture it as he runs. He can't give up. He thinks of his father too, of his admonition not to be afraid.

But that doesn't seem to matter now. He is about to go to his death, the ending of his short time of consciousness on earth. He imagines the mechanism of the ingenious rifle put into action by the great surgeon behind him and the amazing exploding and expanding bullet that the wonderful scientific mind of Alfred Thorne had conceived flying through the air unlike any bird of the skies, anything that God has ever been able to fashion, striking the back of his very own skull and its hot metal imploding inside him, opening up his head like a melon shattered by an axe, exploding his brain, his mind! *Or does your mind live on? What will it feel like?*

But then he sees something that gives him a glimmer of hope. The flat area they are on will come to an end in about another fifty strides and beyond that the mountain falls steeply downward and a glacier grips its surface: a spectacular and dangerous ice-and-snow toboggan run that seems to go on for nearly a mile.

As Edgar reaches it, he glances over his shoulder and sees Godwin gaining on him.

Edgar leaps.

28

Arctic Murder

He makes sure to land on his back and spreads his arms out at his sides to use as rudders. But they are immediately useless, for the speed he quickly reaches is mind-bending. It is the sort of speed that a character might move at in one of H.G. Wells's fantastic stories. He is being fired like a cannonball almost straight downward. In the distance he sees the rocky shore and the gray water of the Arctic Ocean.

He can't look back but imagines that Godwin will be nearing the top of the glacier soon and then standing there looking down, quickly spotting his prey, then leaping onto the ice and allowing himself to be hurtled earthward. It is a scientific fact that the much heavier Godwin will move much faster on this nearly perpendicular glacier. In moments, Edgar will be caught! The monster will hit him from behind like a rocket and carry him at nearly terminal velocity down this slide and into the mountainside, or perhaps the sea, his big hands around Edgar's throat. Edgar is also terrified that he may at any second smash into a protrusion in the glacier and be obliterated. He has no way of steering away and a collision with any of them will shatter his bones or break his skull wide open and leave him a rag doll spinning in this wicked descent. And if he survives all the way to the bottom, there will be no means to arrest his meteoric fall.

He has nothing to lose, so with a great effort of will, he pulls his arms into his sides and makes his resistance to the wind almost negligible. This too is a scientific fact—he will now move at an even greater speed! He becomes an arrow flying down the mountain. He is moving faster than a locomotive, faster than any human invention can make a human being move. He is also wildly out of control.

He cries out as he shoots downward, bellowing for his father, his mother, Annabel, and finally for Alfred Thorne. But he knows only God can help him now.

He tucks his chin into his chest and looks at where he is going, squinting out through blasted watering eyes. The wind makes a whizzing sound, and there are loud thumps and his own groans as he collides with little bumps. It smells like iron and water, and there's a growing hint of salt in the air. Down below in the distance he sees white turn to gray with patches of green and then there is the dark gray sea beyond. As he bounces and bangs along, he glimpses something else—it's out on the water and floating aimlessly toward the shore . . . the whaling ship? That doesn't make any sense . . .

In seconds, it seems, he is approaching the end of the glacier, still moving at rocket speed. He knows for certain now that if he meets the hard ground beyond it at this velocity, he will surely die, and even if he lives, he will be so grievously wounded that he will not be able to function.

He tries to brace himself but realizes that the glacier is scooped out at its foot in a huge concave area like a bowl of milk. But it isn't filled with soft snow as he hoped. It too is hard and icy. He shoots down into the bottom of the bowl and then climbs the other side, slowing down. He puts his arms to the side and arrests his momentum even more. But he is still moving fast when he exits the far side of the bowl and ascends beyond it into the sky. For a few moments he is airborne. It is like absolutely nothing—there is no smell, no sound, no sight, and he has no feelings about it. It is a perfect moment before death and all his fears evaporate and he has the sense that he is safe, in heaven, held gently in God's hand, no small human concerns or desires or false knowledge besetting him. He is flying.

He reaches the apex of his flight.

Then he begins to fall.

Edgar hits the ground with a heavy thud. Miraculously, his landing pad is green and mossy. All the air is immediately forced from his lungs and he cannot breathe. He rolls over, gasping, feeling like this is the end, but now his father's words come to him clearly—*do not be afraid*—and he calms his brain, and his lungs, and slowly starts to breathe.

He lies there for a few moments before he tries to move his legs and then his arms. He sits up. He staggers to his feet. For an instant, he has an overwhelming sense of how wonderful it is to be alive and feels like hugging himself. But then he remembers.

Edgar turns toward the glacier and looks up it. Halfway down, a big black object is hurtling his way. And far up above it, standing at the top, as if trying to decide what to do, he sees two figures—one tall, the other slight and shorter. The tall one is holding something in its arms.

Edgar has no time to think, let alone look. He turns and runs as fast as he can. He races over the tundra, up and down little hills, the sea still out of sight. Then the whaling vessel comes into view. But it doesn't look right. It appears to be tilted and there is no activity on the deck, no one in the crow's nest, nothing. It is drifting toward the shore.

Edgar runs with everything he has, and by the time he nears the edge of the water, the boat is just a few feet from land. He stops and turns to see the top of Godwin's flat head bouncing up and down on the far side of a hill. The creature has made it down the glacier in a flash!

The little ship is listing, tilting sideways as if offering the deck to Edgar, and the shore here is rocky and high. He thinks he can make the leap onto it.

He jumps but loses his footing when he lands and crashes to the boards. He tries to get to his feet but slips and falls again. He looks down. The deck is slippery with blood. But there is no blubber, no pieces of a giant of the sea anywhere on the boat. And he can't spot a single member of the crew. It doesn't make sense. Then, as the little ship floats the last few feet and strikes the rocky shore, he falls again. When he gets to his feet a second time, he looks back toward land and sees Godwin coming up over the last hill. He stops when he gets there. He has spotted Edgar. The monster stands still and stares at his prey. His chest is now caked with red, his forehead black with a bruise. He drops the rifle: he doesn't

265

need it now. There is a look of resignation on his hideous yellow face. Finally, he will eliminate Edgar Brim. He begins to walk toward the ship.

Edgar is frantic. He looks beyond the creature and sees Lucy in the distance, staggering toward the monster, her brother behind her, carrying Tiger's limp body. They are more than twice the distance Godwin is from the boat.

Edgar realizes that his only resources are here on the ship and his eyes dart around the deck. The scene almost turns his stomach. There is not just blood splattered everywhere, but now he sees severed limbs and digits and even a head. He recognizes that the face belongs to the big sailor, his eyes still open in terror, no sign of the ravenous leers he had given Tiger and Lucy. Then Edgar spots two human feet on the deck sticking out from the other side of the big hoist, still in their boots, toes pointed up toward the heavens, the cuffs of thick blue trousers hanging over their tongues. Edgar runs toward the feet, and the legs attached to those boots grow longer until he sees the trunk, then the pea-coat and the arms, and finally the neck and the head. Edgar almost leaps upon him.

"Captain!" he shouts. But the old man doesn't move.

"He can't help you!" booms a voice from the shore.

Edgar turns and regards Godwin, walking very slowly toward the boat now. In a few seconds he will almost step onto the deck. Edgar is beside himself. What can he do? Where can he go? *Flee!*

He runs to the bow of the boat and spots the big black harpoon, pointing out toward the ocean, long and iron and deadly.

He can see it has been loaded and cocked, as if it were abandoned just as it was about to be fired. There is blood all over it and part of a human finger is glued to its surface, right near the trigger.

"EDGAR!"

It's Lucy. She has run ahead of Jonathan and can see the scene about to unfold in front of her, but she is still a hundred feet away.

Godwin turns toward her for an instant. As he does, Edgar seizes the explosive harpoon gun and swings it around on its swivel and, placing his finger right next to the severed one, squeezes the trigger.

The harpoon takes flight like a rocket, exploding from the mechanism in a concussion that rocks the coastline and hisses directly at Percy Godwin as he is turned toward Lucy Lear. It is an unexpected sound and though the creature rotates back and reacts quickly, he's too late. The whizzing harpoon sucks into him in the very center of his chest just below his throat and goes right through him, through his breastbone and out his back right next to the spine, the harpoon's huge tip emerging on the other side, the barbs fully out, dripping red. It knocks him down and pins him to the earth.

But he gets up. He reaches his arms over his shoulders, displacing them in a gruesome manner, and then pushes himself to his feet, the harpoon impaled in him, its attached rope, which had unwound like a spinning top, connecting him to the ship as if it were a tightrope.

Lucy halts.

"Excellent shot," says Godwin. "Bravo!" Then he walks toward the boat.

"EDGAR!" screams Lucy again. She runs toward them. Jonathan stops and lowers his forehead to Tiger's and kneels down with her still motionless in his arms.

Godwin is staggering, the harpoon that sticks out nearly three feet on either side of his chest disturbing his balance. He gets onto the deck and the force of his weight pushing against the boat shoves it away from the shore and it begins to float out into the fjord. The creature walks past the captain, turning toward the bow where Edgar awaits him with his eyes large. Brim cannot believe that Godwin is still alive. He sees the hag advancing across the water behind the boat, walking upon the surface.

"I am designed too well," says the monster, as though he has read Edgar's mind. "I am perfect."

"No you aren't," says Edgar. He points toward Lucy, standing on the shore looking out at the boat with her hands held over her mouth. "You could never do what she did. I saw that it disturbed you."

Godwin hesitates. He is so close now that with another step he could reach out and strike his enemy. "I am an example of science at its zenith. I am the very incarnation of human progress."

"You have no soul," says Edgar.

"SHUT UP!" shouts the creature and he steps right up to Edgar. His horrific face is just a few feet away.

"And you will never have one," says Edgar Brim.

Godwin halts. Edgar sees his face quiver. He stands there silent for a long while, and then a tear drops from a yellow eye. "But perhaps," he says quietly, "I might make one." He looks pleadingly at Edgar. "How . . . how would I do that?"

"There is only one way," says Edgar, "and it has *nothing* to do with science, though much to do with progress, but of an invisible sort. A soul cannot be quantified. There is no physical evidence of it. You do not *make* one. It is far more difficult than that."

"Tell me . . . please . . . and I will try."

"Do what she did," says Edgar, and he nods in Lucy's direction.

Godwin looks over at her, then beyond her to Jonathan, slumping forward with the limp body of his beloved in his arms, and then back to Edgar. The boat is drifting farther out into the water. The monster nods his head pitifully and falls with a crash to his knees and sobs. The harpoon's tip smacks against the deck and shakes him from head to foot. Then he rises again and steps toward the edge of the boat.

"Could you tell me a joke first, a real joke, and see if I can laugh?"

Edgar says nothing and they stand in silence facing each other for a moment. Then Godwin touches his head, running his hands along the scars on his skull and caresses his hideous face and looks down to his attached appendages.

"Perhaps then, Mr. Brim, you might push me?"

Edgar steps forward and shoves Percy Godwin overboard. He hits the frigid water with a huge splash, landing on his back. Edgar looks down upon him. The monster is staring back, his eyes wide open in his ghastly, man-made face. He gazes at Edgar as his body, attached to the heavy harpoon, sinks into the Arctic Ocean. Edgar remembers this creature hugging him, the terror in his eyes when he asked about a soul.

"The sea here, right beneath this boat, is awfully deep too," the captain had said. "I've heard tell it goes all the way to hell."

As Edgar watches those horrible eyes vanish, he hopes it isn't true.

Then he hears a groan. Over near the big hoist, the captain is stirring. Edgar slumps toward him, and by the time he gets there, the old man has gotten to all fours. He looks up at the boy.

"It was a beast of the sea," says the captain. "It came upon us suddenly, as if it were tracking us, as if it wanted revenge, the biggest one I have ever seen! It must have come up from somewhere far below the ocean floor. It sideswiped my ship, lad. It drove its nose into us and knocked several of my men overboard and then it thrashed its giant tail and sent others flying into masts and hoists and weapons, breaking bones and severing limbs. The blood was everywhere. My first mate, he loaded the harpoon, but it was as if this monster knew what he was doing! It came at him with his huge mouth wide and seemed to swallow him up!"

"Calm yourself," says Edgar. "You are safe now."

"It was pale in color," shouts the captain. "I swear this whale was nearly white!"

"We need to get home immediately. Can you take us?"

"Young man, do you believe in the devil?"

"I don't know."

"Do you think that the devil could rise up from the depths and take us to hell for our sins? For I believe that is what happened here. I ask you, do you believe in the devil?"

Edgar looks toward the shore and sees Lucy standing there staring back at him with a longing look. Jonathan is now beside her. He has set Tiger on the rocks at their feet and is bending over her, his hands caressing her face. Edgar looks toward the bow of the boat and sees the hag crouching on the empty harpoon gun, leering back at him.

Then a sound erupts out of the stillness of the gray arctic day. It is unearthly, louder than any animal could accomplish. It echoes over Spitsbergen and across the calm water like thunder from another world. It hadn't seemed to come from anywhere.

"What was that?" asks the captain, fear distorting his face.

Edgar can hear little William Shakespeare back in that room on Drury Lane, apparently hopelessly mad and surrounded by his ghostly friends, telling him that Professor Lear killed the real Grendel, that they destroyed *the* vampire, and that if they kill this Frankenstein creature, something worse will come for them.

Edgar looks toward the hag. She is gone. But he *knows* she is real.

The horrible cry invades the silence again, filling the air around them.

The captain squirms along the boards in the blood as if scrambling to get away from something, his teeth chattering.

On the shore at Lucy and Jonathan's feet, Tiger still doesn't seem to be moving.

What, thinks Edgar, could be worse?

Acknowledgments

This second novel in *The Dark Missions of Edgar Brim* trilogy continues the exploration of a late-nineteenth-century boy who suffers from what we would call an anxiety disorder. He is trying to kill his fears, aided by companions with different approaches to the things that may or may not threaten us.

In my attempt to tell a different and at times complicated sort of horror story, I was fortunate to have as an ally editor Lara Hinchberger, returning for a second time with insightful contributions and sympathetic ways that continued to be invaluable. Copyeditor Shana Hayes again helped us bring our work over the finish line, as did Peter Phillips. And Tara Walker lent her support again, not just as a driving force for the project and for Tundra Books and Penguin Random House, but as an expert in everything Mary Shelley. Jennifer Lum and Rachel Cooper have once more provided us with a stunning cover, a fitting successor to the much-praised first one.

This novel, as was the first, is steeped in classic sensation and horror literature, so there are many authors and books to acknowledge. First is Edgar Allan Poe, who gave not just two parts of his name, but also his inimitable style and works to all of *Edgar Brim*. Of prime importance this time is the immortal Mary Shelley's classic *Frankenstein; or, The Modern Prometheus*, and in companion with it *The New Annotated Frankenstein* by Leslie S. Klinger, whose remarkable work I have leaned on several times before. Miranda Seymour's biography *Mary Shelley* helped make the great lady real. H.G. Wells actually appears in this book and several of his extraordinary creations—*The Time Machine, The Invisible Man, The War of the Worlds* and of course, in a starring role, *The Island of Doctor Moreau*—are featured. Michael Sherborne's excellent biography, *H.G. Wells: Another Kind of Life*, greatly aided me as I tried to make the great man stand up and talk to my characters. Robert Louis Stevenson makes a quick appearance too, as does his extraordinary novel *The Strange Case of Doctor Jekyll and Mr. Hyde*. James Pope-Hennessy's biography of Stevenson was most certainly helpful as well.

As always, I also want to thank my continuing companions in life, Sophie, Johanna, Hadley and Sam, fearlessly sticking by me as I make my way through another endeavor in that horrifying world of the arts.

I look forward to the third Brim book. "What could be worse?" asks Edgar at the end of this novel as he contemplates the emergence of a third and final monster. We shall see.

THE DARK MISSIONS OF EDGAR BRIM

E dgar Brim has suffered from nightly terrors since he was in his cradle, exposed to tales of horror by his novelist father. After the sudden death of his only parent, Brim is sent by his stern new guardian to a grim school in Scotland. There, his nightmares intensify and he is ridiculed for his fears. But years later, when sixteen-year-old Edgar finds his father's journal, he becomes determined to confront his demons and his bullies. And soon the horrific death of a schoolmate triggers Brim's involvement with an eccentric society that believes monster from famous works of literature are *real*.

With the aid of an unusual crew of friends, Brim sets about on a dark mission—one that begins in a cemetery on the bleak Scottish moors and ends in a spine-chilling climax on the stage of the Royal Lyceum Theatre in London.

EYE OF THE CROW

It is the spring of 1867, and a yellow fog hangs over London. In the dead of night, a woman is brutally stabbed and left to die in a pool of blood. No one sees the terrible crime. Or so it seems.

Nearby, a brilliant, bitter boy dreams of a better life. He is the son of a Jewish intellectual and a highborn lady—social outcasts—impoverishment the price of their mixed marriage. The boy's name is Sherlock Holmes.

Strangely compelled to visit the scene, Sherlock comes face to face with the young Arab wrongly accused of the crime. By degrees, he is drawn to the center of the mystery, until he, too, is a suspect.

Danger runs high in this desperate quest for justice. As the clues mount, Sherlock sees the murder through the eye of its only witness. But a fatal mistake and its shocking consequence change everything and put him squarely on a path to becoming a complex man with a dark past—and the world's greatest detective.

DEATH IN THE AIR

till reeling from his mother's death, brought about by his involvement in solving London's brutal East End murder, young Sherlock Holmes commits himself to fighting crime . . . and is soon immersed in another case. While visiting his father at work, Sherlock stops to watch a dangerous high-trapeze performance, framed by the magnificent glass ceiling of the legendary Crystal Palace. But without warning, the aerialist drops, screaming and flailing to the floor. He lands with a sickening thud, just feet away and rolls almost onto the boy's boots. He is bleeding profusely and his body is grotesquely twisted. Leaning over, Sherlock brings his ear up close. "Silence me . . ." the man gasps and then lies still. In the mayhem that follows, the boy notices something amiss that no one else sees—and he knows that foul play is afoot. What he doesn't know is that his discovery will set him on a trail that leads to an entire gang of notorious and utterly ruthless criminals.

THE SECRET FIEND

In 1868, Benjamin Disraeli becomes England's first Jewish-born prime minister. Sherlock Holmes welcomes the event —but others fear it. The upper classes worry that the black-haired Hebrew cannot be good for the empire. The wealthy hear rumblings as the poor hunger for sweeping improvements to their lot in life. The winds of change are blowing.

Late one night, Sherlock's admirer and former schoolmate, Beatrice, arrives at his door, terrified. She claims a maniacal, bat-like man has leapt upon her and her friend on Westminster Bridge. The fiend she describes is the Spring Heeled Jack, a fictional character from the old Penny Dreadful thrillers. Moreover, Beatrice declares the Jack has made off with her friend. She begs Holmes to help, but he finds the story incredible. Reluctant to return to detective work, he pays little heed—until the attacks increase, and Spring Heeled Jacks seem to be everywhere. Now, all of London has more to worry about than politics. Before he knows it, the unwilling boy detective is thrust, once more, into the heart of a deadly mystery, in which everyone, even his closest friend and mentor, is suspect.

VANISHING GIRL

When a wealthy young socialite mysteriously vanishes in Hyde Park, young Sherlock Holmes is compelled to prove himself once more. There is much at stake: the kidnap victim, an innocent child's survival, the fragile relationship between himself and the beautiful Irene Doyle. Sherlock must act quickly if he is to avoid the growing menace of his enemy, Malefactor, and further humiliation at the hands of Scotland Yard.

As twisted and dangerous as the backstreets of Victorian London, this third case in The Boy Sherlock Holmes series takes the youth on a heart-stopping race against time to the countryside, the coast, and into the haunted lair of exotic—and deadly—night creatures.

Despite the cold, the loneliness, the danger, and the memories of his shattered family, one thought keeps Sherlock going; soon, very soon, the world will come to know him as the master detective of all time.

THE DRAGON TURN

Sherlock Holmes and Irene Doyle are as riveted as the rest of the audience. They are celebrating Irene's sixteenth birthday at The Egyptian Hall as Alistair Hemsworth produces a real and very deadly dragon before their eyes. This single, fantastic illusion elevates the previously unheralded magician to star status, making him the talk of London. He even outshines the Wizard of Nottingham, his rival on and off the stage.

Sherlock and Irene rush backstage after the show to meet the great man, only to witness Inspector Lestrade and his son arrest the performer. It seems one-upmanship has not been as satisfying to Hemsworth as the notion of murder. The Wizard is missing; his spectacles and chunks of flesh have been discovered in pools of blood in Hemsworth's secret workshop. That, plus the fact that Nottingham has stolen Hemsworth's wife away, speak of foul play *and* motive. There is no body, but there has certainly been a grisly death.

In this spine-tingling case, lust for fame and thirst for blood draw Sherlock Holmes one giant step closer to his destiny—master detective of all time.

BECOMING HOLMES

I t is the summer of 1870 in London, and death seems to be
everywhere; at least it feels that way to Sherlock Holmes.
Almost seventeen now, he cannot shake the blackness that
has descended upon him. And somewhere in the darkness,
Sherlock's great enemy, the villainous Malefactor, is spinning his
web of evil, planning who knows what.

Only one thing can rouse the young detective from the depths
of despair: the possibility of justice. Holmes uncovers a new and
terrible plot unleashed by his nemesis. Prepared to do anything to
stop Malefactor, Sherlock sets out to destroy his rival, bringing
him and his henchmen down, once and for all. Everything in the
brilliant boy's life changes as death knocks again. . . . In this shocking and spine-tingling conclusion to the award-winning series,
Sherlock Holmes transforms, becoming the immortal master of
criminal detection.